THE SAGA OF WILL STANTON

David Long

Table of Contents

I

Warren Hathaway, the owner, editor, reporter, and sometimes photographer of the *Marion County Banner* was strolling around the courthouse square in Jasper, Tennessee, with his head down and both hands shoved deep in his pockets. He had been racking his brain for days trying to come up with someway to make his paper more interesting. In a rural county such as Marion, nothing much ever happened, and who had given birth most recently just wasn't selling papers. It didn't take an accountant to see that the paper wasn't making much profit. Warren was making a living, but he didn't want to merely make a living. He had a son who might want to go to college someday, and his young wife deserved a better life than he could give her right now. He simply had to come up with some way to sell more papers or get into another line of work.

"Hey, Warren!" this coming from the bench under the maple tree a few feet back from the curb.

Oh, for heaven's sake, thought Warren, just exactly what I don't need today. The way I feel right now, I don't think I can tolerate any more of Tucker's horse trades or 'coon hunts. I really don't want to be bothered—by him or anyone else.

Tucker Walden was the local horse trader and gossipmonger. He was always dressed in overalls and clod buster shoes and always had a quid of tobacco in his jaw, but he would never spit like most chewers do--tobacco was just too precious to waste. Tucker wasn't a tall man, but he was as solid as a brick wall and almost as strong as some of the horses he traded.

"Come on over here and set a spell, Warren, I got sump-in' you jist might be innerested in," said Tucker, while patting the bench where he wanted Warren to sit.

Warren didn't know how he could escape without being downright rude, so he strode over and sat down beside Tucker. "Look, Tuck, I really don't have time to chat, and I certainly don't have anything to horse trade. I've got some important business to take care of," lied Warren. "I can only spare a couple of minutes." Warren's eyes were riveted to Tucker's mud and manure-encrusted shoes--a sure sign of his trade.

"Yeah, shore, Warren, I saw exactly how busy you was. What I got to say won't take more'n a couple o' minutes, so hold yer tater, awright? Then you can git back to rubbin' 'em coins in your pockets together." Warren and Tucker had known each other for years, so this was their usual dialogue.

"Now, dadgummit, where was I? Oh, yeah, as I was gonna say before you innerrupted me, I was up to Cheekville this mornin' buyin' a pig off o' ol' man Jed Thompson. Well, Jed has got hisself some company, all the way from Montana Territory, so he says. A half-breed Injun boy. At least that's what the youn-gun calls hisself. But I tell you sumpin', this here boy don't look like no Injun I ever seed before. Come to think of it, though, I ain't never seed no Injuns before. But anyhow, I know what they's supposed to look like, and this here boy's got real light brown hair—with a kinda reddish tint to it, and his eyes, too, are light brown—almost yaller, and his skin ain't no darker'n mine or yourn. But that ain't what I wanted to tell ye, though. This young

2

feller's pa built the cabin that Jed's boy, Henry, lives in. Course Henry has added on to it over the years."

"You ever heered of a man by the name of Will Stanton? No? Me neither up 'til this mornin'. Don't think he lived in this part o' the country very long. Well anyhow, this here feller, Will, fit fer the South in the war, and I gather he was from a strong Union family, too. Seems this Will lost jist about ever'thing exceptin' his life while he was off afightin'. I don't know all the partic'lars, but I reckon he didn't have nothing much to hold him around here after the war, so he taken off aridin' west. Wanted to see them Rocky Mountains, he said."

"Well, this here Injun boy--his name is Billy Stanton by the way--was atellin' 'ol Jed these stories about his pa. Well, I tell ye, I could o' listened to that youngun all day, but I had to deliver that pig to one o' my other customers. You ought to go and talk to that young feller, Warren, I'd bet my best 'coon hound that you'd hear sumpin' you'd be innerested in."

That sounds like a good idea, thought Warren. Just the fact that someone from as far away as Montana was visiting in the county was news of interest, but it rankled him to admit that Tucker Walden, of all people, might have hit on the very thing that he needed to fill the back page of this week's paper. An interesting story could just turn the trick. He just didn't know why he couldn't have come up with that idea on his own. The fact was that most of the people he knew were just downright boring. Maybe that was why he hadn't thought of it himself. He would have to admit, though, that Tucker Walden was a man that talked to a lot of people.

"You just might have hit on something there, Tuck," said Warren, as he took out his pocket watch to check the time. "What exactly was it that was so interesting about this—what was his name—Will Stanton?"

"Well, Billy was atellin' about his pa's war experiences and some o' the things that happened while he was aridin' out to Montana. He fell in love with this Injun girl, Billy's mamma, and lived with the Injuns fer years. You'll just have to listen to 'im and come to your own conclusion about what's innerestin'. Like I said, I could o' listened to the boy all day."

It had to be very interesting to get Tucker to be quiet long enough to listen, thought Warren. "It's now ten minutes past noon, if I left right now I could be back by supper time. I believe I'll do it. Thanks, Tuck," said Warren.

"Say, Warren, would ye happen to know any body that needs a milk cow or a mule or maybe a good 'coon dog?" asked Tucker.

"No… not right off hand, Tuck, but I tell you what, if I get a story from this Billy Stanton, I'll give you a free ad in this weeks paper. How does that sound?"

"Why, that's right nice of ye, Warren. Thank ye," said Tucker.

"Where can people get in touch with you if they want to buy something?" Warren asked.

"Why, rat cheer at my office. Jist about ever'body knows that," said Tucker, grinning, as he patted the bench he was sitting on.

"How could I have forgotten? I'll let you know how everything turns out," said Warren, as he left to saddle his horse. He stopped by home just long enough to tell his wife where he was going.

It was at least twelve miles to Jedediah Thompson's place, so it would take Warren three hours at a leisurely pace to get there, an hour to get his story, and three hours to get back to Jasper--just in time for supper. He could make better time, but as hot as it was today, he didn't want to push his old horse. The old fellow was just about on his last legs as it was. He hoped that he wouldn't be wasting half a day on a wild goose chase—as if he had something more important to do.

4

Even after twenty years, the Civil War was a subject that could still get people in the Sequatchie Valley stirred up. One-time friends and even families had been split apart by the war, never to reconcile. There were strong feelings still existent that would only die with the people harboring them. The small-time farmers, especially those in the mountainous areas who had strong Union sympathies, greatly resented the more prosperous former plantation owners in the valley, but this was the case even before the war had started. If this Will Stanton's story was colorful enough to get people interested, maybe they would buy newspapers--at least that was Warren's hope.

II

When Warren rode into Jedediah Thompson's yard it was around three o'clock in the afternoon. He figured to spend no more than an hour interviewing young Billy and be back in Jasper by seven. But things have a way of not adhering to the plan. Jed, who was probably around seventy years of age, was sitting on his porch slowly rocking back and forth, with his right hand curled around the bowl of a corncob pipe. There were several chickens scratching around the yard, and a long-legged hound came out from under the house where he had been sleeping, baying out a welcome.

"Quiet down Red! Well, I'll be danged if it ain't Warren Hathaway! Get down Warren and set a spell. I do believe it's been nigh on to a month of Sundays since I last seen you. Just tie the hoss to the porch post there. How's the wife and youngun?"

"They're as fine as frog hair, Jed, how are you and your family getting on?"

"Oh, we'll do, Warren. Could complain about a few minor things, but I won't. What brings you out this way, if you don't mind me askin'?"

"I was talking to Tucker Walden around noon today," said Warren, as he stepped up onto the porch. "He told me about a young man with some mighty entertaining stories. Said this lad was

6

visiting with you. Came all the way from Montana Territory, he says. I thought maybe there might be something that would interest me. What's your opinion of this young fellow and his stories? Do you think he's on the up and up?"

"Have a seat," said Jed, pointing toward a straight back chair, "and we'll jaw awhile. I guess Tucker made hisself a couple of dollars off that pig I sold him, huh."

"He didn't say. We talked mostly about your visitor," said Warren. "Tucker never tells how much profit he makes anyway. To hear him tell it, he little more than breaks even."

"Well, I don't begrudge him a good profit. He has to do a lot of gettin' around for the money he makes," added Jed.

Jed and Warren made quite a contrast sitting side by side on the porch that ran the full length of Jed's log house. Warren was tall, slender, and dark—wearing a pin-stripe suit, patent leather shoes, and bowler hat. On the other hand, the easiest way to describe Jed would be: Santa Claus in overalls. His belly even shook when he laughed.

"Well, to answer your question about Billy, Warren, I've only knowed him for a few days, but I knowed his pa way back before the war, and everything the boy has told me so far pans out. His pappy, Will Stanton, was as honest a man as ever lived, and I believe Billy is every bit his fathers son. I never did hear no news about Will after he left here and went west, so naturally, I'm interested in anything Billy has to say about his pa. Billy and my youngest boy, Gabe, have gone to the spring to fetch a fresh bucket of water. They should have been back before now. They've been gone long enough to fetch the water twice. Listen...ain't that them I hear laughin' around back? Them boys took to one another right off. They act like they've knowed one another all their lives. Gabe has even moved his blankets out to the barn where Billy has been sleepin'."

"Jed, it's none of my business, mind you, but what is this young fellow doing in this part of the country? He's a mighty long way from Montana."

"That he is, alright. He said that he wanted to see where his daddy used to live. And he wants to get the wanderlust out of his system while he's still young. Said his daddy told him it was for the best. Can you believe that youngun has traveled fifteen hundred miles, on horseback mind you, in the last four months or so? Mostly livin' off the land, too, I take it. Got hisself a short-barreled shotgun for rabbits and squirrels. Maybe that's where his Injun blood comes in handy, huh."

"Could be. I don't know much about Indians. But I do know that when I was his age, I wouldn't have had the courage to take off across the country by myself like that, would you?" asked Warren. "not that I would have the courage now, either, mind you."

"Huh, I think you know the answer to that, Warren. I ain't never been more than a hunnert miles from home in my life. I may be built like a bear, but I really don't care what's on the other side of the mountain."

Warren chuckled, then added, "Me either. I've been right here in the valley most of my life. Don't get me wrong now, I've got a certain amount of curiosity, but not near enough to strike out across the country all alone," There was a pause of several seconds as neither of them knew where to go with the conversation.

Jed's wife, Henrietta, came to the door and looked outside. "Why, hello Warren I thought I heard voices. How are your wife and child doing?"

"They're just fine Mrs. Thompson, just fine."

"Would you like a drink of cold water, Warren? The boys just fetched a fresh bucket from the spring."

"No thank you ma'am, I'm fine.

"Well I'll let you men get back to your conversation, then."

"Ain't this some fine weather we're havin'," said Jed, trying to fill the time while they waited for the two youngsters to present themselves.

"yeah, I'll have to agree with that. Could use some rain, though. I'm not a farmer by anybody's reckoning, but I do raise a few vegetables. If we don't get some rain soon, I'll have to fetch water from the well to water my garden," said Warren, as two young men walked around the corner of the house. One of them looked to be at least six feet tall and dressed in buckskin, with moccasins and a headband, although his hair was little longer than average length. There was no doubt in Warren's mind that this was Billy Stanton.

"Come on over here boys and meet Warren Hathaway. He owns the county's only newspaper. You should already know Gabriel," said Jed nodding his head toward the shorter of the two. "This here is Billy Stanton, Warren," indicating the taller, more slender youth. "Billy looks a whole lot like his daddy; however, he's not as heavy in the upper body as Will was, or is, I should say."

"Hello, Gabe. It's been a while. You've grown some since the last time I saw you," Warren said, as he extended his hand. "How are you, Billy? I'm pleased to meet you," said Warren, as he shook Billy's hand. "In fact you're the reason I'm here. Do you remember Tucker Walden, the horse trader?"

"Yes, sir. He was here just this Morning," said Billy

"Well, he said that you could tell a fine story. I'd love to hear some of your stories, and if you wouldn't mind, I might like to run one of them in this week's paper," said Warren, disliking Billy from the start because of his outlandish attire. Warren reasoned that Billy wanted to bring attention to himself by dressing like an Indian. Like Tucker had said, the young man didn't look as if he had a single drop of Indian blood coursing through his veins. Well, he had ridden all this way to get a story; he'd might as well play it through and see what developed.

9

"Mister Hathaway, I really don't have a bunch of stories, sir. There's only one story, and it's about my pa. I've talking about him ever since I got here, and there's more to tell. There are no secrets about his life, so I suppose you can print anything you want to. My pa is just about my favorite subject, I guess. I can talk for hours about him. What in particular did you have in mind?"

"Well, since I don't know anything about your pa, I don't know where to start. If it's alright with you, Billy, I'll ask a few questions, and maybe we can settle on something. Would that be alright?"

"Sure, that would be fine with me," said Billy.

"Let me see now," Warren said, as he took his soft lead stylus and note pad from his inside goat pocket.

"Where did your dad come from?"

"Knoxville. He left home when he was eighteen and came here to the Sequatchie Valley—in '57 I believe it was. He bought a hundred acres of land right there on the other side of the spring branch," said Billy, as he turned and pointed. "He built the main part of the house that Henry lives in."

"How could such a young man afford to buy so much land?" Warren asked.

"My pa worked in his father's warehouse in Knoxville and saved every penny he could from the age of fourteen, and also, it seems that Lady Luck just happened to smile on him that day."

"Then, he was alone when he came here to settle?"

"Yes, sir, he was already on his own."

"It's very unusual for such a young man to be so independent and responsible, too. When I was that age, I was still sowing wild oats," said Warren with a chuckle. "Were his parents still alive at the time?

"Yes, they were still living. My grandmother lives in Knox-ville, now, but the reason my dad left home is practically a story of its own."

"How long did Will live here?"

"Let me see, now. He actually lived there in the cabin four years, and then he was in the war four more. I suppose you could say eight years. At least he owned the cabin for eight years."

This line of questioning went on until the hour that Warren had allotted was up. He had just about filled his notebook, but he still didn't have a coherent story. What he had heard so far had whetted his interest in this Will Stanton character. Then, an idea popped into his mind that excited him!

"Billy, what do you think about going to live with me for a few days? You could tell me your dad's life story, and I could break it down into weekly installments for my paper. I'll even pay you a dollar a day while you are—shall we say—working. I guarantee that you will be well fed, too. My wife isn't as good a cook as Henrietta, but if you tell her I said so, I'll deny ever saying it.

"Well, sir, I had planned to head back west in a couple of days, but what the heck, a few days won't matter one way or the other. I'm not on any kind of schedule, and besides, I could use the money. I'm flat broke."

Warren said farewell to Jed, Henrietta, and little Gabe, while Billy saddled his horse. Jed had listened patiently the whole time Warren and Billy were talking, never once interrupting the interview, something Warren was thankful for, although, he couldn't say so.

After Billy had saddled his mount, he tied his few belongings on the packhorse and in a few minutes was ready to go. As he rode past the front porch, Billy thanked Jed and family for their hospitality and said that he would see them again before he left for Montana.

Warren was more excited than he had been in a long while. Judging from what he had already gleaned from Billy, he would have enough material for several installments. Will Stanton seems to have led a fairly interesting life after all. At least when compared with the vast majority of the people Warren knew, including himself. He was even changing his mind about Billy; for all he knew, everybody in Montana may wear buckskins. Sometimes, first impressions were totally wrong. Billy seemed to be a fine young man, and for someone from the western frontier claiming to be part Indian, he talked as if he had a certain amount of schooling.

There were lots of people who often read the newspaper, but had never in their live read a book, other than a textbook or the Bible, and Warren was hoping that once they got interested in Will Stanton's life story, they would look forward to the next installment. If the experiment were a success, when Will's story ended, he would try to find another interesting character to write about. At the moment it looked as if he would be set up for weeks to come.

Maybe writing about someone's past exploits couldn't be classified as news, but he was the sole owner of the paper and could do whatever he liked. It seemed as if he might owe Tucker Walden his gratitude, but he had no intention of giving Tucker the satisfaction of knowing so. Warren was so wrapped up in his thoughts that he hardly knew when he and Billy rode into Jasper. He apologized to Billy for his silence during the ride home, but Billy said he understood that Warren was in deep thought.

After they took care of the horses, Warren put Billy in the bedroom with his son, Benjamin, since there was nothing else he could do. There were only two bedrooms and he couldn't very well ask an invited guest to stay in the barn. Benjamin was ecstatic at the prospect of having a man who dressed like an Indian share his bedroom. It didn't matter at all that Billy didn't look like an Indian; he was still the most exotic person that Ben had ever seen. He plied Billy with questions about life in the West until Warren had to come to Billy's rescue.

Warren's wife, Mary Beth, was just a little put out at having a stranger in the house without having been consulted before hand, especially one that dressed as offbeat as Billy did. But after Warren explained his plan and assured her that Billy was a fine, upstanding young man, she became quite enthusiastic about the whole project. Even though warren had been too wrapped up in his planning that he had eaten nothing since breakfast, he could hardly wait until supper was over to begin questioning Billy. After everyone had eaten, they all retired to the living room, where Warren again produced a stylus and a new notebook. "Billy, we might as well start with the reason your dad decided to leave the Valley and go west. I'd like to get something in this week's paper. This is Monday evening, and it'll take me a while to get everything formatted and ready to print by Thursday, so we'd better get started. The paper has to be ready to distribute by early Friday morning. You can begin any time you like."

Mary Beth and Ben were patiently waiting for Billy to begin.

"Well, now, let me see," said Billy. "I would say that a good place to start would be down near Selma, Alabama, one week before the war ended. My dad had received a letter from Margaret Smith, Lamar's Smith's wife. Sergeant Smith was my dad's second in command, and also his best friend—actually, you could say his only friend—for several years. The letter said…"

III

His wife was dead! Captain William Forsythe Stanton was sitting on the ground with his back resting against a huge oak tree. He had read the letter in his hands at least a dozen times during the last two days, trying with all his might to find a clue that would tell him that a terrible mistake had been made. But it said the same thing every time he read it: his wife, Virginia had died giving birth to a baby boy. The baby had also died. The letter was dated February 22, 1865; today was April 2. It had taken that long to reach him. The letter could have traveled nearly 500 miles from Cheekville to Nashville, and then who knows what route to Selma, Alabama. He realized it was difficult to keep track of a cavalry unit during wartime, particularly one that moved around as much as his did. Still, six weeks is a long time for his wife to be dead without him knowing about it.

These past few weeks he had been thinking a lot about Ginny and had been looking forward to seeing her again. And now, to know that she had also been pregnant, just added to Will's misery. He had been homesick for quite a while, but now he was heartsick as well. Heartsick and angry! Heartsick because of his wife's death; angry because he had voluntarily left Ginny to fight for this lost cause. He should have been there with her when she needed him most.

It took all his willpower to hold his grief and rage within; however, since he was a leader of men, howbeit in a small way, he put on a stoic front. What he felt like doing was roaring his rage to the world and pummeling the tree behind him with his bare fists. What he did was sit there feeling sick at heart, with his chest actually aching from the pent-up grief and rage.

Recently, Will had been wishing more and more that the war would end, no matter what the outcome, so that he could go home to be with his pretty, young wife. He had been on furlough only a few times in the last four years, but each visit had only whetted his appetite for even more time at home. Over ten months had past since the last time he had seen his wife, and now, there was no one to go home to. After the heartbreaking news he had received, what difference did it make when the war ended—or even if it did?

The small unit of cavalry that Will commanded was lounging around in deep woods on top of a ridge, waiting for the scout to return. Some were dozing; some were talking; and others were playing cards with an almost worn out deck. All talking was done in hushed tones—from habit, not from fear of being overheard.

Will was deep in thought when Sergeant Lamar (Buck) Smith, knowing why his captain was upset, cautiously approached. "Will?" queried Buck, breaking the captain's reverie. "The scout just returned if you'd like to talk to him. He says there is a foraging party of about 25 Yanks, with one wagon, headed west toward Selma. They're about an hour away."

"Yeah, alright, Buck. Bring Corporal Hardy and a map, and we'll see what kind of plan we can come up with.

Right now, Will felt that a good skirmish might be just what he needed to vent some of his anger and get his mind off his problems.

Buck (because he had such a serious overbite) was about five feet and seven inches tall, weighed a hundred and sixty pounds, and was as tough as nails. He and Will had joined the Confederate cavalry together and had been inseparable ever since. Even though they had faced a lot of danger in the last four years, neither of them had received much more than a scratch. Because they were such good friends, there was no formality between them when there was no one else around. Will had never been a stickler about regulations anyway; but to maintain discipline, he tolerated formality from Buck in front of the other men.

Will's unit was in this particular part of Alabama because General Nathan Bedford Forrest's cavalry had been trying to prevent General James H. Wilson's forces from destroying the last munitions depot south of Richmond. There wasn't much Forrest could do except harass Wilson, since it was 6,000 Confederates against twice as many Federal troops, and unbeknown to Will, the Feds were armed with the new Spencer repeating rifle.

Will and his troopers had gotten separated from the main body of Confederate cavalry two days prior, but Will wasn't worried since this had happened many times before. Forrest might have gone back north or even west into Mississippi. Will would find him again; he always had. If trouble arose, such as encountering an overwhelmingly superior force, will's troop would simply break up into individual soldiers riding in different directions. They would then reassemble at a previously designated rendezvous site.

Will and Buck had somehow managed to stay with General Forrest ever since they had joined the cavalry, even though the general's command fluctuated a lot. Will could have been a major now, if he had accepted the promotion, but he liked leading a small unit. That was what he was good at, so he stuck with it. He never had more than 30 men at any given time. At the present he had 21 troopers in his unit, not counting himself.

"Cap'm, this is the best map we have of this area, sir, and it's in pretty bad shape. It's really nothing more than a sketch," said Buck.

"We'll just have to make do, sergeant, spread it out on the ground here."

"Alright, Corporal Hardy, show me where you estimate the Yanks to be about now."

"Well, sir, they was about here when I last saw 'em. My guess is they're about right here, now," said the scout, as he moved his finger across the map.

"Now, sergeant, see this creek that the road crosses? My guess is that they will stop here to water their horses and maybe even take a lunch break. What do you think?"

"It'll be about noon by the time they get there. I think it's a good bet they'll stop," ventured Buck."

"Then we'll be there waiting for them. Get the men mounted, sergeant, and We'll move out."

As it turned out the ambush site that Will had chosen was at the western end of an abandoned farmstead of about 10 acres. The overgrown field was roughly rectangular in shape and the western edge ended at the creek. A chimney was still standing where the farmhouse had been. It appeared that the house had burned, but judging from the size of the young trees that were reclaiming the land, it had happened before the war started.

The road that the Union soldiers would be using entered the eastern end of the field, ran along the southern edge near the woods, and passed close by the chimney before crossing the creek. If the Yanks stopped at the creek, they would be totally in the open. There were no other farms within miles; this being stony hill country, there were easier places to till the ground.

The Confederate troop was divided, with 10 men in the woods to the south, and 12 men including Will across the creek to the west of the field. They didn't have to wait more than half an hour before the vanguard of two Union cavalrymen appeared at the far end of the field. In case the party failed to stop at the creek as he expected, Captain Stanton quietly posted two men—well hidden, one on each side of the road—to take out the vanguard. He need not have bothered. The two Union soldiers dismounted at the creek, drank their fill, watered their mounts, and waited for the rest of their unit to catch up. Will took this as a sure sign that the other men would also be taking a midday rest stop.

When the remainder of the Union troops arrived, they spread out along the open side of the creek to drink and water their horses. They were making so much noise that Will's men were able to lead their mounts, while holding their nostrils closed to keep them quiet, to within 50 yards of the Yanks. Will motioned for his men to quietly mount. Saddle leather creaked, but not loudly, as the men readied themselves for battle.

The 10 troopers on the south side of the road, under the command of Sergeant Smith, waited patiently for the first shot to be fired by the captain before starting their charge. By this time the two men that had been posted beside the road had rejoined the troop. Will looked left and right to see that everyone was ready. He raised his right arm in the air, and with a quick downward motion, he brought his arm level with his index finger pointing forward. At the same instant he brought his heels into the flanks of his mount. The horse leaped forward and 12 men rode as one into battle.

When Will got to within 20 yards of the Union troops, he fired the first shot. One of the men in blue clutched his chest and fell face down into the creek. Each of the Rebels carried two revolvers and a sawed off Enfield rifle, guns that had been captured in various raids, and was trained to make every shot count. After the Enfield had been fired, the men switched to their revolvers. Will raised the Rebel yell and the other men joined in.

The Union Soldiers were taken by complete surprise, and about half of them fell in the first volley before the others began to return fire. Then the 10 men from the south side struck the

Union flank, and more bluecoat soldiers went down. It looked as if it would be a slaughter until a withering fire began from six Yanks who had made a stand near the forage wagon.

They were armed with the new Spencer rifle, something that Will and his men had never encountered before. Each gun held seven rounds that were loaded from the stock and could be emptied in 11 seconds. The only thing that made them slower than a revolver was that the hammer had to be manually cocked after the lever was cycled to load a new round into the chamber. Since the barrel of the Spencer was much longer than a revolver barrel, they were much more accurate at a distance, and the big slow-moving bullet was much more deadly than a revolver round ball. Together, these six men had 42 rounds at their disposal before they had to reload.

The sound of firing was one continuous roar for a few seconds, and the Confederate ranks were being cut to pieces, but the Union soldiers were also taking casualties. The firing stopped suddenly as if by signal. Will looked around the battlefield. He could count only four men that were still moving: two Yankees, Sergeant Smith, and himself. Buck was lining up on a young soldier who had shot his rifle empty and, with muzzle down, was trying to load a cartridge into the chamber, single shot style. At the same time the other Yankee threw his empty rifle aside and mounted a near-by horse. He drew his saber and spurred his mount toward Will.

Out of the corner of his eye, Will could see as Buck pulled the trigger of his revolver; nothing happened. Will now gave full attention to his friend's dilemma. He seemed mesmerized as Buck cocked the hammer and pulled the trigger again; his weapon was empty. The mounted soldier was bearing down on Will, but he seemed incapable of diverting his gaze from Buck. The young soldier had his rifle loaded by this time. He raised the weapon and fired. Will saw Buck's tunic bulge for a split second as the big .56 caliber bullet exited the center of his back. He knew his friend was dead before he hit the ground.

Will's full attention was returned to the charging soldier, but almost too late. The man's arm was beginning the downward swing with the saber when Will fired into the center of his chest. He tried to avoid the saber by dodging backward and to the side, but it wasn't quite far enough. The tip of the blade cut through the brim of his hat and continued down his forehead, through his right cheek to the corner of his mouth, and then glanced off his right shoulder. The blow dazed him and almost unseated him, but he grabbed the saddle horn with his left hand and brought himself to an upright position. Will looked back and saw the soldier he had shot falling to the ground.

Will barely had enough wits left about him to realize the danger posed by the young soldier with the Spencer. In his haste to reload, the young man had dropped the cartridge on the ground. He stooped to retrieve it, giving Will enough time to position himself directly in front of the soldier just as he closed the breech. Will thumbed back the hammer of his revolver as the young man began to raise the muzzle of his rifle. He would never forget the sad look of resignation on the youth's face as he looked at the muzzle of Will's revolver and realized he would be a split second too late. Will pulled the trigger. The Spencer discharged harmlessly into the ground, barely missing one of the horse's hooves, as the young soldier was thrown backward against a wheel of the wagon.

"Will felt a moment of grim satisfaction at having killed the man that had taken the life of his best friend, but almost immediately he felt a twinge of shame. The young man was merely a soldier doing his duty. There was no reason to place blame. If Buck's revolver hadn't been empty, he would have shot the young man first. Still, it hurt. There would probably never be another friend like Buck.

Will surveyed the battlefield a second time. Men with blue or gray uniforms were lying in every direction, but none were moving. However, there were groans coming from near the wagon. From the time of his first survey of the battlefield to the second, no more than a few seconds had elapsed, although, it seemed much longer. He looked down at the front of his tunic and saw that blood covered his chest, stomach, both thighs, and was still dripping from his nose and chin.

Ignoring the wound, he dismounted and stepped to where his friend lay. There was no doubt about his condition. The pang of grief that knotted Will's stomach almost made him vomit. First there was the letter concerning Genny's death, and now, his best friend was also dead. The two people that meant the most to him, and they were both gone. Will's shoulders began to shake, but there were no tears. It was the shakes of raw emotion.

He didn't know how long he had been kneeling beside the body, probably only a few seconds, but suddenly he realized he should get moving. He was out in the opening a vulnerable position. If there had been one wounded Yankee able to shoot, he would now be dead himself. He walked cautiously to the wagon, leading his horse, his gun still in his right hand. There seemed to be none of the wounded that could pose a threat, so Will tried to ignore the groans. There was nothing he could do for them anyway except maybe put an end to their suffering, but he could never do that, not even to a mortally wounded man. War had hardened his heart a great deal, but he hadn't become totally insensitive to human suffering.

Inside the wagon were several flour sacks filled with food, among other things that had been confiscated from farms miles back down the road. There was even a grandfather clock that surely would have to be abandoned. With a war going on, how could a soldier transport such a large object to his home, which was probably hundreds of miles away? Will emptied one of the sacks, and with his knife cut two strips from the bag: one wide and one narrow. The wide strip he folded into a bandage that he placed over the saber wound, covering his right eye completely. The narrow strip he tied around his head to hold the bandage in place as well as possible. The rest of the sack was used to wipe blood from his face. He folded the bloody cloth and shoved it inside his tunic for later use.

Will was anxious to leave the area as soon as possible. The longer he tarried, the greater the chance of someone, maybe even a Yankee patrol, coming by. There was no way he could effectively defend himself with his right eye covered. Since he was right handed and right eyed and had never practiced shooting with his left hand, he would be at the mercy of anyone more than 10 paces away. Knowing that he would have to lie low for a few days, he began checking the food in the wagon. After hurriedly emptying all the sacks into the bed of the wagon, he began making his choices.

Into one bag went one whole cured pig shoulder; into another a side of bacon. Tying the two sacks together, he balanced them across the horse in front of the saddle. He did the same with two jars of canned peaches and two jars of tomatoes, with empty bags as packing material between the jars. One of the sacks had been filled with freshly baked biscuits and pones of cornbread. He stuffed the bread back into a bag. Compared to hardtack, homemade bread was a delicacy.

The new Spencers were especially enticing to Will. He took one and looked for cartridges. Now, he understood why the young soldier was loading single shot style. The tubes of cartridges were in wooden crates that had never been opened. The young man had probably had a few loose cartridges in his pocket. The other soldier threw his rifle aside rather than try to break open a crate.

He took a rifle scabbard from a dead horse, but he would wait until later to attach it to his saddle.

With all the provisions he had gathered, Will needed another horse as a pack animal. The Confederate cavalryman had to furnish his own mount or capture one in a raid, unlike the Union cavalry where all horses belonged to the U. S. government. He took a horse that had belonged to one of his own men; therefore, it didn't have a U. S. brand on it. He had a long way to go to get home; he didn't want to invite trouble. Soon, everything had been transferred to the packhorse.

Will tied the pack animal to his own mount, then he caught Buck's horse and led it to where it's owner lay. At six feet and 185 pounds, Will a much bigger man than his friend, but handling a body by one's self was no easy matter. He managed to get Buck onto his right shoulder. Then, by bending his knees and heaving with his shoulder and knees at the same time, he managed to get the body into the air. He then twisted the body in the air so that it fell across the saddle face down. It wasn't gentle, but it worked, and Buck didn't know the difference. Will used the reins from a dead horse to tie Buck's hands to his feet under the horse, and then he tied Buck's horse to the packhorse. Retrieving both of his friend's revolvers, he put them in a saddlebag, along with his own extra gun.

There was one more task to do before he left. He would surely need some money to sustain himself on his way back to Tennessee. Until this moment, Will hadn't had a conscious thought about what he was going to do after today. He knew for sure that he would never fight in this war again. His wife, best friend, and his whole command were dead. There was nothing left to fight for. Besides, a half-wit could see that the Confederacy was in its last days. Desertion had never before entered his mind, but now, he had no intention of dieing for a lost cause, and he was so sorry that others had died today because of his decision. More specific plans would have to be made later. Right now, he needed a place to hole up and heal.

The leader of the foraging party would be the most likely to have money, he reasoned. Will searched all the officer's pockets and found a small leather purse with a few copper and silver coins in it; he put it in his own pocket. He didn't dare take more time to search. He had lingered far too long already.

IV

Will mounted, looked around for the last time, and then rode to the creek. He paused for a moment, wondering which way he should go. He decided to head upstream. After riding a few hundred yards, he checked his back trail to see if he was leaving much sign of his passing. Only an experienced tracker would be able to follow him, he decided, since the ground was covered with leaves. Besides, why would anyone even look for a trail? How could anybody possibly know that there was only one survivor of the battle, and that he had gone this way?

After riding about five miles, Will came to a steep ridge where the creek gushed cold and clear from under a limestone outcropping. Set about 50 yards back from the spring stood a small, long-neglected log cabin, with a full-length porch and a door hanging askew on leather straps. Will approached the cabin cautiously, with gun in hand. A small rectangular field, overgrown with vines and briars, was at the east end of the cabin. This must have been a hunter's shack. It certainly wasn't large enough for a family, and there was no road leading to it that Will could see. Whoever used it must have walked or ridden a horse through the forest to get here. After calling out a loud hello and getting no response, Will dismounted, and gun ready, peered inside the open doorway. Just as he expected, the place hadn't been occupied for some time.

The cabin was quite small, measuring about 12 by 20 feet. There was only the one door opening into a single room. A small, shuttered window broke the monotony of the rear wall. The cabin was well built, but where the roof had developed a leak, the floor was beginning to rot. There was no furniture except for the remnants of a homemade bed in one corner of the room. A piece of broken mirror anchored to the wall with bent nails hung near the door.

Will's head was beginning to hurt with a dull, throbbing ache. It felt as though his heart was beating behind his eyes. He would like nothing better than to lay down for a while, but he had much to do before he could rest. If he stopped even for a short rest, he was sure he would never get started again before nightfall.

The first task was to find a place to bury his friend. He could have left Buck at the battle site—he would have been buried along with the other dead—but somehow that didn't seem the right thing to do to a friend. And too, Buck would probably have shared a common grave with the other Confederates. This way was better; at least there would be a personal touch. Will walked to the rear of the cabin and scanned the woods. There, he found precisely what he was hoping for: a tree that had been blown down, taking the soil up with the roots. There was a good-sized circular hole left in the ground. It wasn't very deep, but it would have to do. He was in no shape at the moment to dig a proper grave, and as badly as he was beginning to feel, it could be days before he recovered. As warm as the days were getting, Buck's body would deteriorate quickly.

Will led Buck's horse to the site, and cutting the bonds that held the body in place, eased his friend, as well as he was able, to the ground. Since the body had been draped over a horse, it was already set to fit the hole. This wasn't the customary position of burial, but rigor mortis would have prevented one man from straightening the body, anyhow. Besides, what real difference did it make? The body would return to the dust just as well in one position as another. Will searched Buck's pockets to see if there was anything that Maggie would want. He found nothing except three dimes that he put in his own pocket.

Whoever had cleared the small field at the end of the cabin had carried stones and dropped them in a pile. Will unsaddled Buck's horse, took the saddle blanket, and covered the body with it. With a stout stick, he broke dirt from the uprooted tree onto the body. He carried enough stones from the edge of the field to completely cover the body, then he put another layer of dirt on top of the stones. The grave was good enough for now, and not too soon for Will. His head felt as if it were splitting. A wry smile touched his lips at this thought—another inch and it would have been fact.

Will took off his battered hat and held it over his heart. He really didn't know what to say, but Buck deserved a few words. He had been too busy to think much about his friend since the battle, but now his throat began to ache from grief that welled up from deep within his chest; grief for Buck and Ginny; grief for his dead troopers; grief even for the young soldier with the knowing look in his eyes. The sadness he felt for all the wasted years of fighting that had all but destroyed this part of the country made his shoulders droop. Will stood for several minutes oblivious to everything but his own thoughts. If only he could have foreseen the devastation of life and property that the war would bring, he would never have volunteered to fight.

"Buck, my friend," he began. "I am so sorry for everything. If only I had known about those repeating rifles, I would have let this one go. The decision to attack the foraging party was mine alone, and look what has happened—My whole command is gone. I'm sorry we volunteered to fight in this war to begin with. We sure didn't know what we were getting into, did we? I'm sorry about all the lives lost on both sides, but most of all I regret that you were killed. You were the only real friend I ever had. I'm going to miss you. If there is a God, I hope He takes you in. Rest in peace, my friend. Rest in peace."

Will carried Buck's saddle into the cabin and placed it in a corner, where dried leaves had gathered after blowing in through the open door. The sacks of food he stored in another corner. The other two saddles were put with the first one. Next, he hobbled the horses at the edge of the old field; there should be plenty of forage for them there.

Once the heavier chores were over, Will walked to the creek, taking a canteen with him, and washed his face in the cold water, soaking the bandage so that it would come off more easily. The cold water felt so good to his throbbing face that he submerged his whole head for as long as he could hold his breath. At first the cold helped to relieve the throbbing behind his eyes, but after he surfaced, the pain rushed back with a vengeance. All he could do was hold both hands over his face until the pain subsided once again into the dull ache.

He removed his boots, tunic, shirt, holster, and pants. Rubbing the clothes with sand in cold water wasn't a very effective way of removing bloodstains, but there was no help for it. Putting on his boots and holster (he then remembered that he hadn't reloaded his revolvers) he draped the wet clothes over some low bushes near the cabin to dry. The holster, revolver, and canteen Will left inside the cabin. Wearing nothing but boots and hat, Will took the Spencer and walked downstream looking for willow bushes. He went only a short distance before finding a willow thicket. In a few minutes he had all the twigs he needed. He made his way back to the cabin, so tired and weak that he could barely put one foot in front of the other. The constant throbbing behind his eyes had not only sapped his strength, he was also becoming nauseated.

His only cooking utensil was a frying pan into which he scraped willow bark. In one of the saddlebags he managed to find a few sulfur matches. With dry leaves and twigs, he soon had a small fire going. After adding water from the canteen, he put the frying pan over the fire. In a few minutes there was a greenish-white liquid boiling in the pan. He set it aside to cool. Willow bark makes a mild analgesic. Maybe, at least he hoped, it would alleviate the pulsing pain in his head.

After pouring more water on the bandage, he went to the piece of mirror to look at the wound. The mirror was so small that he could see only part of his face at any time. The bandage came off with a little coaxing. It was still stuck in places, causing the wound to bleed a little. The area under the right eye was so discolored it looked as if he had connected with a prizefighter's fist. The eye was swollen so much that there was only a narrow slit left open. The edges of the wound were swollen and beginning to curl back, making the cut even wider than it should be. Will bandaged the wound again, adding as much pressure as he could stand to hold the edges as close together as possible. He needed stitches, but that was out of the question. He had a needle and thread in his saddle bags, but he knew he could never stand the pain. The scar would have to be accepted however it turned out.

Will took the three bedrolls that were with the saddles, and using his saddle as a pillow, prepared a pallet on the floor. Before lying down, he drank the willow bark tea; it tasted so bad he shuddered. He had to fight the urge to vomit. Quickly opening a jar of peaches, he drank some of the juice to quiet his stomach and rid his mouth of the bad taste. He had eaten nothing since early morning. After eating some of the fruit, he felt much better.

Placing the Spencer within easy reach, Will finally lay down, covered himself with a blanket, and fell asleep almost immediately. He slept like a dead man until his bladder forced him awake. He was weak from hunger, and the throbbing pain had abated little if at all. Pain gnawed at his face like a hungry rat. The cut itself probably wouldn't have been so painful if the saber hadn't chipped the bone in his forehead and cheek. He had to steady himself with the wall as he walked to the end of the porch to relieve his bladder. His legs felt as if they were made of rubber as he made his way back inside.

He took a knife and cut a fist-sized chunk from the pig shoulder. On his way back outside to sit on the edge of the porch, he bit down on the meat. He almost cried out from the acute pain that jolted through the right side of his face! Gingerly, he clamped his teeth together; he wouldn't be able to put much pressure on his teeth for a while. The teeth on either side of the upper right canine were extremely sensitive, and his upper lip was swollen until it protruded.

After slicing the meat into thin slivers, he slowly ate the whole chunk, as well as more of the peaches, not so much from hunger as from a desire to strengthen his weakened body. Will drank tepid water from the canteen rather than trying to walk to the spring. He wasn't sure he could negotiate the slight slope back to the cabin. He lay down and was soon fast asleep once again.

When next he awakened, Will deduced from the position of the sun that it was about eight o'clock in the morning. It looked to be the beginning of a beautiful day. His headache was not markedly better, and he still could not think clearly. The throbbing caused a sort of delirium, but he was pretty certain there was no fever. The willow bark tea hadn't seemed to lessen the pain very much, if any at all. There was no need to drink more of the disgusting stuff if it didn't help.

Deciding to fill the canteen with fresh water, he took the rifle and walked to the spring, still wearing nothing but his boots. On the way back he gathered his clothes, which were now thoroughly dry. He glanced at the horses; they had hardly moved. After putting on his pants and shirt, Will led the horses to water, and then hobbled them in a different spot at the edge of the field.

After going back inside, Will cut more slivers of meat that could be easily chewed. Rinsing the frying pan, something he hadn't done after boiling the willow bark, he put in four dried and hardened biscuits and emptied the contents of the peach jar over them. After the bread softened, he ate slowly, relishing each bite. This was the most he had eaten since he had arrived at the cabin; small wonder he had felt famished.

Taking powder, ball, and caps Will loaded both revolvers. He would never fight in another war, but he would defend himself if the need arose. Thinking that the flap on his military holster would make drawing the revolver much slower in an emergency, he cut it off. Since he had no intention of ever being in another heated battle, the gun wasn't likely to be lost.

Will soaked the bandage again then lay down to wait for the scab to soften. In his mind he began to recount the events of the previous days, He had never been one to feel sorry for himself, but he had been dealt some bad hands recently. His wife dying, his only friend getting killed, losing his whole command, and being wounded for the first time, these were some pretty bad blows. Oh, come on. Who was he kidding? Of course he was feeling sorry for himself. Ginny, Buck, and the others were dead; he was still alive; however he felt that there wasn't much to live for any more.

He still felt a deep burning anger, toward what, he didn't know—God? Fate? Himself? He wasn't sure. It would be nice to have someone or something to blame. All he knew was that the anger was there. Instead of venting the anger, the skirmish at the creek had only intensified it. Because of his decision, many people had died. But , even with all the anguish within, there was still an innate desire to survive.

When Will removed the bandage, he found that his right eye was swollen completely shut, and the discoloration had spread even more. There was an angry red color along the edges of the wound, but there was still no fever. He could see that the wound would not yet stay closed—it was scabbed over, but still seeping—so he put another bandage over it.

Lying down once more, he drifted off to sleep, but this time more slowly. Did that mean he was getting better? When Will next awakened it was dark. He walked outside and sat down on the porch with his back against the wall and listened to the crickets chirping and the owls hooting their haunting calls into the night. After awhile he ate again and slept some more. Throughout the night, his dreams were filled with images of Ginny and Buck. The next morning he was no more rested than when he lay down, but the pain was noticeably less. He forced himself to get up and add to Bucks grave. He didn't put up a marker—no one in this area would know Buck anyway, even if they were to read his name. Probably no one but he would ever know where Buck was buried or that this hump was even a grave.

Will ate, and since there was nothing else to do, lay down again. One day turned into another—and each day brought more improvement in his condition—until the day came when he felt that he was ready to move on. He removed the bandage for the last time. The area around his eye was still discolored, but the swelling had shrunk a great deal. The pain was hardly noticeable any more, but the wound itself was sore to the touch. A scab at least a quarter of an inch wide ran from his forehead to the corner of his mouth. He would never win any beauty contests, he decided.

V

That evening about an hour before dark, Will saddled the horses, looked around to make sure he was leaving nothing behind, and after visiting Buck's grave for a final goodbye, rode back to the battle site. He figured to ride all night and sleep during the day, hoping thus to avoid army patrols—whether blue or gray. At the edge of the old field, he stopped for a minute to look around. There was no one around that he could see. In the growing dusk, the only signs that a skirmish had taken place, other than trampled briars and grass, were the bones of horses that had been picked clean by scavengers. He remembered that it had rained one night when he was in the cabin. That would have washed away much of the sign, and time would have done the rest. How much time? He wasn't exactly sure—could be eight, could be nine days.

Will headed east away from Selma, intending to take the first road that branched off to the north. He knew that he was on the road between Selma and Montgomery, but the road he needed to be on connected Selma with Birmingham. Will had traveled only a few miles when he came to a narrow, rutted road that exited to the left; he hoped it wasn't a dead end. If the road ended at some isolated farmstead, he decided not to backtrack but to strike out northwest through the woods instead. Eventually, he would have to come to the Selma-Birmingham road. Only a few miles after crossing a small river, he intersected another road running in a northeast-southwest direction.

The northeast road, unless it curved, would take him in the general direction of home, but these small back roads were badly rutted and hard to travel. Will decided to take the southwest direction. Surely it would lead him to the main road he wanted to be on. He had every intention of avoiding Selma, that being where the main body of Union cavalry was located, but he wanted to get to a better road where he could travel faster.. After crossing the same small river once more, but at a different location, he traveled only a few miles before he came to the road that he was looking for. He headed north once more.

Will figured he had gone only about twenty-five miles since leaving the cabin, but he and the horses were tired. They all had done nothing for at least a week, except eat and sleep. There were only two choices: take a nap or fall out of the saddle. There was no way he could stay alert in this condition. He took the horses about two hundred yards into the woods and tied them to a bush. He loosened the cinches but left the saddles in place. Rolling himself in a blanket and placing the rifle at his side, he was soon fast asleep.

After about two hours Will awoke, and since it was still dark, he decided to put a few more miles behind him. After riding a short time, he topped a rise and could barely distinguish in the distance a small cluster of buildings. As he drew closer he could see that one was a general store and directly across the road was a livery stable. The other two buildings appeared to be dwellings.

Not wanting to be seen on the road after daylight, he would buy a few food staples and then find a place to sleep for the day. There was smoke coming from the back of the store, so someone must be up and about. He hoped the store would be open this time of the morning; he needed to get his business over with quickly.

Dawn couldn't be far away. Dismounting and tying the horses to the hitching post, he knocked on the door.

A very large woman—not obese, but tall and heavy--wearing an apron and carrying a large butcher knife, cautiously opened the door enough to peer outside. She looked Will over from head to foot and then took a step backward. Putting her flour-covered fists on her hips, she asked, "Are you a customer or do you just like bothering people in the middle of the night?"

Will smiled with the left side of his mouth. He knew it couldn't be long until dawn; it was already getting lighter. "I apologize, ma'am. I can wait until later if you'd like. What time does the store open? I need a few supplies."

"Nonsense! You are here now, are you not? You might as well come on in. I am cooking breakfast if you wish to eat with us. My husband iss in the back. We live here in the store. It is more convenient that way. Sit yourself down here in front of the window. I will go light for you a coal oil lamp. Be sure to keep an eye on your horses. There haf been some unsavory characters hanging around the last two days. I will be back in a moment."

Will shook his head and smiled. This was a no-nonsense woman to be sure. The clipped sentences made her sound foreign, and he thought that he could detect a slight accent as well. While he waited, he scanned the large room. There were shelves--mostly empty--along the walls, a short counter by the door, and barrels and baskets--also mostly empty—in neat rows across the floor. There was a lone double-barreled shotgun leaning against the wall beside the door leading to the back room. From the looks of it, the store had seen more prosperous days.

When the woman returned with the lamp, she introduced herself. "My name iss Gretchen Barger. My husband iss Hans. Breakfast will be ready shortly. If you wish to wash your hands there iss a water pump around back."

"Glad to meet you ma'am. I'm Will Stanton."

"How do you do, Will Stanton? I will be back with a plate of food in just a minute. You will eat what Hans and I eat; there is nothing else."

"I'm sure everything will be to my liking ma'am."

Will went to the pump and worked the handle twice. Before the water stopped flowing, he washed his face and hands. He was surprised to find a fresh towel hanging by the pump. He gingerly dried his face--there was still a lot of soreness around the wound.

Back inside, Will met Gretchen and a man, whom Will took to be Hans, coming from the kitchen into the dining area. The man was big, but Gretchen was even bigger. After an introduction and a handshake, they sat down to eat. Will picked up his fork and was about to dig in, when he was stopped by the sound of Hans saying grace. He silently laid the fork down and bowed his head. In the past four years of living among coarse soldiers, he had forgotten how decent people lived. Even though faith meant little to him personally, he respected the beliefs of others.

They were having eggs, bacon, grits, and pancakes with honey. Will thought the meal tasted heavenly--the best he had had in many months--and told Gretchen so. She blushed like a schoolgirl.

Will was self-conscious about the wound on his face, but neither Gretchen nor Hans seemed to even notice it. With the slash in his hat brim in alignment with the wound and the stains on his uniform, it probably wasn't hard to figure out what had happened. A soldier with a wound was nothing out of the ordinary.

It was coming on to full daylight by the time they were finished eating, and Will was anxious to be on his way, but he had to have a few supplies. As he looked out the window, he noticed a man walking around his horses and paying especial attention to his gray. He stood up and started toward the door when Gretchen said, "That iss one of the men I haf told you about, Will

Stanton. The other two are standing in the livery stable door. They are bad men to be sure. Because of them, Hans has been keeping the shotgun close at hand. Be careful Will Stanton. I do not like these men at all."

Will went quietly outside and walked up behind the man who was bent over rubbing the gray's left front leg. "You lose something, Mister?" Will asked in a flat voice.

The man slowly straightened, showing no surprise that Will was behind him. He was extremely dirty, and the stench of his unwashed body was almost stomach wrenching. When he grinned at Will he showed a mouth full of rotting teeth, and his beard was stained at both corners of his mouth with tobacco juice.

"Nope, I ain't lost nothin'; I'm jist admirin' this here gray. Had me one jist like him onct. Best horse I ever had. I'm gonna buy this here 'un off of ye."

"This horse is not for sale," said Will, firmly, hoping the man would go away but knowing better.

"Reb, I do believe ye've been standin' too close to them cannons. I didn't ask ye if 'at horse was fer sale, now, did I? I said I'm gonna buy 'im off of ye."

"Fellow, I'm only going to say this one more time--the horse is not for sale. Now, you'd best take some good advice and move on while you're still able," Will said, with his hand hovering over his revolver.

The man casually looked down at a dung beetle struggling with a ball of horse manure, and, working up a mouthful of saliva, spat at the beetle. His aim was perfect. The beetle was knocked onto its back, legs thrashing. Righting itself, it scurried away, forgetting about the object of its labor.

"Awright, Johnny, I'm goin', but ye can bet I'll be seein' ye agin 'bout the horse," he drawled, grinning out of one side of his mouth, while working at the quid of tobacco with his tongue..

Will watched the man cross the road and join the other two men, who looked like copies of the first. He could imagine the stink of the three of them together. The first man said something to the other two, and all three looked at Will and laughed. He had a feeling that he hadn't seen the last of these men.

Will stepped through the open door and found Hans holding the shotgun. As he put the gun away Hans said, "Come, let us haf some coffee. Of course it iss not real coffee, but it iss hot." Gretchen placed three cups of what proved to be parched acorns on the table. It was hot.

"Are you on your way home, Will Stanton, now that the war iss over?" asked Gretchen.

Will almost dropped the cup! He hoped the Bargers hadn't noticed. "Uh, yes... yes. I'm on my way home. It seems strange to be going home to stay, after being away for so long." He was making conversation to give himself time to think. The war was over? "Do you have a newspaper?" asked Will. " I haven't read one in weeks." Could the war actually be over? He couldn't believe it! The war was finally over! But how could he have known? He hadn't talked to anyone in over a week. He didn't even know for sure what day it was. He needed information without letting these nice people know why he was so ignorant of recent events. He certainly didn't want to try to explain why he had been hiding out for the last week.

"Yes," said Hans. " We haf yesterday's paper from Montgomery. We did not get it until late yesterday afternoon. I will find it for you."

The front page was covered with news about Lee's surrender on April 9. The paper was dated April 10, so today had to be April 11. He quickly scanned the columns, finally finding what he was looking for: the terms of surrender. All public property was to be turned over to the U.S. Army--battle flags, guns, muskets, wagons, everything. Officers might keep their side arms and horses, but the

Confederate army and everything it owned was to go out of existence. Every enlisted man that wanted one was to be given a horse
or mule to work on his farm. That meant the Spencer rifle and the
extra horses could potentially pose a problem. He could continue to
travel at night or get other clothes and pretend to be a civilian. What
was he thinking? With a face like his, he would look like a civilian?
Besides, where would he get enough money to buy clothes?

No! He would discard the two extra saddles--it would draw
attention having two saddled horses without riders--but he was
keeping everything else. The way he looked at it, Buck's horse
belonged to Maggie; the other one he would make use of as a
packhorse. The rifle he would keep wrapped in a bedroll. There
must be thousands of other soldiers on their way home--one more
shouldn't draw too much attention. He would just have to stay alert
and avoid all Union soldiers.

"Thank you. What do you have in the way of traveling food,"
asked Will, as he handed the paper back to Hans.

"Nearly everything iss scarce these days. Most of what we haf,
we kept hidden from the Union army. I can let you haf a small slab of
bacon, some potatoes, a pone of cornbread my wife baked yesterday,
and some eggs. Gretchen will boil the eggs for you if you wish."

"That will be fine, thank you. What do I owe you?"

"You do not owe us anything. Gretchen and I want to do this
for you."

"All right, but I'm going to have to discard two saddles," said
Will. "I want you to take them and sell them for whatever you can
get out of them. That should be more than enough to cover the
cost of what I'm taking."

"If that iss what you wish," said Hans, as they shook hands.

It took Will a few minutes to put the saddles in a shed around
back, and when he returned to the front, Gretchen had his food
bagged and ready to go.

"How far must you travel to get to your home?" asked Hans.

"I don't know exactly. Probably two hundred or more miles. My home is in Tennessee."

"Promise me you will be careful, Will Stanton. Those bad men are watching you. If they follow you, then they mean to do you harm," cautioned Gretchen as she hugged him. "You would be welcome to stay with us until these men go away."

"Thank you for the offer, but if I let every stranger slow me down, I'll never get home. Gretchen, Hans, I don't know why you've been so nice to me, but from the bottom of my heart, I appreciate it. I'll tell you something. If those men follow me and try to do me harm, their horses might just happen to come back this way without riders. If they do, keep the horses or sell them if nobody claims them after a few days." With that, Will smiled, tipped his hat to them, and headed north once again.

They stood and watched until Will rode out of sight, then Hans said, "Gretchen? Does this Will Stanton remind you of someone? To me it seemed as if our Erwin was back with us for a while, God rest his soul. Gretchen… we haf been trying to come up with a name for this community, other than Barger's Store. What do you think of Stanton as a name?"

Gretchen pursed her lips and nodded her head. "Why not? I like the sound of it."

As they turned to go inside, they saw the three men across the road mount their horses and ride north. They stopped and watched the men as they rode by. "If those awful men try to harm Will Stanton, I hope the good Lord strikes them down without mercy," said Gretchen. "Let us go right now and pray for him, Hans. I feel that he will need the Lord's protection."

"Yes, Gretchen, we will pray for Will, but I haf a feeling that those men are the ones that need the Lord's protection," said Hans, nodding his head sagely as the three men rode out of sight.

VI

As soon as Will was out of sight of the buildings, he urged his horses into a gallop. He kept this pace until he came to the end of a long stretch of straight road. Stopping on a slight rise, he looked back; no one was in sight. Good, then no one would see him leaving the road. If the three men followed and tracked him into the woods, then they would have to be looking for trouble. He rode about two hundred yards into the forest and tied the horses to a sapling. Then, taking the Spencer and checking the chamber, he walked back to within sight of the road and sat down on a log to wait.

Being more of a guerrilla fighter than regular cavalry these past years had given Will a lot of experience at ambush and surprise tactics. He would much rather ride on in peace than to confront these men, but his instinct told him that this was not to be. To face them now under conditions that he controlled would be much better than taking a chance later of letting them get the upper hand. If these men wanted trouble, he would try his level best to give them more than they had bargained for. There were too many people in this world, such as the men he was now waiting for, who would rather take what they wanted than to work for it honestly. Well, let them try. He didn't have much, but what he had, he intended to keep—or die trying.

In a few minutes three horses went by at a gallop. They shouldn't go far before seeing that his trail had ended. Will got up from the log and walked back to where he could see his own horses. A few feet to the right stood a huge oak almost four feet in diameter. Will positioned himself behind the tree and waited. The oak would be to the right of the three men if they followed his tracks into the woods, making it more difficult for them to aim at him, presuming of course that they were all right handed.

He didn't have long to wait. Seeing that the tracks that they had been following were no longer in the road, the three riders had backtracked and found where Will had gone into the woods. They made their way cautiously into the woods looking right and left.

Will had removed his hat and was peeking around the tree with one eye. He kept the tree between himself and the riders, being careful not to rustle the leaves or snap a twig with his feet as he moved. He could see that they were all armed with double-barreled shotguns, a very effective weapon at close range, especially if they were loaded with buckshot. They were riding abreast and very closely spaced, making it more difficult for them to maneuver, which was to their disadvantage. Just as the men came even with the tree, they saw Will's horses only fifty yards ahead. The one on the right motioned to stop. They were so close that Will hoped their horses wouldn't hear his wildly beating heart. Will stepped out from behind the tree, putting him directly behind the apparent leader of the group.

"You gents looking for me?" Will asked, aiming the Spencer at the man on the right--the one he had confronted at Barger's store.

"Git 'im boys," the man said as he jerked his horse's head violently to the left, almost unseating the rider in the middle.

Will fired, hitting the man in the left side, the bullet angling upward into his chest. By convulsive action, the man fired one barrel of his shotgun, barely missing the man in the middle. Working the lever to chamber another round, Will fired into the man on the

42

left, knocking him out of the saddle. The man in the middle had righted himself enough to succeeded in turning his mount and was bringing his gun to bear on Will. Taking a quick step to the right Will fired, hearing the man make a sound as if the breath had been knocked out of him. Then he ducked behind the oak, just as a load of buckshot tore bark from the tree only inches behind him. The man had been hit in the stomach, but he was still able to fight. Will sidestepped to the right from behind the tree and fired without aiming, and in one motion, stepped back behind the tree. Just as he had planned, the man also fired, cutting the air where Will had been only a split second before.

Will heard the shotgun hit the ground. "You got me Reb... my gun's empty...you might as well finish me off."

Will peeked around the tree to see if the man had another weapon, then stepped out with his rifle at the ready. "Get down off the horse," ordered Will, having no sympathy at all for the wounded man.

The man was leaning forward and holding his stomach with both hands. He took hold of the saddle horn and dragged his right foot over the horse's rump. This made the horse start, throwing the man to the ground where he landed hard on his back. He stayed in the position he had fallen, holding his stomach and slowly wagging his head from side to side. "I'm shot...real bad, Reb. Do me a favor...and finish me off... will ya?"

"Not until you tell me something first. Why did you follow me? Why did you want to kill me?" asked Will, sure that he already knew the answer.

"Look, it weren't...nothin' personal, Reb...me and my brothers...we been takin'... what we wanted...ever since the war started. We wanted your guns...and horses...and money... if you had any. We never figured... one man...would be any problem. Looks like...we was wrong. You got any water, Reb?"

Will went for his canteen, but when he returned, the man was dead. He went through all their pockets and saddlebags, finding nothing worth keeping except a few coins. They couldn't have bought a horse even if they had wanted to. Taking two of the shotguns and tying them to the men's saddles (keeping one--with shot, wads, and powder--for himself) and leading the horses to the road, Will headed them back the way they had come. Maybe they would go back to the livery stable--the last place they had stayed. If Hans and Gretchen saw the three horses, they would know what had happened. He left the bodies of the three men where they had fallen, if no one found them, the buzzards would take care of them. He felt no obligation to do anything with them; they should have left him alone. Walking back into the woods, he recovered his hat and horses and once again resumed his journey toward the north.

The next town was Clanton, the seat of Chilton County. Will rode through the tiny crossroads community barely giving it a cursory glance. He stopped a few miles north of town to make camp on a small tributary of the Coosa River. Having had only two hours of sleep since leaving the log cabin, he was more than ready for a rest. After the several days of recuperation at the cabin doing no strenuous activity at all, Will's muscles were trending toward softness. Even sitting in the saddle all day, something routine only a short time ago, had completely fatigued him. He was so tired his mind would hardly function. To take the time to build a fire and cook a meal wasn't an option, even though there was time enough before nightfall. His supper was a half a dozen boiled eggs and cornbread washed down with water.

He had kept the extra bedrolls when he left the saddles with Hans. They made his bed a little bit softer. He placed the blankets in an open space between two small trees that was clear of sticks, stones, and undergrowth, inadvertently tearing down a spider web in the process. Sleep overcame his weary body long before the events of the day could be fully recounted in his mind. He spent the night in dreamless sleep.

Bright sunshine on his face brought Will slowly to consciousness the next morning. He couldn't remember the last time he had slept this late. As the fog of sleep slowly lifted from his mind, he noticed that a large yellow and black spider had rebuilt the web he had torn down the evening before. The web was above his midsection between him and the sun. A heavy dew had fallen, making everything including his blankets feel damp. Droplets of dew clinging to the spider web sparkled like many tiny diamonds in the sunlight. The intricate design of the web, as well as the sunlight refracted into rainbow colors in the tiny dew droplets, was really quite beautiful.

Stupid spider! Will felt around until he found a stick with which to tear down the web. As he brought the stick back over his head intending to strike the spider and destroy the web at the same time, he realized that he would be undoing in one second what had taken the spider hours to build. Have I become so callous that I can destroy life so easily? Haven't I seen enough death and destruction to last a lifetime? That spider wants to live just like every other creature. Having had a change of heart, he put the stick down and slid backward out of the blankets. Walking around the spider web, he pulled the blankets from between the two trees and draped them over a bush to dry while he prepared breakfast.

Building a fire near the damp blankets, Will fried bacon and most of the potatoes. The other potatoes he would keep until later, as he didn't want to take the time to prepare them at the present. The morning was wearing away, and he wanted to be on the road headed north. As he saddled his horse, he glanced toward the spider web. The dew had evaporated, and the spider was still waiting patiently for a meal. Will gave the spider a mocking farewell salute, but in his heart he actually felt better for having let the creature live.

The day was peaceful and quiet as the miles rolled away behind. The aches from yesterday's riding were slowly being worked from his body by the motions of the horse. Then, late in the afternoon he heard the rumble of thunder to the southwest. Since the wind was coming from that direction, he began looking for some kind of shelter. Finding none, he continued to ride. The sky darkened until a pall was cast over the whole landscape, making the lightening that was striking all around especially bright. The boom and rumble of thunder was an almost continuous sound. The very ground seemed to vibrate, making his normally docile horse jittery. Will patted and rubbed the horse's neck to keep him calm.

The full force of the storm soon caught up with Will, and the wind was blowing so hard that the rain was coming almost horizontally. He had donned his oilskin in preparation for the storm, but the rain was blowing in around his collar. He had pulled his hat down as low as possible, but still, after a time, he was soaked to the skin. The temperature had dropped several degrees, and with the wind and wet clothes, he was shivering by the time the storm finally passed.

Will rode into the woods a few hundred yards and chose a campsite on a slight rise near a small creek. Before unsaddling the horses, he looked in the saddlebags for a match. He found two, but both of them were too damp to strike. Well, there was another way to get a fire started, and he had to have a fire. He searched until he found a piece of pine, rich with rosin. With his knife he cut away the wet outside, then whittled his hat full of shavings from the dry inside of the stick. Then, he gathered an armful of small dead twigs from cedar trees and yet another armful of bigger wood.

Going back to the saddlebags, he got a piece of greasy cloth that had once been wrapped around the slab of bacon. Next, he took a powder flask and poured about a tablespoon of powder on the cloth and worked the powder into the grease. Next, using the knife, he pried the bullet from a Spencer cartridge; he replaced the bullet with a small piece of powder-impregnated cloth tamped in over the powder left in the cartridge. Using the shotgun ramrod, Will pushed the larger piece of cloth into the barrel of the rifle until it contacted the empty cartridge. Then, placing the muzzle close to the ground, he pulled the trigger.

The cloth was afire! Adding shavings, then twigs, he soon had a small fire going. Adding more wood, he had a roaring fire in no time. At first he stood so close to the fire that his clothes appeared to be smoking. He had to pull his wet pants legs away from his skin to keep from being scalded. After he was finally dry and warm again, he finished preparing his camp for the night. Will placed several potatoes in the hot ashes of the campfire to be left overnight. After finishing the eggs and cornbread that Gretchen had packed, he placed the oilskin under his blankets and was soon fast asleep.

Each evening Will tried to find a spot where the horses could eat their fill, but this wasn't always possible, so in Pell City he bought as much hay as the horses could eat.

Will took a left hand turn near Gadsden to cross the southern portion of Sand Mountain on the way to Guntersville. Before he reached the ridge of the mountain he rounded a sharp turn in the narrow road and came face to face with a small Union patrol. There were five soldiers strung out in a line, one behind the other, but upon seeing Will, they quickly bunched into a group in order to block the road.

Will had known since reading the terms of surrender at Barger's store that having three horses could possibly lead to trouble, but he had hoped to avoid all patrols. If he had seen these men in time, he would have ridden into the woods and let them pass, but the meeting had been so sudden that he had had no chance to do anything at all. His horse was almost nose-to-nose with the leader of the group, a burly sergeant, who looked very unfriendly. The Spencer rifle was wrapped in his bedroll out of sight and out of reach. One revolver was stored in a saddlebag; the other was in its holster under his tunic.

The sergeant urged his horse a couple of steps forward toward Will's right, and a private did the same on the left, effectively hemming Will's horse. The only way open was to the rear, but it was useless to try to back the gray; the soldiers would simply follow.

"Where you going with all them animals, Johnny Boy?" the sergeant said, with a sneer.

"The war's over. I'm going home, if you'll get out of my way," said Will.

"Well, now, you men hear that? This horse thief here must not know he's a loser. Talks like he ain't never been whipped, don't he? I say we give him a little taste of defeat. What do you fellows say, huh? De feet. Get it? De feet."

The other soldiers laughed their appreciation of the pun. Will knew that if these soldiers got their hands on him he would be a dead man. He had to make a move, no matter how desperate, and do it soon.

When the sergeant turned to grin at his men, Will slipped the knot that held the pack horses, slammed his heels into the ribs of the gray, and at the same time drew the revolver from under his coat. As the gray slammed into the sergeant's horse, Will put a ball through the man's sternum at point blank range. He fired another round into the face of the next man in line and immediately turned his mount to face the remaining three soldiers who were busy trying to get control of their excited horses and draw their weapons at the same time. Will shot another man from the saddle, and was lining up his fourth target when a bullet tugged at his sleeve, burning a path across the inside of his left arm. Will's bullet took the shooter in the throat, toppling him to the ground.

The last of the soldiers was hightailing it around the curve in the direction Will had come from. Will fired a quick shot at the fleeing man, but the bullet went wide. There were still many miles to travel before Will reached home. He couldn't afford to let the only witness that knew his description get away. Urging the gray into an all out run he sped after the fleeing Yankee, who by this time had at least a hundred yards lead. The gray had cut the lead by a quarter before Will managed to work the Spencer from the bedroll. He levered a round into the chamber and waited until there was a long straight in the road ahead before bringing the gray to a skidding halt. Hurriedly dismounting and going to one knee, he took aim at a point between the retreating man's shoulders and squeezed the trigger. When the smoke cleared enough to see, the horse, with an empty saddle, was slowing to a trot.

Will assured himself that the man was beyond talking before riding back to check on the others. That he had shot the soldier in the back bothered him not at all. He felt it was a necessity and let it go at that. When he came to the sergeant, he gave the body a hard kick in the ribs, saying through gritted teeth: "A little taste of de feet, sergeant."

Will immediately rode into the woods and took a generally parallel course with the road for at least five miles before making a fireless camp. Even though it was early afternoon, he would try to sleep for a while before moving on. Instead of continuing on to Guntersville, he now intended to travel north along the top of Sand Mountain to its end, and only at night. That way he could avoid the concentration of soldiers at Stevenson, and also, the mountain would be sparsely populated, lessening the chance of any more encounters with Union patrols.

When Will reached the northern end of the mountain, he descended by a steep narrow trail down Scratch Ankle Hollow to the railroad above Running Water Creek. Making his way westward around the mountain until he could look down on the Tennessee River, he sat down and waited. When it became light enough to see clearly, he checked the site of the Rankin Cove ferry. As he expected, there were several blue uniformed soldiers milling around.

Will continued along the railroad bed until it neared the river south of the ferry. As cold as the water must be this time of the year, he was going to have to swim the river. Gathering three small logs about three feet long, he lashed them together with rope to make a small raft. Shucking his boots and clothes, he piled them on the raft, along with his revolvers, rifle, and saddlebags.

He waded into the water up to his thighs, stopping to tie the raft lead rope around his waist. The raft swung slowly downstream, creating a drag that Will thought was manageable. The horses reluctantly followed him into deeper water. When the water became deep enough for the animals to swim, Will held onto the pommel of the saddle, holding the reins tight to keep the gray horse from turning back toward the bank.

By the time they were half way across the river, Will began to wander if he would be able to make it to the other side. The tug of the raft seemed to have gotten stronger, threatening to separate him from his horse. His grip weakening by the minute, Will knew he had to do something or drown. He was already too weak to pull his body across the saddle. Crooking his right elbow around the pommel, he wrapped the reins tightly around his arm and the pommel, securing himself to the saddle. He pulled the raft in close enough to support part of his weight on his left arm.

Will closed his eyes, he thought for only a moment, but his next conscious memory was of his horse's hooves striking solid ground. As the horse struggled for firm footing on the muddy slope of the shore, Will tried to stand, but his legs wouldn't respond. He realized even in his stupor that he couldn't remain hanging from the saddle for fear the horse would step on his dragging feet. The other two horses were clamoring for firm footing, making the gray horse unmanageable. Fumbling with stiff fingers, he somehow managed to unwind the bindings from his right arm. Without the support of the saddle horn, Will plopped onto the narrow beach, with his feet still in the cold water. He was barely able to drag his body by his elbows far enough to clear the water before he lost consciousness.

Luckily, the warmth of the sand and sun together brought sensation back to his body before his exposed skin burned. His teeth were chattering uncontrollably as he pulled the raft onto the narrow shore. After many fumbling attempts Will was able to dress himself. He walked, stumbling, up and down the beach until he developed enough control over his muscles to mount his horse, but he was so completely fatigued that he didn't know whether or not he could remain in the saddle.

A short distance away, Will could see a ridge covered with cedars. He made his way into the trees just far enough for conceal-ment, tied the lead horse to a tree, rolled himself in a blanket, and was instantly asleep.

The next morning he woke feeling surprisingly refreshed and ready to ride, with no obvious ill effects from the previous day. Before he rode away, he looked across the river at the place he had entered the water. He was surprised at the distance he had been washed downstream. The river didn't look that swift.

The horses badly needed something to eat, but surely they could make it another dozen miles.

Will had been in the saddle ten or more hours each day and averaged about forty miles per day, except for the delay at the river, so in the early afternoon on the sixth day after leaving the little cabin in Alabama, he rode past the Cheekville courthouse. His mind turned to his own home only two more miles up the road. He didn't know what to expect at the cabin. What if someone had moved in without permission after Ginny had died? It might not be prudent to ride in unprepared.

As the cabin came into sight, he felt no elation at being home again. In fact, there was a feeling of dread, knowing that Ginny would not be there to greet him. As he dismounted, a large brown dog came slinking around the corner of the cabin, with head lowered and fangs bared, growling threateningly at Will. Without any conscious thought, Will drew his revolver and aimed at the big dog. "Rex? Is that you boy?" The big dog stopped growling, but he was still wary. He didn't recognize this stranger, even though the man knew his name. "You were just a big puppy the last time I saw you, boy. Come here. Come on. Come on, boy." The dog cautiously came closer, half-heartedly wagging his tail. When he got Will's scent, he was overcome with joy. He almost bowled Will over when he put his paws on his chest and began to lick his face. Will had to laugh at the dog's exuberance. He could hardly reholster his gun since he needed both hands to fend off the dog.

The door of the cabin opened and Henry Thompson stepped outside. "What's agoin' on out here? Rex, what's the matter with you?" When Henry recognized Will, he became almost as excited as the dog. "Will Stanton! We've been expectin' you, Will, now that the war is over!" exclaimed Henry as he pumped Wills hand. "I've been stayin' in your cabin since Ginny...well, you know. We--my family and me--didn't want nobody botherin' your stuff, you know.

"Thanks, Henry, I appreciate your concern. Thank you, too, for taking care of the dog. He seems to be in pretty good shape.

"To tell you the truth, Will, ain't nobody takes care of that dog; he takes care of hisself. He was Ginny's dog--real devoted to her--and when she, uh, you know.

"Died, Henry. Ginny died," said Will.

"Yeah. Well, with Ginny gone, that dog never took up with nobody else. He's shore enough glad to see you, though. Don't see how that dog could recollect you. You was here only a few days, and he was just a pup then, you know."

"Yeah, but he did follow me everywhere I went the whole time I was here. He must have imprinted on me," Will ventured.

"Well, He's yore dog, now. That's for shore. Won't have much to do with any of us. He just sort of tolerates us. Say, Will, let me help you with the horses, then we'll mosey on over to the house. Ma oughta have dinner ready about now, and I know Ma and Pa will be glad to see you."

"We can put the roan packhorse in the corral, but I'm going to need the other two later on. All of them could use of some hay, though. Your mother still know how to cook?" Will asked, teasingly.

"When you take a gander at Pa, you'll know the answer to that," said Henry.

"I take it that Jed hasn't slimmed down much then," said Will, laughing.

"Not so much that you'd notice."

Henry had grown into a stocky man, but Jed Thompson, as Will well remembered, was fat--very fat.

"I'll be with you shortly, Henry, I want to visit Ginny's grave for a few minutes."

"Shucks, Will, you'd think I would o' knowed that. Sorry."

As Henry took the packhorse to the corral, Will walked toward the wooded ridge behind the cabin. A clump of short, blue flowers were growing by the wayside. Using a stick, he dug the flowers up by the roots. Though he hadn't been told, Will knew exactly where Ginny was buried. They had sometimes sat on the exposed root of a giant oak in the cool of the evening and talked about how beautiful the view was from the ridge. He would have built the cabin on that very spot if it hadn't been so far from the spring.

Will found the gravesite without any trouble; the red clay soil heaped over the grave drew him like a beacon. He planted the flowers by the unmarked headstone that someone had placed at the western end of the mound.

He stood silently for several minutes staring at the mound of earth, yet not actually seeing it. Finally, he knelt beside the grave and began to tell Ginny how sorry he was about not being with her when she needed him the most. He told her about Buck and his whole command being killed and how it was his decision to attack the foraging party, taking all the blame for what had happened upon himself. He had been wounded, he explained to her, but he probably had deserved to die along with the rest of his men. He poured his heart out, but after his confession, he didn't feel one bit better. He still felt sadly burdened and completely alone in the world.

Crossing the spring branch Will arrived at the kitchen door just as Jed was sitting down at the dinner table. And just as Henry had stated, Jed and Henrietta were very happy to see him. They all talked as they ate, and afterward, as they sipped hot parched-corn coffee—real coffee being almost nonexistent in the South--the whole family, except Gabriel, the baby, swamped Will with questions. They asked him about everything except the wound on his face. Will knew they were being tactful, because the scar had to be the most noticeable thing about him at the present. They were very sorry to hear about Buck Smith, and they didn't envy Will for having to carry the news to Buck's widow. At four o'clock Will had to beg away; he had the dreaded task to do before the day ended.

He thanked Jed and Henrietta for the meal, walked back to his cabin, and went inside. He stood in the middle of the living room and looked all around, as if this were the first time he had ever seen it, then he did the same in the bedroom. Without Ginny he felt like a stranger here; he felt no attachment to the cabin at all. He went outside, mounted his horse, and headed for Hicks Chapel on the other side of the Sequatchie River. Rex trotted along in front sniffing at every briar patch and clump of bushes.

VII

When Will rode into Maggie Smith's yard, she was using a shovel to break up the sod in her garden plot, making ready to do the spring planting. She dropped her shovel and walked to where Will was standing, holding his horse's reins and looking like a shy schoolboy.

"He isn't coming back is he Will?" said Maggie, without so much as a how-do-you-do and showing no emotion at all.

"No, Maggie, he's not coming back," said Will, just as flatly.

Maggie covered her face with both hands, and Will thought that she was about to break into sobs. He put his hands on her shoulders and drew her close to his chest, but when she removed her hands from her face, there were no sign of tears. She looked him in the eyes, and then, slowly, her gaze followed the line of the scar across his face.

Will self-consciously turned his face away.

"Were you with him when it happened, Will?"

"Yes, and if it's any consolation, Maggie, he didn't suffer," Will said, as he released her.

"Yes… yes, Will, that's good to know. Did he have a decent burial?

"I buried him myself," said Will, not going into any detail. She probably wouldn't have approved of his method.

"Is that when... you got your face cut?"

Will's right hand came automatically to his cheek to touch the wound. "Yeah, it was the same battle."

"Where did it happen? Not that I would ever get to go there, mind you, but I would like to know."

"It was about twenty miles east of Selma, Alabama, one week to the day before the war ended. That somehow seems to make it worse, being so close to the end, I mean. I brought his horse and his guns back. I thought you could maybe use the horse for plowing. That's all there was that was worth anything--except for his saddle. I had to leave it behind."

"That was kind of you, Will, to bring them so far. A horse will be a whole lot better and faster than that shovel, that's for sure. So, he's been gone only about two weeks. You may not believe this, Will, but I knew in my heart that this was the way it would turn out. I've been expecting to get word of Lamar's death for weeks. Don't ask me how I knew; I just did. Come, have a seat on the porch while I get us some buttermilk." Will was glad to see her walk away. He felt much more comfortable with some space between them.

So far Maggie had shown no signs of grief, but then, she always had been a strong woman. Being Buck's best friend, Will knew that she and Buck had been devoted to one another, making it harder to understand her attitude. Yet, he hadn't shown any outward grief himself when he had gotten the news about Ginny, even though, at the time, he had been torn apart inside. But then, he had to put on a front because of his men.

It could be that Maggie had gotten used to Buck being away from home these past four years. If Buck had been in her presence when he had died, her reaction might have been different; the sense of loss would have been more acute. From the way things had shaped up, he need not have dreaded bringing Maggie the news after all. She was taking it all so well--too well to suit Will.

At the very least, he had expected some kind of reaction to the news—a few tears maybe.

Maggie returned with two tall glasses of buttermilk and two wedges of cornbread. They ate in silence.

For some reason he couldn't define, Will felt very uncomfortable here alone with Maggie. He decided the best thing to do was to put even more distance between them. Standing up and handing her the empty glass, he said, "Thanks, Maggie, I'd best be going."

"You really don't have to rush off, Will. What are you going to do now? Now that Ginny is gone, I mean?"

"Up 'til a couple of hours ago, I really didn't know. There's no way that I can live in that cabin any more--too many memories. It doesn't even feel like home to me any more. I'm thinking seriously about going west. I've wanted to see the Rocky Mountains ever since I first saw a picture of them when I was still in school. I don't know what else to do. All I know is that I can't stay around here."

"I think I understand what you mean. If you...uh...If I were a man I'd go with you."

"Is there anything I can do for you before I go, Maggie?"

"No, you've done more than enough already, Will. You've provided me with the means to get out of debt at Griffith's store. I never did like being beholden to anyone. I'll keep one of the guns, though, just in case I might need it."

Will didn't have to ask if she knew how to load and shoot; he had seen her handle guns before. Maggie Smith was one of the most competent women he had ever known.

"Good-bye, Maggie, I hope the future is kinder to you than the past has been."

"'Bye, Will, and good luck. I'll ask God to watch over you."

That statement held no comfort for Will. He wasn't at all sure that God cared one way or the other what happened to him, or anybody else for that matter. He hadn't taken very good care of

Ginny and Buck or his men. In fact he hadn't seen much evidence that God even existed. If He really loved mankind, why did He permit the misery, pain, and cruelty that was so prevalent?

Will had had no choice but to attended church with his parents for the first eighteen years of his life. And later, he had attended willingly enough while he was courting Ginny, but there was no way he could be called a person of faith--too much had happened. His father had been a regular churchgoer, but judging from the tyrannical way John had ruled his family, Will wondered about his faith. In patriarch days, the man was lord of his household, but those days were far in the past. Maybe he was way off base, Will thought, but he had his own idea of how a believer should treat others, and it wasn't the way his dad had done.

Will made a detour on his way back to the cabin to visit Ginny's parents. Mrs. Morgan broke down and wept profusely at the sight of him, and Will had to struggle to keep his own composure. Carl maintained a stoic attitude, but Will could see unshed tears glistening in his eyes. They talked some, but without Ginny around they really didn't have much in common any more. Carl had aged mightily since Will had last seen him--no longer was he the lusty, out-spoken man of the pre-war years. He now seemed quite subdued—maybe, like Will himself, regretful, now that it was too late--for getting involved in the war in the first place. During their conversation, the war was never mentioned at all.

There was one small consolation that Will got from the visit: Mrs. Morgan had been with Ginny throughout the whole ordeal. Having a family member present to comfort Ginny during her travail seemed important to Will, especially since he wasn't there himself. The atmosphere at the Morgan home, at least for Will, was one of unpleasantness—a feeling that he really didn't fit in any more. He left at the earliest possible opportunity.

Will stopped at a secluded spot on the Sequatchie River and took a cold bath, his first since...he couldn't remember when, unless one counted the crossing of the Tennessee as a bath. He didn't have any soap, but using sand, he rubbed his skin until it was pink. His clothes would have to wait until later.

It was dusk when he got back to the cabin. He gave the horses some hay, and taking his blankets to the barn loft, he made his bed there. There was no way that he would even attempt to sleep in the cabin. In fact, sleep was a long time coming as it was. His mind just wouldn't let go of the memories of Ginny and Buck. It was still hard to realize that he would never see either of them again. He and Ginny would never again walk in the woods in the cool of the evening. Buck would never go hunting with him again or set another trap along the river. He had to get away from this place as soon as possible if he was ever to have peace of mind. When sleep finally came, so also came haunting dreams of the two people he had cared for the most.

Rex made his bed at the foot of the ladder; his master was never getting away from him again.

The next morning Will went to talk to Jed Thompson. "Jed, I've been doing some thinking, and I've decided to leave here and go west. I don't think I can ever be happy here again, so I'm going to give Henry the cabin, the land, everything. It won't be many years until he'll be getting married, I would think. With a house and land, he'll have a good head start on life. We'll need to draw up a bill of sale and get it notarized, and then you can get it registered later. You can hold everything in your name until Henry comes to legal age."

"What do you mean, Will, you're goin' west? You plannin' on leavin' for good?"

"Yeah, Jed, that's what I'm saying. So much has happened in my life that I'm not the same man I was four years ago, and there is nothing at all that can hold me here any more. Without Ginny the cabin just doesn't seem like home to me."

"I hate to see you go, Will, but if your mind is made up, I can't keep you here. Now, about your place, you've got way too much invested in it to just give it away. I can't pay you near what its worth, but I'll have to give you what I can, or I won't feel right about it. I've got a young thoroughbred bull that old Sam Pickens wants real bad. I bought that bull when he was just a little feller for almost nothin' after his momma died. Fed him milk from a homemade teat on a bucket. If you need the money today, I can send Henry to get it, and Sam can get the bull later. It'll just be a hunnert dollars, but it's the best I can do."

"I wasn't asking for anything at all, Jed, so a hundred dollars is fine. If you remember, that's exactly what I gave for the land in the first place. And yes, I would like to leave just as soon as possible; this place is not my home any more."

"I remember like it was yesterday when you first come here. You give a hunnert dollars for the land, but you got a lot of work tied up there, too. I can't begin to pay you for your time."

"I don't expect you to. I enjoyed the work, since it was my own place, but things are different now."

The war changed a lot of people, Will. It split some families right down the middle. In the Steve Layne family just south of Cheekville, two of his boys fit for the North and two fit for the South. It'll take years to heal some of the wounds—if at all. I'll go get Henry started right away. If you ain't got nothin' else to do, set yourself down on the porch here and we'll gab a while. I'll be right back."

"How did folks around here manage to hold onto their stock, Jed?" Will asked, after Jed had returned. " In Georgia, Alabama, West Tennessee, everywhere I have been, I know from experience that the Union boys took whatever they wanted. They just about turned northern Mississippi into a desert. People will never forget Sherman and his march to the sea, but he wasn't the only one to adopt a sack and pillage policy, in fact, he wasn't even the first. On my way home this past week, the desolation caused by the war could be seen everywhere. You wouldn't believe the number of burned houses I've seen, with their chimneys still standing like monuments to the destruction. Sherman's monuments, some people call them. Fields overgrown with saplings and briars are everywhere. I'd venture to say the innocent suffered the most. This area looks virtually untouched in comparison to some places I've seen."

"We have been blessed for sure. The way I figure it, since Union sympathy ran close to fifty percent here in the valley, the Feds didn't want to drive ever'body to the Southern cause, so they mostly left us alone. And besides that, most of the activity was over on the eastern side of the valley, that bein' where the main road to Chattanooga is. The supply depot they had at Stevenson, Alabama, had to help some too. Havin' supplies just thirty miles away probably helped keep them off us. But just in case, though, me and Henry had us a corral built up there on the mountainside where we kept most of our animals. We couldn't allow fresh tracks to be seen near the house; that would have been a dead giveaway. We did have a couple of pigs that disappeared, but overall we fared pretty good."

"There was some folks, though, that was knowed to be Confederate sympathizers that lost all their animals, down to the last chicken. Still, it's been rough on ever'body, since just about ever'thing is scarce. And of course, besides the soldiers, there was rabble on both sides that didn't care who they took from, or who they hurt."

"Yeah, I've had some experience with some of them," said Will, with the image of the three brothers still fresh in his mind.

"I tried to stay neutral as best I could," explained Jed. "It ain't always been easy, and some people don't like me to this day 'cause

I wouldn't declare either way, but I've got friends on both sides. I've been called a ridge runner, fence straddler, copperhead, and a bunch of other names that ain't nearly so nice. The first couple of years, I spent many a sleepless night on guard duty. I always kept my two double barrels loaded with buckshot within easy reach, even when I was out workin' in the fields. Never had to shoot nobody, but I come close enough to scare a few. After a while they left me alone altogether. Some folks, though, got burned out completely. Lots of barns was burned to the ground; wells was contaminated with coal oil; animals was shot. It was almost like a war within a war, but finally folks seemed to come to the conclusion it was better to live and let live. Feelin's still run pretty high, though. It ain't hard at all to git a good fist fight started if the right people git together."

"If the people who voted for secession could have looked into the future and seen all the destruction, this war might never have taken place," said Will. "But since we did have war, if the destruction hadn't been so complete, the South would still be strong enough to fight, and with a good chance of winning. There is no way of telling how long the war might have gone on. It's a little late to be saying this, but if I could back up four years, I would do whatever was necessary to stay out of the war altogether. If I could have seen the future, I would have left the country back then, just as I intend to do today."

"I personally know men who hid out under rock shelters on the sides of both of these here mountains to keep from bein' conscripted into the army on either side, North or South," said Jed.

"There was a time when I would have called such men cowards, but not any more. What has anyone gained by all the suffering and dying and destruction? Nothing, as far as I am concerned," said Will, sadly shaking his head. "It's all been a total waste."

"We didn't have a whole lot of fightin' around here," added Jed. "There was a Union wagon train destroyed straight across the valley yonder. It was loaded with supplies for the Union army at Chattanooga. We could hear the gunfire and see the smoke from the burnin' wagons, but the battle, such as it was, didn't have no effect on the folks on this side of the valley. The people over yonder around Hicks Chapel got a real boon from it, though. They carted off nearly ever'thing that didn't burn, and some folks that was gettin' pretty low on vittles had fresh mule meat for a while there. I been told it ain't half bad."

"I've had it myself, more than once," said Will, grinning. "It'll do when you're hungry, but I prefer beef. It's probably just the thought of it being mule meat that doesn't set too well with a man. There can't be anything wrong with it; a mule eats the same stuff a cow does, but it's sort of like eating a dog, I would guess. If you didn't know you were eating dog, you might think it was good."

"Probably. I heard tell about a few dogs disappearin', but not anywhere close by. They probably didn't get eat though, but like I said, some folks really had it rough. Thanks be to the good Lord, I managed to come through it all without too much trouble, but it'll be another year or two before things get close to resemblin' normal again. Ever'thing is still scarce around here. No doubt, though, it's the same ever'where else, too."

But, I was tellin' you about that wagon train that was destroyed over yonder. I give ever'thing a couple days to settle down, and then I took my wagon and rode over there to the battle site. Like you said, war sure is a waste. There was pieces of wagons, barrels, mule carcasses stinkin' to high heaven, just about ever'thing you can think of scattered around. I guess that train must have been over a mile long. I can only imagine what it looked like before people carried off most of it. I come back home with a couple of good kegs and enough wheels, axles, and boards to build another wagon. I figured I was just as entitled to have that stuff as anybody else."

Little Gabe came tottering outside and climbed onto his father's lap. "What do you think of my little man here, Will?"

"Looks to be a fine boy, but there's quite a spread of years between the little one and Henry. Almost like having a grandson, isn't it? What got into you after all these years, Jed? You and Henrietta have a second honeymoon?"

Jed laughed. "Naw. It's just that after so many years we thought we couldn't have any more kids. Then, surprise, surprise!" They both laughed, while little Gabe grinned and looked quizzically from one face to the other.

"Jed, I've got something to do before Henry gets back," said Will, as he got up to leave. "I'll stop by again later." Will was happy for Jed, but he wanted to get away from him and his son. If things had been different, he would now have a son of his own--just one more reason for quitting this place.

Will walked past his cabin and made his way to a small knoll overlooking the spring. At the very top of the knoll was a large hollow beech tree. He knelt at the foot of the tree, and reaching inside, began scooping the soft soil aside. After digging down about a foot, he uncovered a quart fruit jar. In the jar was his life's savings--money he had made trapping for furs when he had first come to the Sequatchie Valley.

He went to the cabin and poured the money, all gold and silver coins, onto the bed. There was three hundred and twenty-five dollars total, meaning that Ginny had spent only fifty dollars in all the time that he had been gone. She had planted vegetables every spring and canned produce in the fall, so she probably hadn't needed much money. He divided the coins into two equal piles, and wrapping them in two separate cloths, took them to the barn and put one bundle into each of his saddlebags. With the money that Henry would be bringing, he would be carrying what would amount to a year's wages for the average man.

Will walked up the mountainside and searched until he found a flat, smooth fieldstone that was big enough to shape into a grave marker. He had to stop and rest twice before he got back to the barn with the heavy stone. Taking a hammer and chisel, he chipped Ginny's name and dates into the stone. By the time he had the stone in place at the grave, it was almost noon.

Henry returned a little past midday, bringing Will five twenty-dollar gold pieces. Confederate money had been near worthless long before the war ended, greenbacks, gold, and silver were scarce, and so people who had hard money were very fortunate. Sam Pickens was considered a well-to-do man in these parts--he always seemed to have money no matter how hard times were--so these coins had probably been cached away for many years. Will looked at the dates on the coins. They were all more than a dozen years old.

After Will and Jed got all the legalities taken care of, there was nothing more to delay his departure. He visited Ginny's grave again to say goodbye for the last time. The blue flowers he had planted were doing well. Now all he had to do was pack his belongings, which would take only a few minutes, and be on his way.

Though his mind was made up to leave, he felt a sadness that he couldn't explain. He would be leaving behind everything that was familiar to him and heading into the unknown. It was just a little bit scary, but he had done the same thing once before, and he had been only eighteen at the time. His plans were no more definite now than they were then, and even as inexperienced as he had been at that time, he had survived, so he would make it now, for sure.

Although he and Ginny had planned to be buried together on the hill of red dirt, now that would never be. He probably would never see this part of the country again, and certainly no one would ever bring his bones back here for burial. He hoped that Ginny would understand and forgive him.

When he was all packed and ready to go, he mounted and rode into Jed Thompson's yard. Jed had been plowing, but at the moment he was in his favorite spot: the rocking chair on the porch.

"Been waitin' on you, Will. Henrietta's got everything ready to go on the table. You got to eat dinner with us before you leave."

"What do you think I stopped by for, Jed, to see your pretty face? I know about what time you folks eat. I would never pass up a meal that Henrietta had cooked. Let's go and wash up; I'm hungry." Will knew that it was well past the Thompson's usual meal time and that they had been waiting for him, but he was trying to keep the mood light by making jokes.

After the meal was over, good-byes were said all around, and Will mounted to leave. "Folks, I may never see any of you again, so I'm saying now that you've been the best of neighbors, and I hope all of you have the best of luck, always. I'm going to miss your cooking most of all, Henrietta. If I stayed around here for long, I'd be as big as Jed."

"Same to you, Will. It's not too late to change your mind about leavin', you know. I could let you stay in my cabin," said Henry, grinning from ear to ear.

"Thanks, Henry. I hope you'll be happy in the cabin, but leaving is something that I feel I have to do. I can't fully explain how I feel, but this place just doesn't seem like home any more." Then looking at the big dog, Will said, "You going with me, Rex?" The dog wagged his tail and barked once. When Will looked back, Henrietta was dabbing at her eyes with the corner of her apron. Will could hardly hold back his own tears.

Will rode to Griffith's store to get supplies, and while he was there, he decided to pay Maggie Smith's bill, which amounted to thirty-seven dollars and change. Besides, she would need the horse for plowing; the extra revolver she could sell. After loading the supplies on his packhorse, Will rode to Cheekville and turned his horse toward the steep road that wended its way up the side of the mountain. Near the top of the mountain the road had been changed some since the last time he and Buck had ridden this way on their last hunting trip. From the fresh look of the bank dug into the mountainside, this new addition had to have been made during the war years. This must be what Jed had referred to as Gray's road that wound its way through the coves and over the mountains to Sewanee. Will had already decided to take the less torturous northerly route through McMinnville.

When at last he topped the mountain, Will stopped and looked back at the beautiful valley, a place he had never dreamed of leaving until yesterday. There had been times when he and Buck, while out hunting, had admired the scenery from this very spot. Sometimes in the early morning, the sun would be shining brightly here at the top of the mountain, while in the valley, thick fog would have settled. The sun shining on the fog gave the appearance of a huge lake extending up and down the valley, as far as the eye could see. In Will's opinion, there could be no more beautiful scenery anywhere in the world. This late in the day, there was no fog, and he could pick out individual farmsteads interspersed with forest. He searched for the cabin he once called home, but it wasn't visible from this spot. He sat and looked for several minutes, as if to fix forever in his mind the details of the valley, then he reined his horse, almost violently, to the left and headed westward.

VIII

Warren Hathaway had written so much the previous night that he had developed writer's cramp, but he was very pleased with the way everything was going. He wished that he could write faster. It must be difficult for Billy to go so slow, but there was no help for it. However, he had developed his own personal type of shorthand. He had so many abbreviated words that no one other than himself could possibly make sense of his notes. Now, after a good night's rest and a hearty breakfast, he was eager to begin anew.

"Billy, did your dad ever tell you for sure why he felt he couldn't live around here any more? I don't mean just in the cabin. I'm referring to the general area. Or, is what you have told me your own opinion?"

"I don't recall that he ever spelled it out," said Billy, "but I've done my own surmising, and, in my opinion, as long as he was in familiar surroundings and could see familiar faces, he was reminded of everything in his life that made him sad. Without Ginny and Buck, he had no real ties to this area any more. Jed Thompson and his family came closer to being friends than anyone else did, I suppose, but they just couldn't take the place of a friend and companion such as Buck had been."

"Although my dad had been a loner much of his life, in time he could have made new friends and maybe even remarried, I'm sure, but he would have been constantly reminded of Ginny as long as he lived in the cabin. Of course he left before any change could take place in his life. I think he just wanted to get away from everything that held any kind of memory at all and completely isolate himself from the world. The guilt from not being there when Ginny most needed him was always present. I believe that he felt that only in completely new surroundings could he start a new life."

"The Rocky Mountains seemed to be the only place that had captured his imagination, so that is where he decided to go. At least he would be more isolated there and probably never meet anyone that he had ever seen before. Some people would probably say that he was a coward and trying to run away from his problems. I can't think of him in those terms. I have tried to picture myself in his position. He must have been a very lonely, confused, and frustrated man for a while there. I hope that I never have to experience anything like that."

"That pretty much mirrors my own thoughts on the subject," Warren said. "You told me once that your dad came from Knoxville, Billy; let's go back and pick up on his earlier years. You can start at any age you want," said Warren.

"Well, I suppose that my dad's early childhood would have been considered normal by most standards. He went to school; he went to church with his parents; he played with the neighborhood kids. As a child there were certain chores that were assigned to him around the house, but when he was twelve, his father said…"

IX

"Will, It's about time you stopped playing all the time and learned what it's like to work a little bit. You're not going to remain a child forever, so it's best that you get a taste of what grown-up life is going to be like. From now on you're going to the warehouse with me on Saturdays, and you'll sweep the floor and take out the trash and learn a little something about the business. There's more to life than playing games, and someday the business will be yours. I figure you're old enough to start learning something about it, don't you?"

"I guess so, sir," said Will, not really having any choice.

John Stanton owned a large warehouse on the bank of the Tennessee River. There were moorings for boats of all sizes and booms with block and tackle to facilitate the loading and unloading of heavy loads. John made money two ways: by transferring freight onto and from boats and by storing freight until someone claimed it. Years of heavy toil had made him into a bear of a man.

For the next two years, Will spent every Saturday at the warehouse, earning ten cents per day that he could spend on whatever he wanted. He saved the dimes toward the day when he would have enough money to buy a particular hunting knife that he had seen at the local hardware store. His dad would ask him sometimes what he had bought with his money. Usually, Will would say that he had bought candy, and John would frown and shake his head. John never said anything, but Will could tell that his dad disapproved. In fact he couldn't remember his dad approving anything he had ever done. John would probably have approved if he had saved the money to start a bank account. There was no way Will could let his dad know the truth about why he was saving the money. He would surely tell Will that twelve was just too young to have such a dangerous item as a hunting knife. To him candy would be the better investment. At least candy wasn't dangerous.

The chores that Will had to perform at the warehouse were so boring that his mind was usually any place other than on the job. One day toward the end of spring two men paddled up to the warehouse in a large flat-bottom boat that was loaded with bales of pelts. They had spent the previous fall and winter along the French Broad River hunting bear and trapping beaver in the Appalachian Mountains. They wanted to store the furs for a few days until a buyer came for them. Will was so absorbed by the stories that he overheard the men telling another client that he had ignored his chores. He had to rush to finish before the warehouse closed. His dad would have really ranted if he hadn't completed the sweeping.

That night--and many nights thereafter—Will's mind was filled with fantasies of bear hunting and trapping in the mountains. Since there wasn't much time to spend playing any more, Will's main pastime was to escape into a fantasy world that he had created in his own mind. There were times when his school homework suffered because of this fantasizing, but he would then study even harder to make up for the slack times.

On most Sunday afternoons while his dad was napping, Will spent all the available free time he could in the woods near his home. He found a rock outcropping with an overhang that created a cave large enough to accommodate his body with some room to spare. Here, Will would pretend to be an Indian or mountain man living in the wilderness. When he was finally able to buy the knife he wanted, he didn't dare take it home, for fear his father would find it. He wrapped it in an oily rag and kept it buried in the dry soil at the rear of the little cave until he wanted it again.

With the knife on his belt and a self-made bow and arrows in hand, Will stalked squirrels and birds in the woods. He was never successful in his hunting, but that mattered little. Pretending to be a hunter was satisfaction enough. The happiest hours of his life were spent alone in the woods beside the river in his own make believe world.

Will slowly turned into a loner who seldom had contact with the other boys in town. He loved slipping through the woods as silently as possible watching the animals at play, something that was impossible to do with others around. He would have enjoyed having a friend, but there was no one that he felt like sharing his secret world with. The other boys weren't interested in his silent world; they seemed much happier when playing with a ball and making lots of noise.

As time passed, Will withdrew farther and farther from his dad, seldom speaking even at mealtime. The warehouse was his father's favorite subject and dominated most of his conversations. Clare, his mother, tried to join in, but she knew little about the intricacies of the business. Will had nothing positive to add to the conversation, so he kept his mouth shut rather than risk making his father angry.

There was nothing in John Stanton's life that could be called a pastime or a hobby--no hunting, fishing, camping, anything. He went to church on Sunday morning, dozed or read the Bible Sunday afternoon, and worked at the warehouse the rest of the time. Everything else was considered frivolous and any member of his household who disagreed with him was in for a heated reprimand. The man seemed to have no sense of humor and never joked and seldom smiled. He was totally honest and fair in his dealings with his clients, but he was quite strict and severe with his wife and child.

Will was expected to follow in his father's footsteps and to agree with him on every point. His wife, Clare, was expected to keep house, cook, sew, and anything else considered woman's work. John never once allowed Clare to voice an opinion of her own. For a man who claimed that slavery was wrong, John Stanton came close to making slaves of his own family, but unbeknownst to his father, Will had every intention of someday leaving this hated life behind and becoming his own man.

When Will turned fourteen, John told him that he had enough education. He could read and write and do figures well enough. Too much learning would just muddle his mind. It was time to go to work full time, and since he still lived at home, he would be paid a half-wage. Will had no choice in the matter, so six days a week he worked at the warehouse, loading and unloading boats and wagons and moving heavy crates and boxes and learning to keep records and take inventories. The heavy work added muscle to his arms, back, and thighs. He would become a muscular man because of this heavy toil, but not burly like his father. He didn't want to spend his whole life doing this type of work. It was strenuous and extremely boring, so Will continued to daydream about a more exotic way of life. He began saving every penny that he could and looking forward to the day when he would be old enough to strike out on his own. The money was used to start a savings account at the local bank. His dad thoroughly approved, thinking his son was beginning to follow in his footsteps.

The years seemed to drag by slowly, and it was difficult for one so young to be patient, but in the next four years Will managed to save well over four hundred dollars. On his eighteenth birthday he decided the time had come to make his move. He didn't say anything to either of his parents, nor did he show up at the warehouse for work. Instead, he bought a horse and saddle and a used thirty-two-caliber squirrel rifle. After buying all the supplies that he thought he needed, he found that one horse couldn't possibly carry everything he had bought--and a rider too. He bought another horse, an older and less expensive one, for a packhorse. He had never owned a horse before and had ridden but little in his life, but the horse was gentle, so there shouldn't be any problem. He intended to leave Knoxville even if he had to walk.

When everything was loaded and ready to go, Will mustered all the courage he could find in order to face his father. He could simply have left without telling anyone anything, but he didn't want his mother to worry about what might have happened to him. And besides, that would be the cowardly way, and Will didn't consider himself a coward. His father had never hit him, so Will wasn't afraid of his father in a physical sense, but John sure had blistered him with words many times.

That evening just before dark he went home, dreading what was to come. When he went inside, his father, who was sitting in his favorite chair, jumped to his feet, livid from pent-up rage, and began ranting immediately. "Where have you been all day, boy? You go off without telling anybody anything. What kind of man are you going to be if you can't be responsible now? Tomorrow, after you had turned eighteen, I was going to start paying you a full wage, but you've proven that you don't deserve it. You can just..."

"Dad, I'm leaving. I wouldn't work at that warehouse the rest of my life for a double wage," said Will, trying to make his voice as steady as possible.

"You're what! Leaving! Let me tell you something young man, if you walk out that door, don't ever come back. You won't be any son of mine. I'll disown you."

"I've never been treated like a son anyway—actually more like a servant or a slave in my opinion."

"Oh, Will, what are you saying? Please, Son, think about what you are doing," his mother pleaded.

"Mother, I've done little else but think about it—for years. I'm being slowly smothered to death, and you, of all people, should know exactly what I'm talking about. I've never once been allowed to think for myself, and neither have you. I can't see things changing any time soon, can you? I've got to have some freedom; a life of my own choosing. I won't—I can't—continue to live this way."

"Everything that I have ever done, I did for you, boy," John began again. "I built that business--and it's a good business--from scratch, intending to turn it over to you someday. Now, you're throwing it all away. Well, if that's what you want to do, then have at it. I won't lift a finger to stop you."

"Dad, I never wanted the business. You never asked me if I wanted it. In fact you never asked me anything; you always told me. Tell me one decision that you have ever let me make in my whole life. Huh? There isn't one is there? Well, I'm making one now, for better or for worse." The more he talked the stronger his conviction became.

"And just where are you going and what are you going to do when you get there?" asked John.

"I don't know, and I really don't care, Dad. But I swear to you that I would rather live under a tree and grub roots for a living than continue this type of life."

Will hugged his mother and then extended his hand to his dad, but John turned his back saying, "Get out! You're no son of mine. Go waste your life gallivanting around the country. You just wait and see what I'm telling you. You'll be sorry, but don't come running back to me at the first sign of hardship. It won't do you any good." He then plopped down in his easy chair and stared at the floor, so angry the veins on his forehead were standing out in bold relief.

As Will turned to go, his mother was sobbing uncontrollably. He didn't want to hurt her--she was as much a victim of John's dominance as he was--but he couldn't stay. He actually thought that he would rather be dead than continue life in this same vein, with no hope of escape. It was just as bad to stifle a person's mind as to restrain his activity, and John Stanton did both. Why should he live in misery? If his dad liked his own life that was great, but Will detested his, and beginning today, for better or for worse, he was starting a new one.

It was dark when he rode away. He recovered the hunting knife from under the little rock shelter. It had probably been months since he had used the knife, but it was still in good condition. Since he had grown so much bigger in the last two years, the overhang was too small to sleep under. The only place he knew to go for the night was to a well-used campground about a mile down the river—a place used by fishermen and weekend poker players. He would sleep there tonight and make a fresh start in the morning. It took only a few minutes to travel the mile to the camping area. This being a weekday, the campsite was deserted. This suited Will just fine. He really didn't want company at the present time.

Will had built a fire and gathered cedar boughs to make his bed softer, but it was a long time before he could go to sleep, being apprehensive as well as excited at the prospects of his new life. He was a little fearful at leaving the only life he had ever known, but the feeling of relief in his newfound freedom was overwhelming. He had enough money to last a good long time, but after the money was used up, he would have to find a job, at least for a while. What that would be, he didn't know, but there was one thing he knew for certain: he would starve if need be before he would go back home to live. His one regret was leaving his mother to take the brunt of his father's wrath. Her life would undoubtedly be even more miserable now.

Even though he hadn't slept much, Will was eager to be on his way as soon as the sun came up, but first he wanted to familiarize himself with the rifle. After an hour of loading and shooting, he was able to consistently hit a target the size of a walnut at fifty yards. The former owner of the rifle had sighted the gun in well, which was a blessing, since Will had no experience at this task. He had shot a rifle only a few times before today, but he knew the principles of shooting, and he had a steady hand. He was confident that he would get by."

X

After he saddled up, Will headed westward toward the Cumberland Plateau. He had heard that there were still some elk in the more remote sections of that area. He wanted to try his luck with one of those large animals. The valley of the Emory River offered what looked like an easy access to the plateau, but after less than a mile the going got pretty rough. There was a trail of sorts that ran along beside the river, but in places it was quite narrow, and he didn't seem to be getting any closer to the top of the mountain. He had never been in mountainous terrain before, in fact, he had never been very far outside of Knoxville before.

There were wagon roads that he could have taken to the top of the mountain, but the reason he had left home was to live in the wilderness. Roads always led to towns and farms and people. From the looks of the narrow trail he was following, there weren't many people, if any at all, in this area. There were plenty of deer tracks in the trail, and over them, the tracks of a single horse going in the opposite direction from Will, but nothing else.

As the shadows began to lengthen, Will knew that he must find a place to camp soon. He didn't know what time it would get dark in this narrow valley, so the sooner he found a suitable site the better. He had so very much to learn, but he was undaunted by his inexperience. Even though, as a boy, he had read everything he could lay hands on about outdoor life, there probably wasn't anybody less prepared to live the life he intended to live, but he had one thing going for him: determination.

He didn't get very far into the valley of the Emory before the sun dropped behind the mountain. He began to look more earnestly for a campsite. Dusk couldn't be far away. The site that Will found for his second night away from home was near a small spring that flowed from under a limestone outcropping. Many others had used this spot in the past, judging from the mound of old ashes in the center of the small clearing. From the number of flint chips lying about, Will deemed this to be a very old campground indeed. More recent campers had already gathered all the dead logs in the area, making it necessary for Will to take his horse and drag firewood from a distance.

After his camp was made ready, he took his rifle and slowly made his way upstream, hoping to shoot a squirrel for his supper. The valley was so narrow that the trail had to follow close to the river, staying, in most places, just above the high water mark. Will had gone maybe a quarter of a mile, when a doe and a yearling, intending to drink from the river, stepped cautiously out of the woods onto a sandbar on the far side of the stream.

Stalking through the woods as a boy server him well this day, for the two deer had no idea that any danger was near. Will didn't want to harvest more meat than he could eat before he chose a more permanent place to stay, so he decided to take the yearling. Steadying the rifle against a tree, he aimed just behind the shoulder, and pulled the trigger. He stepped around the powder smoke in time to see the little deer fall in its tracks. With a flash of her tail, the doe bounded into the forest and disappeared.

Will was ecstatic! He had made his first kill! After dragging the carcass across a shoal to the trail, he walked back to camp for his horse. The smell of blood made the horse skittish. Instead of trying to load the deer on the horse, will decided to tow it back to camp. He built a fire, skinned out one haunch, and hung it over the flames to cook. Slices of liver woven onto withes were propped by forked sticks over the fire to cook. Meanwhile, he built a small rack from saplings, and after slicing the rest of the meat into thin strips, draped the strips over the rack to dry, just like he had read about in books.

It was now well after dark, and the only light was from the flickering campfire. The dancing shadows cast by the fire combined with the hooting of owls just added spice to the thrill of camping alone. As he sat with his back against a boulder, Will could hardly believe it. He was actually living the life that he had fantasized about as a boy. He was a now a mountain man and these mountains surrounding him were the towering Rockies. There, roasting over the fire and sending out a tantalizing aroma to a hungry hunter, was the leg of an elk. He was happier than he could ever remember being before in his life. Sitting on the ground with his back against a boulder, he closed his eyes and sighed his contentment to the night.

Will was brought back to reality with a start, when out of the dark came: "Hello the camp!" Since the man was coming from the same direction that will had come, he thought it possible the man could be following him for some sinister reason. With his heart racing, he dived forward and scrambled on hands and knees to reach his rifle, which was leaning against a tree ten feet away. Will had forgotten to reload the gun, but the intruder didn't know that.

"Come on in!" said Will, as he scrambled back to the boulder, making sure the rifle across his lap could easily be seen.

The most unkempt person that Will had ever seen emerged from out of the darkness. The man obviously hadn't bathed, washed his clothes, shaved, combed his hair, or anything else for a long time. He smelled like rotting flesh. A battered rifle was cradled in his left arm, and he was leading a packhorse loaded with traps and dead animals.

"I smelled that there meat acookin' a good ten minutes b'fore I ever got here. Name's Junior Hawkins. I trap the Emory an' the Obed an' ever' side stream that runs into 'em. I been down the river takin' in what traps was down that way. What're you doing way out here in the middle of nowheres, young feller? I hardly ever see a soul in this here little valley."

"I'm elk hunting, if you must know," said Will, a little chagrined at the man's prying.

"Don't get your dander up, son, it's just that I don't see many folks up this way. I stay out here all by my lonesome so much that I almost forget how to talk. Besides, I can save you a heap o' trouble. There might possibly be a couple o' elk left up around the Kentucky line, but they's been gone from around here for a long time. An' besides, that peashooter you got there ain't no elk gun. You'd need at least a fifty caliber for elk. Where you from, son?"

"My name is Will Stanton and I'm from Knoxville," Will said with emphasis.

"Yep, city boy. It figures. Seeing as they's no use to go elk huntin', Will Stanton, what're you goin' to do now?"

"I might just do what you're doing, set up a trap line somewhere. Maybe right here," said Will, getting more irritated with each prying question.

"I ain't being nosy, son. I'm just making conversation. Besides, it's mighty hard to make a livin' now a days just trappin' alone, an' besides I don't see no traps. If I was like you, and just startin' out, I'd get me some fertile land som'ers that I could farm in the summertime, and then I'd trap in the winter--fer fun an' to make a little extry cash."

"And just where would you consider a good location? I mean, if you was just starting out, that is," said Will, interested but trying not to seem too obvious.

81

"Why, I can't think of no better place than the S'quatchie Valley. It's fillin' up with people, but they ain't so many of 'em trapping no more. Still a lot of mink and muskrat an' a few beaver left along the river. Ever' once in a while you might get a fox or a bobcat, but mostly muskrat. The soil is better'n mountain soil, too."

"Where exactly is this valley you're talking about," asked Will, hopefully.

"Probably no more than thirty miles south and a little bit to the west o' here to the head of it," said Junior.

"If I was to decide to go to this S'quatchie Valley, there'd be somebody there who sells traps I suppose."

"Yeah, I suppose. You ever do any trappin', son?"

"No. Why?" asked Will, resenting this man more each time he was called son.

"Nope, I didn't think so. They's a lot to know about traps an' trappin'. You've got to know how an' where to set 'em, and you've got to use the right trap fer certain animals. Trappin' is over fer this year, though. I'm gonna run mine one last time an' take 'em up. Already took in the ones down the river. Tomorrow, why don't you run 'em with me, and I'll give you some pointers as I take 'em in?"

Will didn't want to seem too eager, so he paused as if he were thinking it over. "All right, I'll do it. I don't have anything better planned for tomorrow. That liver looks to be about done now. At least it smells pretty good. Let's have some of it."

Taking one of the withes, he handed one to Junior. The liver not being enough to fill two hungry men, will sliced two chunks of meat from the haunch, one for each of them. Will did the slicing because he didn't want Junior touching any part of the meat. The inside of the haunch near the bone was still red, so he hung it back over the fire to cook a little longer. Will savored each bite, chewing slowly to prolong the enjoyment of his first kill. After they had eaten, they talked for a while, with Junior hogging the conversation, then decided to turn in. Will put his saddlebags under his saddle and used the saddle for a pillow. All the money he had worked years for was in the saddlebags, and if Junior got to them, he would have to get past Will. He laid his rifle by his side, along with his hunting knife, though the rifle was useless for anything except a club. He would try never again to forget to reload immediately after shooting; it could prove to be a very costly oversight, he decided.

Will intended to stay awake most of the night feeding the fire for the light and to facilitate the drying of the meat. As soon as Junior began to snore, he quietly as possible reloaded his rifle. The night passed slowly, as there was nothing much to do except listen to the crickets chirping and the owls hooting. Will was happy to see the gray forms of trees emerging from the darkness as dawn finally arrived.

He was quite puzzled by Junior. The man looked and smelled like worthless buzzard bait, but the way he talked belied that. A completely worthless man wouldn't be running a trap line, which was obviously hard, cold, lonely work. That didn't make Will any less wary of him, nor did it deter his own determination to someday become a trapper. The night passed without incident, and if Junior knew that Will hadn't slept much, he didn't mention it. They ate the rest of the haunch with hardtack biscuits for breakfast, and then set out up the Emory. Will walked and led his horses; he didn't want to ride while Junior walked--the man looked to be sixty years, if not older.

Junior showed Will how to set beaver traps, so that after a beaver was caught, it would drown. Beaver would sometimes chew off a foot in order to escape the trap, if they were snared on land. The castor glands were kept to lure other beaver into the traps. Will learned where and how to set traps for beaver, fox, mink, muskrat, and bobcat. By the time all the traps were in--Junior had remained dry while Will waded in the cold water--Will felt that he would be able to run his own trap line, learning even more as he trapped.

Even though Junior had used him to take in the traps, Will truly was glad that he had met the man, as irritating as he was. Providence seemed to be with him. There would have been no way he could have successfully trapped anything without the knowledge he now had. He even learned how to skin the animals—with Junior's guidance--and how to stretch and flesh the hides. Of course, there were things to learn that only more experience could teach him, but he was learning fast.

They made their way to where Junior had his permanent camp under a rock overhang. It was dry and plenty big enough for a man and a horse, with space left for furs and a big heap of firewood. Blankets had been strung up as windbreakers around a sleeping cubicle that had a fireplace toward the outside. Will thought that he wouldn't mind spending a few days here himself once the taint of Junior wore off the place.

"Well, since we've got all of your traps in, we can load your furs (now Will knew why Junior smelled like rotting flesh) on the horses, and just swing by your place. There's no way you could have carried all that load on one horse is there?"

"Not in one trip," said Junior. "Actually, I've never carried the traps home b'fore. I've always stored 'em here under this here rock shelter--slept here too, right there on that 'ol bearskin. But I'm goin' to have to give up trappin', so I'm takin' 'em home with me this time. This has to be my last season. These old bones of mine just can't take the cold like they used to. Wadin' that icy water just ain't fer a man my age. You're goin' to need traps, son, if you're goin' to be a trapper. I'd be willing to sell you mine at a bargain price. Fifty traps fer just a hunnert an' fifty dollars."

"I don't know about that, some of these traps have seen better days. Besides that's a big investment for somebody just starting out. I don't know if I could even make my money back," said Will, figuring Junior was trying to skin him like one of the animals that he trapped.

"Yeah, I guess you're right about that; I have got a lot of use out of 'em. How does an even hunnert dollars sound to you?"

"You never did say where you lived," said Will, wanting to give the impression of bargaining experience that he didn't have. "Can we get there before dark?"

"Awright! Awright! My final offer is seventy-five dollars, if you won't give that much, I'll just have to keep 'em."

"All right, you've got yourself a deal. Now, which way to your place?" Will wasn't at all sure that he had made a good deal--he didn't have any idea what new traps cost--but at the worst, it was only a half-bad deal.

"We'll take the next trail to the left. That will get us to the top of the plateau, then southeast fer about ten miles to the foot of the Crab Orchard Mountains." They had to walk the whole way--the farthest Will had walked in a single stretch in his life. He was tuckered out and footsore by the time they got to the top of the mountain, and they still had ten miles to go.

Will was curious about the bearskin and asked Junior where he had gotten it. "Well, son, it was like this. Late one winter about five year ago the weather turned real warm. I reckon that old bear came out of hibernation a little early, and he must o' been real hungry, 'cause he started raidin' my traps. I tried fer several days to get him in the early mornin's, then I switched to the evenin's, but that old rascal was doing his raidin' at night."

"They's a curve in the Obed where the river has deposited a long sand bar on the inside o' the bend. This sand is real light in color. I put a ripe beaver carcass on it, so the scent would carry a long way. I figured that under a full moon that ol' bear would stand out pretty good against the lighter sand. I stopped trappin' fer a while, so that ol' bear would get real hungry, but it still took three nights b'fore he showed up. When he finally did, I was right there awaitin'."

"I couldn't see the sights on my rifle none too good, but I taken a chanst anyhow an' only wounded him. When I found a blood trail on the sand, I knowed fer shore I'd hit him, but I didn't know how bad. I was about as skeered as I'd ever been in my life. I didn't want to be out in them woods with a wounded bear, so I hightailed it back to camp an' kept a big fire going fer the rest o' the night, an' my gun acrost my knees. There was no need to've worried though, the next mornin' I found that ol' bear no more than two hunnert yards from where I shot 'im. I eat bear meat 'til I got sick of it, and I've been sleepin' on that there hide ever since."

"Are there any bears left around here any more?" Will asked hopefully.

"A few. A man needs some good dogs to hunt bears though. Since they ain't no more elk around here, you plannin' on goin' bear huntin' now, son?" asked Junior, grinning like a 'possum.

"Maybe I'll just do that someday, but I've got more important things to do first." Will was so mad that he refused to say another word the rest of the way to Junior's cabin. He was furious because Junior didn't take him seriously. Sure, he was inexperienced, but he was determined to learn, and in time, he was sure he would earn the respect of even an experienced woodsman. He was relieved when they finally sighted Junior's cabin.

The cabin, if it could truly be called that, looked hardly livable from Will's point of view. It sat under a huge oak tree, the only tree left standing in a clearing of maybe an acre. Junior had built walls of logs, with a tarpaulin stretched tight over a ridgepole for a roof. There was no way it could be much warmer than the rock shelter where Junior made his winter camp. Every type of junk imaginable was strewn around the weed-choked clearing. The place was just as unkempt as the owner was. There were pieces of beds, furniture, mounds of broken jars and tin cans, and even a three legged stove, with a stone replacing the missing leg. The only thing that looked salvageable was the stove.

"What are you planning to do now that you're giving up trapping, Junior?"

"Well, son, I got a sister what married a man that was a big landowner down in Alabama. I said was a big landowner 'cause in her last letter, Sis said that her man had passed on, and I should come and live with her. She says she would feel safer with a man around, but she ain't got no intentions 'o gettin' married agin. There ain't no way that woman would ever share what she's got with another man, that's fer shore. I can't see no man bein' innerested in her anyway. She ain't that good lookin' in her old age, but then agin, she never was. She's got some darkies on the place to do the heavy work. I reckon my presence there is all she wants; a place to live out the rest of my days is all I want. I reckon it was made to order."

"I wrote her back and told her I would finish out this trappin' season and then I"d come on down. After I sell my furs, I'll be on my way. Shouldn't take me long to pack up ever'thing that's worth takin', huh?

After seeing the condition of Junior's cabin, Will had intended to give the man a hundred dollars for the traps, but now, it appeared that the man had a more secure future than he had foreseen and wouldn't need the extra money after all. So, with all haste he paid Junior, said his farewell, and headed south. He appreciated all the information that he had gleaned from Junior, but he was glad to be getting away from the man. No one in his eighteen years had ever irritated Will quite as badly as Junior had.

It was getting close to dark, so he camped at the very next creek, making sure his rifle was still primed before going to sleep. After staying awake most of the previous night and walking so much today, he was more than ready for a good night's sleep. But first he had to build another drying rack, since the deer meat hadn't thoroughly dried the night before.

XI

The next morning, he skirted Grassy Cove and rode to where the road dropped off into the head of the Sequatchie Valley. To the south of him was one of the most beautiful sights he had ever seen: as far as the eye could see there was a broad, flat-bottomed valley between two parallel mountains. For the first few miles, the individual smoke columns from the scattered homesteads could be distinguished, but in the far distance, the smoke became a blue haze that sight couldn't penetrate. In the far distance, the mountains seemed to fade into nothingness and become one with the smoky haze. Judging from the haze, every wife in the valley must be cooking breakfast at this time of the morning. Somewhere down there between those two mountains, he intended to make his home.

As the road leveled out at the head of the valley, the forest became so dense that Will couldn't see the mountains on either side. With tree trunks crowding in from the sides and limbs intertwined overhead, the road was actually a tunnel through the forest. When Will came to the first homestead, he could see the mountains from a new perspective. They didn't appear quite as high from below as they did from the top. The day's ride took him past the little settlement of Pikeville. That night he made camp beside the Sequatchie River, although, to Will, it seemed little more than a creek at this point. Come next winter, if his plans came to fruition, he would be trapping along this very river.

The next day he began asking everyone he met about the availability of land. There was land to be had, but nothing that Will really liked. All of the better spots with springs and creeks had been claimed. Good water was not only necessary for drinking, but a cold spring could be used as a cooler for milk and other perishables. The inquiries slowed his progress to only a few meandering miles that day, but that still put him well south of the community of Coops Creek. That night he made a dry camp in a patch of woods.

He was beginning to desire something to eat other than deer jerky and bacon, so the next morning he stopped at a little country store to see what was on the shelves. When Will entered the dimly lit store there were three elderly men gathered so close to a pot bellied stove it looked as if they were trying to keep the stove warm. Will was wondering why the men were so close to the stove; the weather was much too warm for a fire. Then he saw one of the men spit tobacco juice into the ash pan. The two that were seated had a checkerboard set up on a keg between them. The one that was standing slowly made his way to where Will was waiting. Yes, sir. What can I do for you, young feller?" asked the old timer.

Will, having surveyed the canned goods, placed his order, then made the usual query about land, not really expecting anything positive, when the storeowner said: "You just might be in luck young feller. Man by the name of Ted Weems was in here t'other day and said he was alookin' fer somebody to sell his land to. Don't know what the place looks like. Didn't ask no questions 'bout it, since I warn't interested in it personal like. Weems come to the valley about a month or so ago from up Virginny way. Well, sir, his wife don't like it here. Don't like it none at all, he says. Told Weems, she did, that if he didn't take her back to Virginny, she was leavin' on her own—walkin' if she had to. His place is on down the road about five or six miles. Don't know exactly where. You'll have to ask fer directions onct you get in the neighborhood." Will paid for his goods, thanked the man, and left.

Will had no trouble at all finding the Weems place, having to ask for directions from only one person. The man told Will that he would like to have the place for himself but couldn't come up with the money.

After Will made a quick scan of the surroundings, it seemed to be the very place he had been searching for. There was a spring at the head of its own miniature valley, with plenty of clear, cold water flowing out of the mountainside. There was more than enough level land beside the spring branch for planting, and trees to build a cabin with, and also, it was only a short distance from the Sequatchie River. Ted Weems had already started building the walls of a cabin, but he hadn't gotten very far along with them. He had snaked in several logs, though, that were ready to be notched and laid in place.

A man that Will took to be Ted Weems, sitting on a stump in the shade of a large oak mending harness, looked up as Will approached him. There was a canvas-covered wagon parked nearby and a rope corral with two horses inside. "Are you Mister Weems? My name is Will Stanton," said Will as they shook hands. "I hear that you've got land for sale."

"Yep, that's right young feller. Not that I want to sell, mind you, but I got m'self a little bit of a problem. My woman ain't been weaned yet. She insists on goin' back to Virginia so she can be close to her mama. That's the very reason I wanted to leave there in the first place. She was always at their house--never would spend no time at home. I tell you, son, it ain't no fun at all livin' that close to yore in-laws. That ain't what you asked me about, though, is it?"

"Well, anyway, they's a hundred acres more or less that I need to get shut of. Already sold sixty acres to Jed Thompson acrost the spring branch there. I need to sell out purty quick, so if you want the place, you can have it fer a dollar a acre. One thing, though, you'd have to share the spring with the Thompsons. I already made the same deal with Jed. What do you think?"

"Seems to me there's plenty of water for everybody. Write up a bill of sale, and you've got yourself a deal."

"We'll have to ride down to the Cheekville courthouse to get the bill of sale legalized; it won't take long."

"Mister Weems, I was told that you have been in these parts only a month or so, if you don't mind my asking, sir, how did you come by such a nice place as this. Every place I've come across with good drinking water has been settled for a long time," said Will, as they rode slowly toward Cheekville.

"I inherited the place from an uncle who was granted a quarter section way back when the Cherokees was moved south across the Tennessee River. He could o' took a much bigger grant if he'd awanted mountain land, but he wanted this place here. He come down here and registered his claim, but he never done nothin' to improve the place, though. He went back to Virginia and stayed there 'till he died. Kept the taxes paid up right to the end, he did. What little work I done here is all I got in the place."

"What exactly are you talking about when you mention this grant?" asked Will. "Oh, I'm sorry, I figured you knowed what I was talkin' about. Well, you see, it's like this. Men that fit in the War for Independence was granted land by the gov'ment for their services. The land around here belonged to the Cherokees at the time, but that never made no difference to the gov'ment. Some of them grants was fer as much as five thousand acres. Of course, most o' them big tracts was the most worthless of mountain land and in the hardest places to git to," explained Weems.

"Well, lucky for me your uncle took this place; it's exactly what I've been looking for."

"I like it a lot m'self, but if I'm ever gonna see any peace, I gotta keep my woman satisfied, I reckon."

After the legalities were finished, Ted Weems was ready to leave. He had stopped working on the cabin days ago, knowing that he was going to have to abandon it. He and his wife had been living in the wagon, so everything was already packed--except for a few articles of clothing that had been hung out to dry close by the spring branch. As Mrs. Weems gathered the clothes, Will got a good look at her. She was barely more than a child, while her husband had to be at least thirty years old. Will could better understand why she wanted to return to her parents. From Wills point of view, she shouldn't even be married yet, much less to a man twice her own age. It looked as if Ted Weems had married into a future chocked full of trouble.

XII

Will was as proud as a young rooster as he went to meet his new neighbors--Jed, Henrietta, and little Henry. After talking to them for a while, he believed that he and the Thompsons would get along just dandy; they seemed to be fine folks. The Thompsons were also living in a wagon at present. After some discussion, they decided to work together to clear enough of Jed's property to put in a crop of corn, beans, and other vegetables. It took several weeks to clear enough land, and as it was getting on toward early summer, they planted as they cleared. Will agreed to work with Jed until he and his family were settled in, and then Jed would return the favor. Henrietta did the work of a man in the field as well as cook and watch over little Henry.

After enough ground was cleared and the crop planted, they used the suitable trees that had been felled while clearing the land to build the Thompsons a two-room house. It would be well along toward winter before they could finish the cabin that Ted Weems had begun for Will to live in. He ate nearly every meal that summer with the Thompsons, practically living with them until his own cabin was erected, and he was sure that Henrietta was the finest cook he had ever known--even better than his own mother.

Will missed his mother dearly, but his dad he seldom thought about. These past few months he had drawn closer to Jed

Thompson than he ever had been to his own father, and Henry, who was eight, was almost like a little brother.

From the day he had bought the land, Will had been sleeping under a shelter made by pegging down a canvas tarpaulin draped over a rope tied between two trees. After his cabin was erected, He used the canvas to build a temporary shelter for his horse. The old packhorse had been sold since it was no longer needed, and also, it would have been difficult to stretch the meager supply of hay to feed two horses through the winter. Will had never worked so hard in his life as he had throughout the past spring and summer, but it was work that he actually enjoyed. This land was his; he could put his sweat into it without any regrets.

Since the weather was now turning cooler, Will went over all the traps that he had bought from Junior Hawkins to make sure they were in good working order, and then he took his rifle and walked to the Sequatchie River. Working his way upstream he began checking for signs of different animals and where would be the best places to set traps for them. At this time of the year the river was very low and could be crossed at any shoal, but later, after the winter rains began, it would be almost impossible at times to cross anywhere without a boat. The river was only about fifty feet across at most places, but when running full, it was quite swift.

Will intended to trap only the western side of the river; any animal that wanted to cross over from the eastern side wouldn't have any problem doing so. Any aquatic animal could easily swim across the river, and for the others, there were logjams or tree limbs that grew far enough over the water to touch each other at mid-stream.

Before the weather turned really cold, Will built a fieldstone chimney and finished chinking the cracks between the logs of his little cabin. Now, in his spare time, he was working on chairs, a table, and a bed. He was using skills that he had no idea he possessed. Anything that he could picture in his mind, he discovered, he could build. The single room, which was only twelve by twenty feet, wouldn't have any spare space once he was finished with the furniture. Next summer, he had plans to add a bedroom to the north side, but right now he was comfortable with what he had. He was never more contented than when he was sitting before the fireplace, watching the flickering flames and absorbing the warmth that radiated into the room.

One day, while browsing at Griffith's store, south of Cheekville, Will met another trapper by the name of Lamar (Buck) Smith, and they began to talk. They liked one another immediately, starting a friendship that lasted until Buck's untimely death. Buck, an experienced trapper, gave Will quite a bit of good information. He didn't seem one bit resentful that another trap line was being set up on the river. They mutually agreed to stay out of the other's territory--Buck agreeing to trap farther down stream and on the eastern side of the river, since that was the side he lived on.

Trapping the animals turned out to be the easy part. After that came the skinning, the scraping, and the stretching. Will took care not to let the rancid odor from the curing hides permeate his clothing; he didn't want to end up smelling like Junior Hawkins.

Will began putting his money from the sale of furs in a quart fruit jar that he kept buried in a secret location. After selling the packhorse, he had a hundred and fifty dollars left from the original four hundred. Adding seventy-five more after three month's of trapping brought the total to two hundred and twenty-five dollars. He didn't cache all the profit away, holding some out for spending money. It didn't take much money for him to live on, since he got nearly all the meat he could use from the animals he trapped during the winter, and he and Buck hunted on the Cumberland Plateau or Walden Ridge in their spare time, which wasn't often. He spent a lot of time drying meat, since that was the easiest method to preserve it any length of time. Will ate a lot of muskrat, raccoon, and beaver. Some people claimed that beaver tail was a delicacy, but he never developed a taste for it.

Trapping during the winter and drying and preserving what he grew during the summer kept Will busy most of the year, but in the early autumn, he and Buck always managed to find time for a hunting trip. He was never happier than when on a two-week excursion into the mountains, hunting, camping, and living off the land. Buck seemed to enjoy these times just as much as Will, causing their friendship to grow. They would camp under rock shelters that had been used by Indians in times past, reminding Will of his childhood in the woods behind his Knoxville home and his fantasies of living like a mountain man. The hunting trips taught him much about subsistence living, and from the tracking of animals, he acquired skills that were useful later in life.

A bedroom had been added to the cabin, and a small three-walled barn with a pole corral had been built. Will worked from daylight until dusk six days a week but was much happier than he could have ever been at his father's warehouse. Trapping wasn't making him rich, but after the third season he had three hundred and seventy-five dollars cached away. In his opinion, that wasn't anywhere near bad.

His life continued in this manner until the summer of 1860, when Buck asked Will to go to a church social with him. Buck had met a young woman named Margaret McGowan some weeks earlier, and they were seeing each other on a regular basis. Come Sunday morning, Will dressed in his very best clothes and rode to Hicks Chapel. He looked the crowd over before dismounting, trying to find Buck in the throng. Then, seeing his friend on the far side of the crowd, with an attractive brunette keeping him company, Will made his way to where Buck was sitting as quickly as possible. Since most of the people surrounding Will were strangers to him, he felt very conspicuous. Both Buck and his companion had plates heaped with food and urged Will to fill one for himself. Finding a plate, he went to the long makeshift table filled with more food than he had seen since he had gone to church with his parents in Knoxville.

When he returned with his food, Buck introduced him to Margaret and to Virginia Morgan, Margaret's cousin, who had joined them. Will was instantly stricken with the beauty of the dainty blonde. The four of them talked until after everyone else had gone home. This was one day that Will didn't want to end, but the young ladies said their fathers would come looking for them if they didn't get home soon. With the four of them on the seat of a wagon, Will had to sit very close to Virginia; this was something he didn't mind at all.

Will untied his horse from behind the wagon when they arrived at Virginia's house. After good-byes were said all around, Buck drove away with Maggie, leaving a self-conscious Will standing with reins and hat in hand. He had a feeling that his meeting Virginia wasn't a total accident, but that was just fine with him. He hadn't seen a prettier girl in a long time--if ever.

"Miss Virginia, uh, do you reckon it would be all right if I, uh, called on you again some time?" stammered Will, feeling as if his heart was in his throat choking off his breath. He had never had a girl friend before and didn't know anything about courting, but he liked this pretty girl, and he hoped that she liked him, too.

"First of all, you must call me Ginny; and if you were to come by here next Sunday morning about half past nine; and if you just happened to be on your way to church, I don't see why we couldn't walk together, do you? My parents don't go to church on a regular basis, but I seldom miss a Sunday. The next Sunday-- and every one thereafter for weeks--Will walked by Ginny's house, leading his horse, at precisely nine thirty.

Will was attending the church services only to be with Ginny, but he couldn't help but hear the preacher's sermons. Most of them went in one ear and out the other, but one sermon in particular stuck in his mind. He couldn't remember the exact words, but the gist of it was that when a person had sunk as low as he could go, there was an ever-present help in the time of trouble. If you felt as lowly as Job and you had no way to look but up, the preacher said, then call upon the Lord and turn your life and problems over to Him, and He would bring you out of despair.

Why this particular message stuck in his mind Will didn't know; he had never been in such a lowly condition as Job had apparently been. True, he had been extremely unhappy as a teenager at home, but he had known that just as soon as he was old enough, he would be free to make his own way in the world.

Will and Ginny kept the Sunday routine for about two months, and then Ginny invited him home for Sunday dinner. Will had briefly met her parents but he hadn't talked very much with them. The Morgans seemed like nice enough people, and they had no objection to Will calling on their daughter. Buck was a well-known and respected figure in the Hicks Chapel community. Obviously, being Buck's friend was all the credentials that Will needed.

Since the whole country was presently in an uproar over the issues of slavery and states rights, Carl Morgan used the dinner as an opportunity to air his opinions. He was a strong state's rights advocate, though, on the issue of slavery, he was less outspoken, as Will found out. Carl felt that since slavery had been an institution in this country for the past two hundred or so years it was up to the individual states to decide whether to keep or abolish it. Personally, he had no slaves, and even had an aversion to one man owning another, but he was willing to fight for the right of each state to decide its own destiny within the Union.

As a child growing up in Knoxville, Will had not been closely associated with any black people. There weren't very many slaves in the area, and the ones that were present were strangers to him. He had never been exposed to the plight of the black man and had no strong opinions about slavery. As far as he could recall, his father had never discussed the issue at length at the dinner table but had made many generalized statements about his opposition to slavery.

Will had never had any reason to think very deeply about either issue, but his own beliefs were, nevertheless, somewhat stronger than Carl's concerning slavery. Will took pretty much the same position as his father did concerning that issue. He agreed with his dad that no human being should be owned by another, and that slavery should be abolished, but he was not fanatical about it. For Ginny's sake, Will allowed Carl to win any discussion concerning the subject.

With the issues of slavery and state's rights taking precedence in almost all conversations wherever people met, discussions were really heating up. Fistfights were common, church members began to segregate according to their viewpoints, and one man, Josiah Anderson, was shot and killed as he was giving a political speech in the Hicks Chapel community.

As the country seemed to be splitting apart, Will and Ginny were drawing closer together, and in March 1861, were married in Hicks Chapel. Buck and Maggie had gotten married the previous December. South Carolina had already seceded from the Union and hostilities had begun with the bombardment of Fort Sumter in Charleston harbor. Nine other states followed South Carolina's example and formed the Confederate States of America.

The secessionist movement in Tennessee, on the first vote, failed to carry the state, but many influential men were working to bring the issue before the people once again. The citizens of

Franklin County were so outraged at the failure that they threatened to secede from Tennessee.

After a week of marriage, Will and Ginny decided to rent a carriage and make the trip to Knoxville so that she could meet Will's parents. They planned to spend one night there and then head back home, taking one week for the round trip. They arrived in Knoxville late in the afternoon of the third day and spent a pleasant two hours visiting with his mother. Clare was very happy to see Will again and took to Ginny right away.

Shortly after six o'clock, John came home from the warehouse. Rather than greeting his son, John began immediately with: "So you've finally come to your senses have you? I figured you wouldn't be able to hack it in the real world. Looks like I was right. I guess you are expecting your old job back aren't you? Well, you'll just have to prove yourself worthy first."

Will was seated when his dad began his tirade, but he came quickly to his feet. Anger such as he had never felt toward his father drained the blood from his face. With his throat so constricted by anger that he had difficulty speaking, Will said, "I came here thinking that you might like to meet your daughter-in-law, but you haven't changed one bit. You've still got only one thing on your mind, haven't you? Take a good look at my face, Dad, because you'll never see it again as long as you live. Come on, Ginny, let's get out of here." He was so angry that he didn't even say good-bye to his mother.

Ginny was so surprised by the turn of events that she couldn't speak. Silently, with her mouth hanging open, she followed Will outside. Before words ever came, she began to sob. Will held her close and tried to console her, but to no avail.

"He hates me doesn't he, Will?"

"No, darling. It has absolutely nothing to do with you. Come on, let's go find a place to stay, and I'll try to explain what just happened."

Will and Ginny found a room for the night and then started the trip back home the next morning. Up until yesterday, Will
had believed that the rift between his father and himself could be
mended, but now, after the way his father had acted, he decided
that he would never try again, for as long as he may live, to mend
the fence that separated them. The next move, if there were one,
would have to come from his dad.

After Will and Ginny had walked out the door, Clare said
something that she had never dared to say before, something that
completely astonished her husband: "John Stanton, after four long
years you should have been happy to see your son again, but you
have let your stupid pride drive him away forever. You are nothing
but a fool."

XIII

Carl Morgan joined the Confederate army and urged Will, Buck, and any other man that he had any influence with to do the same. He even gave his son-in-law his very best horse, a fine gray gelding, as an incentive to join the Southern cause. Ginny didn't actually want Will to enlist but neither did she protest when he told her of his decision to join the cavalry. He felt that his loyalty lay with Tennessee rather than with the Union, and he was naive enough at first to think that there was a glamorous side to making war.

Will showed Ginny where the money jar was buried and urged her not to forgo anything she needed while he was away. He really didn't expect to be gone from home very long--believing that the Union's determination to fight didn't run very deeply.

They spent every minute they could together of the time that was left before Will had to leave. Several times Will's determination wavered, but in the end his father-in- law's persuasiveness won out. Leaving his young wife behind was the most difficult thing that he had ever done in his life, even though, at the time, he believed the war would be short lived.

Will tried to persuade Ginny to move back home with her mother for the duration of his absence, but Ginny had such an independent spirit that she refused.

Will was pleased that Buck had decided to join up with him; it would help to have his friend beside him. There were other young men from the Cheekville area who left home to join the Union Army. Since Will had always been such a loner, many of them were mere acquaintances, but still, he hoped that he would never meet any of them in battle.

Many Tennessee men were being sent to Virginia and other out of state locations. Will was hesitant to offer his services to the Confederacy if he couldn't fight closer to home. Carl had been sent to West Tennessee as part of General Leonidas Polk's Army of Tennessee. Knowing that Will had his heart set on being a cavalryman, Carl wrote him a letter telling about a new cavalry unit being formed in the Memphis area by a wealthy businessman named Nathan Bedford Forrest.

Will and Buck bought tickets in Bridgeport, Alabama, and rode the train along with their horses to Memphis. Forrest was equipping a cavalry unit at his own expense; he readily accepted the two new recruits.

Nathan Bedford Forrest, Will later learned, was a millionaire businessman who enlisted as a private in the Confederate army, but after raising the cavalry unit at his own expense, was quickly commissioned a colonel. He had had no formal military training, but as it turned out, he became quite a strategist. Later he became a general over thousands of troopers but sometimes had to capture arms and horses to equip his men. He was the only soldier in the Civil War to rise through the ranks from private to general.

Because of his experience at record keeping and knack for organization at his father's warehouse, Will was made sergeant over ordinance in short order. And after a few months of battle-tried experience, he showed such an aptitude at hit and run tactics, sabotage, and harassment of the enemy that he was made captain of his own troop of Forrest's Independent Scouts.

When Will's commanding officer called his men together and read to them from a Nashville newspaper the account of the recent battle at Bull Run, the men cheered for a full ten minutes. Since the Union army had been chased back to Washington in disarray, Will was more assured than ever that the war would be a short one. But before the first year was up, he had given up on the idea of a quick ending. In his earlier naiveté he had grossly underestimated Union tenacity, and he found that this had been a common mistake, even among the top leaders of the Confederacy.

The first major action that Will was involved in didn't go well at all for the Confederacy. In February 1862, Federal troops under General Grant attacked Fort Donelson on the Cumberland River—the Union had already taken fort Henry on the Tennessee--and the Confederate commanders decided that the fort must be surrendered. General Pillow, the top commander at the fort, decided to personally escape, leaving his men to be taken prisoners, so he handed over his command to General Floyd, who also escaped, passing the command on to General Buckner, who surrendered to General Grant.

Unwilling to leave his men to be taken prisoners, General Forrest, with 4000 men--his whole contingency plus some others--managed to find a hole in the Federal lines, and floundering through icy, waist-deep water, managed to escape to safety. After the fort changed hands, General Grant, learning what had taken place, held nothing but contempt for General Pillow because of the cowardly way that he had shunned his responsibility.

General Forrest made his way to Nashville and removed what military stores he could, as well as several valuable machines that were needed for the Confederate war effort. Time was short and railroad cars were few, however, and as a result, the Confederacy lost most of its much-needed supplies in Middle Tennessee.

The next major engagement was at Shiloh in early April, where more soldiers died than in the whole Revolutionary War. Forrest's only distinction came after the battle as his cavalry fought a rearguard action until the Southern army could escape.

In July, Forrest, with 1,000 troopers, attacked the Union garrison at Murfreesboro, capturing 1,200 Union soldiers and a quarter of a million dollars in military stores. The railroad bridges over Stone's River were burned, shutting down the Union supply line for two weeks.

Forrest was winning acclaim with his uncanny ability at leadership. His successful raids and repeated victories over opponents that outnumbered him were widely renowned. The most celebrated of his victories over a superior force was the defeat of Samuel D. Sturgis at Brice Cross Roads in Mississippi. Sturgis had over eight thousand men; Forrest had less than half that number. Forrest whipped the Union cavalry while the infantry was six miles to the rear. Then, after the two Union contingencies managed to join, Forrest defeated the combined force and ran them in disarray all the way back to their base. It took Sturgis ten days to get to the battle site but only sixty-four hours to return to base. There were 2,500 hundred Union casualties in this battle to 492 Southerners killed or wounded.

Forrest's ability as a leader was not recognized until far too late in the war. Both Jefferson Davis and Robert E. Lee later lamented this fact. He remained undefeated in every battle where he was commander until the final days of the war, making one defeat in 54 engagements, and then only by overwhelming odds.

It seemed to Will that his beloved general tried to be everywhere at once. But after all, Forrest's strategy was: "Get there first with the most men." As his fame spread, men were actually deserting their own units and joining up with him. He petitioned the war department to let the men stay with him. His reasoning was that if they were sent back to their own units they would just desert again. If they were allowed to stay, he could make an effective fighting force out of them.

Forrest left Mississippi after defeating Sturgis and swung way up into West Tennessee hitting several Federal supply bases. There were so many horses and arms captured that every trooper had his choice of mounts, and they were better armed than at any other time since the war started. They also burned railroad bridges and destroyed telegraph lines so completely that the Union army in Mississippi had absolutely no communication with the rear echelon.

For Will and Buck, the first two years of the war were spent campaigning mostly in Middle and West Tennessee, and even though he was usually within two hundred miles of home, Will might as well have been in South America. There always seemed to be another raid to be staged, another depot to hit, or another skirmish to fight.

He missed Ginny very much, and while both North and South were juggling for position just before the serious fighting began in the Chattanooga-Chickamauga campaign, he and Buck managed to have a few days at home. The furloughs home were too few and far between, but Ginny and Maggie seemed to be managing quite well alone. It was springtime, and Ginny was planting vegetables. Will would have liked nothing better than to have stayed and helped her, but the war stopped for no one. Although, he would be in the Chattanooga area for quite some time, it would be months before he would see Ginny again.

Forrest's cavalry was attached to Braxton Bragg's army at the battle of Missionary Ridge, where the fighting was so intense that his cavalry dismounted and fought as infantry. Will and his unit took a position in a thicket, and with trees and fallen logs for cover, laid down such a deadly fire that the Union advance in that particular area was completely halted.

Confederate General Hill, who normally considered cavalry as a non-fighting army given to useless riding and sashaying around, found new respect for these stubborn fighters after he was told they were part of Forrest's cavalry.

The next day the South lost its last chance to win a significant victory, when Longstreet broke through the Union ranks at Chickamauga, a few miles south of Chattanooga. Bragg had lost so many men the day before that he refused to take the advice of Longstreet and Forrest to pursue the fleeing Yankees and not give them a chance to regroup. The ensuing argument between Forrest and Bragg resulted in Forrest's transferal, without his command, back to Mississippi, where he had to start raising a new troop from scratch. Bragg was ultimately defeated and retreated to Georgia, where he was removed from command because of his failure at Chattanooga.

The fighting drifted southeast toward Atlanta as General Sherman began his march across Georgia. Will and Buck decided to ride away from the army that was confronting Sherman and to go home for a few days before finding and joining up with General Forrest's new command. They could have been shot as deserters, but they were willing to take the chance just to be back with the only leader they trusted. When Will left home this time, he had no way of knowing that Ginny was pregnant.

Before long, they were back in Middle Tennessee attached to Hood's army at the battle of Franklin, just south of Nashville. When Hood also refused to heed Forrest's advice, he too was defeated. Forrest's cavalry fought a rear guard action against General Wilson's cavalry--again fighting as infantry from behind cover--so that Hood and his army could escape. They were successful at holding Wilson back, but now the only thing between Wilson and the last major munitions depot in the Deep South, at Selma, Alabama, was Forrest, and he was outnumbered more than two to one.

XIV

"You don't have to write this down Mr. Hathaway, but I want to relate to you some of the more interesting things that my dad told me about General Forrest and his men," said Billy. "For instance, there was the time that Forrest sent one of his subordinates with a small force to capture the fort at Union City, Tennessee, while he, with the rest of the cavalry, went on to Paducah, Kentucky. The fort was too strong to be taken by a frontal assault with so few men, so a little trickery was necessary to get the job done. The front wheels were taken from under a wagon, and a black log was attached to them. Since it was getting dark, there was just enough light to make the log look like a cannon to the men inside the fort. A letter, with Forrest's signature forged on it, demanding unconditional surrender, was sent to the Union commander of the fort. He requested one hour to make up his mind; he was given twenty minutes. The fort was captured without a shot being fired."

Warren laughed heartily, then added, "I'll bet that Union commander felt mighty foolish after he saw that cannon, didn't he?"

"In his place, I know that I would have," said Billy.

"Forrest decided early on that the Union forces at Paducah were too strong to take, but he came away with a herd of horses and mules. On the way back to Tennessee, one of Forrest's generals happened to read in a local newspaper the story about their raid at Paducah. According to the paper, the animals they had taken belonged to private citizens; the army's animals were safe at another location. The general asked Forrest if he could go back and get those animals, too. Forrest said, "Go ahead."

"Later at Fort Pillow, Forrest had three horses shot out from under him as he rode reconnaissance around the fort. The Union was trying, unsuccessfully, to reinforce the fort by steamboats on the Mississippi River. After the fort was taken by Forrest, the guns at the fort were turned on the boats, driving them away. During the course of the war, a total of 29 horses were shot from under him."

"He was very daring, or very foolish, in his exploits, putting himself in dangerous situations time after time. Once, after Sturgis was defeated at Brice Crossroads, General A.J. Smith was sent after Forrest with orders from General Sherman to: 'Kill him, for there will never be peace in Tennessee until Forrest is dead'. While Smith's force was bivouacked for the night, Forrest and one of his aides rode past the Union pickets and reconnoitered the whole camp from within. However, on the way out another picket challenged them. 'How dare you challenge your commanding officer', yelled Forrest, giving himself and his aide a chance to spur their horses into a run. They were fired at, but the bullet went wide."

"I had already heard a few tales of his exploits, " said Warren, "but I thought they were just folklore. He must have been quite a character."

"My dad said the men loved him and would do anything that he told them to do. The main reason for his success was that he had his men fight as infantry, using horses only as a fast means of transportation. He was one heck of a leader. Soon after the war was over, a Union officer asked Lee to identify the best soldier he ever commanded. Lee replied: 'a man I have never met, sir. His name is Forrest.'"

"One more anecdote and I'll stop about the general," said Billy. "Forrest's health had deteriorated to the point that boils were breaking out on his body, probably from a lack of vegetables in his diet. Since he was always exposing himself to enemy fire, his staff was urging him to be more careful; whereupon, he said, 'It might do me good to get shot. It might bust one of these boils.'"

All the anecdotes about Forrest had captured Warren's interest. This just might be his next colorful character to write about. He would have to do some intensive digging, though, to come up with enough facts to make a life story. It wouldn't be as easy as interviewing Billy.

"You mentioned the capture of Fort Pillow, Billy. What did your dad tell you about the aftermath of the capture of that fort? It sure enough got a lot of publicity back near the end of the war, and afterwards," said Warren. "I was very young then, but I can remember people discussing the newspaper articles about the incident."

"According to my dad, the whole thing was blown way out of proportion. He said that there was some unnecessary killing by individual soldiers who were angry because they had been jeered at by the black soldiers before the attack began, but there was no concerted effort to wipe out all the blacks at the fort. It was called a massacre mainly for propaganda purposes by the northern newspapers, and of course, other papers picked up on that. Public support for the war effort at that time was lagging in the North, so this incident was perfect for publicity purposes. As you probably already know, the loss of life at Fredricksburg, Shiloah, and Antietam had caused Union desertions by the thousands, giving the South false hope, and encouraging Lee enough to go on the offensive into Gettysburg. Something to bolster Union morale was badly needed, and it was found. There was an inquiry after the war, as you probably know, but no formal charges were ever brought against Forrest. He was cleared of any violations of the rules of war."

"Yeah, that does make sense, I'll admit. I do know that nothing developed from the inquiry, but it's still called a massacre even today," said Warren, still not completely convinced by Billy's explanation.

"It probably always will be. There was a lot of misinformation circulated about Forrest, though the general was by no means a saint, no matter how much his men might have revered him. My dad had much respect for him, but mostly because he was a great military leader. He hated the way the general had made his fortune before the war. He was a slave trader, as you may already know, something my dad could never support. But he had a good reputation even as a slave trader, refusing to sell any slave to a known abuser. Some slaves begged Forrest to sell them, knowing that he would find a kind master for them."

"I know it sounds like I'm whitewashing the general, but everything I'm telling you can be verified with a little investigating."

"My dad told me so much about the general that I feel like I know him personally. Most of what he told me runs contrary to what is commonly believed about Forrest. To satisfy my own curiosity, I stopped in Memphis and Nashville on my way here and did some research concerning the general. Everything Dad told me turned out to be true. It's not that I thought my dad would actually lie, but that maybe he was just so taken with the general that he couldn't see him in a true light. Am I making any sense?"

"Yes, you are making perfect sense, Billy. What you are trying to say is that you thought your dad couldn't see the Forrest for the trees. Isn't that it?"

"Actually, that's just about perfect," said Billy laughing.

"To get back to Fort Pillow, the casualties were certainly high among the defenders, with 80 of the 262 blacks surviving the battle and 164 of the 295 whites. There were quite a few atrocities committed, as verified by some of Forrest's own men, but they were not at the general's orders. The fact is, he was incensed at the deeds committed by some of his men."

"Another bit of misinformation is that Forrest founded the Ku Klux Klan for the sole purpose to harass and persecute blacks. That is totally false. General Lee was first asked to take the leading role in the Klan, but refused because of his age and health. He did, though, give his support. The Klan was in existence for a year and a half before Forrest was asked, at Lee's suggestion, to take the leadership position. And it was founded solely to combat the carpetbaggers and scalawags during Reconstruction who were preying on whites and free blacks alike."

"Forrest actually sent word to President Grant to do something about the reign of the carpetbaggers, or the only alternative would be a repeat of the Civil War. With half a million whites and several hundred thousand blacks backing him, the U.S. government took him seriously."

"From what I have read there was an actual guerilla war going on between the Union backers and the various secret societies, of which the Klan was the largest. The White Camillas, the White League, the White Brotherhood, and the Red Shirts were some of the other secret organizations. Most of the members were white, but black people were also allowed to join these groups."

"As you know, President Lincoln intended to be extremely lenient with the conquered South, but after his death, radicals, who wanted the South to be punished for its rebellion, took over, bringing on the conditions that made the Klan a necessity. The ex-Confederate's citizenship was taken away, in fact, it was stated that his only right was to be hung. In a secret meeting between Grant and Forrest, the president promised to return full citizenship rights to former Confederates, along with home rule, if Forrest would disband the Klan."

By the time 1869 rolled around, the Klan's purpose had been achieved and Forrest ordered it disbanded. However, the other groups, in which he had no part, ignored that order and continued to function until about 1880. Since the Klan had been the most prominent of the secret societies, its name, as well as Forrest's name, continued to be used, no matter who might have committed a depredation. The carpetbagger era, however, finally did come to a close, but by that time the damage had been done to the general's reputation."

"Yeah, I lived through a lot of what you are telling me, and I'll have to admit, Forrest's name has certainly been smeared with mud," said Warren.

"In North Dakota and Montana there was no such thing as Reconstruction. Most of what I have told you, Mr. Hathaway, I learned at the Memphis courthouse and library. Memphis is where the general spent his last years. He died only nine years ago, so lots of people who knew him personally are still living there. They are saddened, blacks and whites alike, by the bad publicity the general has received, but they don't know what to do about it."

"The belief that he hated black people is also unfounded. At the beginning of the war, Forrest owned 45 male slaves. He told them that if they would stay with him and fight beside him that he would give them their freedom after the war, no matter what the outcome. Only one of them chose not to fight. The other 44 stayed with the general throughout the war, despite numerous opportunities to escape."

"Forrest had an elite command escort called the green berets, and eight of them were black. There were 65 black soldiers with him when he surrendered. Now I ask you, does this sound like a racial bigot to you? Do you think he would trust his life to men that hated him? Do you think those men would have protected a man they hated?"

"Well, Billy, judging from what you have told me, it looks as if history has done the man a terrible wrong," said Warren.

"The records are there for anyone who is interested enough to search them out. Most people are all too willing to believe the worst about the general. I now know that common knowledge isn't always the truth. If my dad hadn't known the man personally, I too would have believed the lies about him. There wouldn't have been any reason not to."

"After the war, Forrest was given the directorship of a Memphis railway. He hired blacks and whites alike because of their abilities and qualifications, not because of color. When Forrest died in 1877, over 10,000 people formed a funeral procession two miles long. Three thousand of those people were black. That bit of information alone should tell us something about his relationship with former slaves."

"I'll have to admit that in the beginning I was skeptical, but you've convinced me that the general was a much better man than I ever considered him," said Warren.

"You don't have to take my word for it. If you ever get the chance, go to Memphis and search the records for yourself. Somebody needs to set the record straight."

The conversation lapsed for a few seconds as Warren seemed to be entranced by all the information that Billy had expounded.

"Mr. Hathaway," said Billy, breaking into Warren's thoughts. "Tomorrow I'd like to take a break from all this and ride up to Hicks Chapel to visit Maggie Smith. I'm sure she would like to hear that my dad is alive and well, after all, they were friends for quite a while.

"Why sure, Billy, that would be fine with me. My fingers sure could use the rest. We're getting far enough ahead with the story that a break will do us both good."

The next day Billy had to ask directions to get to Maggie's house. He discovered that she had remarried and was now Margaret

Warner. He found the house without too much trouble, however. When he rode up to the front gate, he thought at first that no one was home. It was a very warm day, yet the front door was closed, and there was no kind of outside activity that he could detect.

The house was a board and batten frame structure that from all appearances had never seen a coat of paint. It was about the right size for a four-room house, which was very common in these parts. The yard was swept bare, dirt only, with not a blade of grass growing anywhere. Though quite plain, the whole place was neat and clean.

Billy knocked on the door and waited. He was about to turn away when the door opened and there stood a young lady so beautiful that Billy was struck dumb for several seconds.

The young lady seemed to be awestruck also. She and Billy stood with mouths agape until both became embarrassed. She recovered first and blurted out, "Who in this wide world are you, and why are you dressed like an Indian?"

"I--I'm Billy Stanton, Miss. I am half Indian, but I know I don't look like it. I'm looking for Margaret Smi—uh, Margaret Warner's residence."

"Well, Mr. Stanton…Stanton! Your name is Stanton?" She almost screamed, as she covered her cheeks with her hands, mouth agape. "You are--are you Will Stanton's son?"

"Why, yes I am. But I'm afraid you have the advantage, Miss…"

"Oh, forgive me, please. I'm Gracie Warner; Margaret is my mother. Won't you please come in? Mother is next door visiting. If you will have a seat for a few minutes, I'll go fetch her. Oh my goodness, she is going to be totally delighted! She has told me so much about your father that he seems like an old friend."

When Billy had ridden up, there hadn't been another house within sight. He wondered how far Gracie would have to go to fetch her mother.

"If you would like, I could get you a glass of water or buttermilk to drink while you wait."

"Actually, some buttermilk would really hit the spot."

"Is that something you inherited from your father? Mother said he loved buttermilk."

"He still does," said Billy, never taking his eyes off this beautiful girl.

She brought Billy a tall glass filled to the brim with cool buttermilk. "I'll be back in just a few minutes," she said, as she ducked out the back door.

Billy hurried to the back door and watched as Gracie disappeared into the trees behind the house, holding her skirt away from her feet with both hands. At least, he now knew in what direction the other house lay. Carrying the glass, he went to the front porch and sat down on a bench to drink the buttermilk.

Gracie was winded when she got to the neighbor's house, causing her mother some concern. " What's the matter, Gracie? You're all out of breath, and you look as if you've seen a ghost."

Not wanting to miss a chance to have a little fun, Gracie exclaimed, "Oh, Mother, you won't believe what I'm going to tell you! There's an Indian at our house and he's looking for you!"

Both Maggie and her neighbor, Betty, gasped at the same time. "What? An Indian? I don't know any Indians! What are you talking about? What does he want? What does he look like?" Maggie blurted.

Thinking she had gone far enough, Gracie said in a demure voice, "He is probably the handsomest man I have ever seen in my whole life." Then a little more animated and clapping her hands she said, "His name is Billy Stanton, Will Stanton's son, Mother. Can you believe it?"

Maggie aimed a playful blow at Gracie's derriere, but Gracie skipped away, laughing.

"You come in here out of breath and scare me half to death; I ought to make you go to bed without supper," said Maggie, smiling.

"Everything that I said was the truth, and besides it's only ten o'clock in the morning."

"Well," said Maggie, eagerly. "Take me to meet this handsome Indian." Turning to her neighbor Maggie said, "'Bye, Betty, I may see you again later."

Billy heard female voices, so he went back inside the house. With a thank you, he handed the glass to Gracie, who turned to take it to the kitchen. The other woman--whom he presumed to be Maggie, appeared to be around forty years old but already with streaks of gray in her hair--had yet to say a word. She was quite a striking woman, Billy decided, as she stood there with her hands on her hips. Then she walked up and placed her hands on his shoulders, and looking him square in the eyes said, "My, my, except for your size and hair color you would be a young Will Stanton. I believe that I would have known you were Will's son if I had met you on the street somewhere. Come, let's sit down, you've got a lot of talking to do. How is Will doing these days?"

"He was just fine when I left Montana, ma'am."

"Let's get this ma'am business out of the way immediately. All my friends call me Maggie. I expect you to be my friend just as your father was."

"Yes, ma'am...uh, Maggie."

The day Will left here he said he was going to the Rocky Mountains; it looks like he made it."

"Yes ma'am. Uh, I'm sorry, Maggie, I can't help doing that. It's the way I was raised. Yes, it took him several years, but he finally made it. It's really beautiful country out there. We all love it. This valley here is quite beautiful, too, but the mountains here are nothing in comparison to the Rockies. Their snow caps sometimes seem to pierce the belly of the sky."

"That's something I'll only see in pictures I suppose," said Maggie, plaintively.

The conversation soon turned into questions and answers about Will, and they talked until three o'clock, when Maggie excused herself to start the evening meal. Maggie would have liked to continue with her questions until Billy was drained of all information concerning Will. They had lunched around noon on cold meat and cornbread washed down with buttermilk, but Herman Warner worked as a logger and he would be hungry when he came home. No mere snack would do for him. Billy got up to leave, but Maggie would have none of that; he had to stay for supper, and no argument out of him. That meant riding back to Jasper in the dark.

Herman Warner was built like one would expect a logger to be built: shoulders and biceps bulging with muscles, his neck as thick as a woman's waist. From his dad's description of Lamar Smith, Billy thought this man must be his opposite. Yet, he seemed to be as gentle as a lamb, and he and Maggie showed great affection for each other. Billy was made to feel right at home and was the center of attention at the supper table. He could hardly keep his eyes off Gracie, and if Herman and Maggie couldn't see that he and Gracie were stricken with each other, then they would have to be blind.

After they had eaten, Billy once again tried to leave, but all three Warners pleaded with him to stay, and if he wouldn't be offended, he could sleep in the barn. Billy assured them that he had slept many times in less comfortable places and wouldn't be the least bit offended. And besides, he relished the idea of seeing Gracie again tomorrow.

While it was still light enough, he took his horse to the barn, which was made of logs, unsaddled it, forked down some hay from the loft, and went back to the house. They talked until around nine o'clock, when Herman said that he had to get to bed. He had to rise before dawn and be in the woods on the side of Waldens Ridge soon after daybreak.

Though Billy could easily have found his way to the hayloft blindfolded, Gracie insisted on taking a lantern and seeing him to the top of the ladder. After they had said goodnight and Gracie turned to go, Billy said in a low voice, "I wonder how you're going to like living in Montana beautiful lady?"

"What did you say, Billy?" asked Gracie.

"Nothing. I was just thinking out loud. See you in the morning."

"I'll come and wake you; it'll still be dark when we eat breakfast."

Billy lay on his back in the hay, and though he was quite comfortable, it was some time before he could go to sleep. He just couldn't get the picture of a beautiful dark-haired girl out of his mind. He was going to marry that girl if she would have him. He had no way of knowing it, but much the same thoughts concerning him were going through Gracie's mind. Also, Herman and Maggie weren't blind. Maggie was so thankful that Will was alive and safe and had found someone he could love. She had said many prayers for him, and now, to her delight, he had a son right here at her house, and that son had obviously fallen in love with her daughter, and vice versa. Nothing would please her more than to have Will Stanton's son as her son-in-law.

The next morning Gracie came with the lantern and found Billy sitting with his feet on the top rung of the ladder.

"Why didn't you come on inside, Billy, since you were obviously already awake?"

"Because I wanted the most beautiful girl in the world to escort me to the house."

Gracie was immensely pleased, but she said, "Well, I'm sorry, Billy, but I guess you'll just have to settle for me." They both laughed and Billy thought Gracie's laughter sounded like tiny bells ringing. He was completely enamored of this beautiful girl, and it was the most wonderful feeling that he had ever had.

After they had eaten breakfast and Herman had left for work, Billy had to take up where he had left off the night before. He was covering essentially the same ground as with Warren Hathaway, but he was moving much faster because no one was writing anything down. Around two in the afternoon, Billy decided that he must leave or Warren would think that he had gone back to Montana. When he went to the barn to saddle his horse, Gracie went with him. When he had his mount ready to go, Billy turned to Gracie, and so nervous that he could hardly breathe, took both of her hands in his. The mere touch of her hands sent his blood racing through his veins.

With his heart beating so loudly that he was sure Gracie could hear, Billy began searching for the right words to tell her how he felt about her. "G-Gracie, you may think I'm being too bold or maybe even a little bit crazy, and maybe I am. It may be entirely too soon to say what I'm about to tell you, and if it is, then just say so. I-I believe I have fallen in love with you. I fell for you the moment I laid eyes on you. I've never been in love before, never even had a girlfriend before, but you are undoubtedly the most beautiful woman I have ever seen, and I want you to be my wife. Am I being too rash? Am I being completely silly, since we met only yesterday?"

"Well, Billy Stanton, if you're crazy and silly, then so am I, for I feel the same way about you. I believe that I would have surely died if you had ridden away without telling me." When they kissed, Gracie felt as if she were soaring above the clouds. They parted reluctantly.

"When I finish at Mr. Hathaway's, I'm going to Knoxville to visit my grandparents. I'll stop by here on the way. It should be only two or three more days, then I'll see you again."

"'Bye, Billy, I'll be counting the hours."

Gracie watched until Billy was out of sight, then she skipped into the house like a little girl; she had never been so happy before.

When she saw her mother, she locked elbows with her and sashayed around in a circle, then switching arms she went in the opposite direction.

"Whoa, there, little filly, settle down. What has gotten into you? As if I didn't know." Maggie teased.

"I'm in love, Mother, and he said that he loves me, too," Gracie exclaimed. Then, her mood changing dramatically, she asked: "Is that possible, Mother? I mean, is it too early to tell if it's love, real love that is, or is it just infatuation? I've had crushes on boys before, but this isn't the same. What do you think, Mother?"

"There's no way that I can answer that for you, my darling girl. You'll have to decide that on your own, but I do know it's possible to have a lasting love at first sight." Realizing that she might have said too much, Maggie said nothing more.

"Mother? Did you love Will Stanton?"

Her daughter had caught on to what Maggie had never told anyone. Well, her little girl was a baby no longer; maybe it was time to confide in someone. "Yes… yes, I fell for Will the first time that I ever saw him, but he never considered me as more than a friend. More like a sister, I would guess. I was going with Lamar Smith at the time. Lamar was Will's best friend, and then, I even helped arrange it so that Will would meet my cousin, Virginia. That pretty well cancelled any chance that I may have had with him. Any way, I would never have hurt Lamar. He was a good man, but I don't think that I was ever truly in love with him."

"If Will had asked me, though, I would have ridden away with him the day that he brought the news about Lamar's death, but the first move would have had to come from him. It would have killed me if I had made an advance toward him and then been rejected. Gracie, you must never divulge to anyone what I have just told you. Promise me right now that you won't."

"I promise, Mother." Somehow, this secret between them made Gracie feel closer to her mother. In a way she was glad that her mother had loved Will. Now that she was in love with his son, it seemed like a fulfillment of an unrequited love.

"Gracie, don't think for one minute that I don't love your father, because I do, very much."

"Oh, Mother, don't be silly. No such thought ever entered my mind. Anybody can see that you love Daddy." Then after a long pause Gracie said, "Mother? What if Billy asks me to marry him and go to Montana with him? If I accept, I might never see you and Daddy again."

Maggie took Gracie's hands in her own, saying, "Darling, there comes a time when a baby bird has to leave the nest if it's ever going to learn to fly. If you're mature enough to be in true love, and he asks, then you'll know what to do."

Warren Hathaway hadn't worried about Billy at all; he figured anyone who could travel all the way from Montana alone could take care of himself for two days. He didn't even ask Billy what he had been up to. Warren simply wanted to get back to the story. He had already gotten some favorable comments about the first installment in the paper, and once word got around, he believed sales would increase.

That evening after supper Warren said, "What do you think, Billy, are you ready to start again? We got to the point where your dad had topped the Cumberland Plateau and was headed west."

"Well now, let's see. He left in the middle of the day, so he was still atop the plateau when night fell. He had passed a little community called Barkertown and was on the stagecoach road that led to McMinnville when he came to a small stream and decided to make camp. He got far enough off the road so that…"

XV

No one would be able to see the small fire that he had built, Will decided, and the slight breeze would carry the smoke scent away from the road. He didn't want to advertise his campsite, even though Rex would warn him of any intruders. That is, when Rex decided to make his presence known. The last time Will had seen the dog was at an old abandoned field a few miles back down the road, a good place to hunt rabbits, he supposed.

There was just enough daylight left for Will to finish eating and lay out his bedding. Then he lay back against his saddle, and since he wasn't yet sleepy, he watched the fire burn down to glowing coals. Rex came into camp wagging his tail, and judging from the swell of his stomach, he had eaten quite well.

Will was about to doze off when Rex emitted a low growl. "Ssh! Quiet, boy," whispered Will. He too had heard the snap of a twig. Slowly removing his revolver from the holster, he waited. Since Will was lying on the ground, the silhouette of a boy or a small man with a rifle or shotgun was outlined plainly against the lighter background of the sky. When Will cocked the revolver, the click of the hammer sounded, in the stillness of the night, as loudly as the twig breaking. The hunched figure froze in the act of making a step. Will watched the person closely. If the gun swung toward him, he would have to fire, but thankfully, the figure never moved a muscle. "Lay the gun on the ground very, very carefully," commanded Will. The figure obeyed without delay. "Now put a handful of leaves on the coals." When the leaves blazed brightly, Will could see that he had captured a boy about twelve years old. He put sticks on the fire, and after they caught fire he began to question the youngster.

"Young fellow, what in this world was you trying to do? I could have killed you, you know that?"

"I--I'm real s-sorry, Mister. I—I was j-just hungry. I thought if I c-could get the drop on you, I could t-take your food. I wasn't g-goin' to hurt you. Shucks, my old g-gun ain't even loaded. I already s-shot all my pow-powder up. M-me and my m-ma have b-been livin' off w-what I could k-kill, n-now we ain't even g-got that, and no m-m-money to buy no more pow-powder with. The n-neighbors have done g-got tired of us always bor-bor-borrowin' and n-never givin' n-nothin' back."

Will checked the old shotgun, and the kid was telling the truth, there was no cap under the hammer. "You took an awful chance, son, coming in on me like that. Say you're awful hungry, huh? Well, let's see what we can do about that." Will sliced bacon into his frying pan and opened a tin of beans. The boy started on the bacon before it even had a chance to cool properly then practically drank the beans from the can, hardly chewing them at all, before Will even had a chance to warm them. He was afraid the kid would choke.

When the boy had finished eating, Will rinsed out the bean can and poured the boy a drink of water. From his canteen. "Now you take this blanket and you lay down right there in those leaves and you go to sleep. If you move, that big dog there will tear your throat out." The boy was looking wide-eyed at the dog and didn't see the slight grin on Will's face. As if he understood what was said, Rex growled from deep within his chest and moved closer to the boy and lay down again. Will lay down on the saddle blanket, drew his hat down over his face and was soon fast asleep.

The next morning they had more bacon and a can of peaches each, then Will said, "Now, let's go see where you live." Will placed the boy at the front of the saddle so that the youngster could more easily carry his old shotgun across his lap while they rode.

On the way, the boy told Will that his dad had been killed at Shiloah, fighting for the Union, and things had gotten progressively worse for him and his mother since that time. Now, they were on the verge of starvation. By the time the boy had finished talking, Will had backtracked the mile or so to where the youngster lived.

"I-I didn't see no d-dog when you p-passed me yesterday, Mister. I was h-hidin' in the woods right along here s-somewheres. If I'd a kn-knowed you had a dog I wouldn't o' even t-tried to sneak up on you."

"You shouldn't have anyway, but that's all in the past now. Let's forget it. By the way, what's your name?"

"J-Jimmy. Jimmy Cleek, my m-momma's name is S-Sarah."

When they rode into the yard of a surprisingly well-kept house and yard, a scarecrow of a woman came out of the house to meet them. She was clean, but her faded dress was practically nothing but patches. Obviously, Will thought, from the looks of her, she has been depriving herself of food so that the boy could eat.

Will dismounted and lifted the boy down.

"Jimmy, Son, I've been worried sick about you. Where have you been all night?"

"Mrs. Cleek, you'd might as well know the truth," said Will, answering for the boy. "Jimmy tried to rob me of my food last night. I made him stay the night with me. Jimmy told me what a rough time you two are going through. Ma'am, pardon me for asking, but what are you going to do? What I mean is, how are you going to get by? You can't live on squirrels and rabbits the rest of

126

your lives. Surely, you must have some kind of plan. Both of you will starve before the summer is over if you continue on like this."

"We've managed to make it this far, Mister. I'll have to admit it ain't been easy, but we're alive," said Sarah, with as much pride as she could muster.

"Look, Ma'am, I'm not trying to rob you of your dignity, but I am concerned about this boy here. He could have been killed last night. Now, if you will, please, tell me what you plan to do.

"Well, I don't have no plow horse, but if I had some money to buy seed, I know I could manage to break up enough ground with a shovel and hoe to raise enough corn and beans and taters to live on, with Jimmy's help of course."

"How would you live until harvest time?"

"It wouldn't be much of a problem if Jimmy had powder and shot; he's quite a hunter for his age. They's wild plants and roots that I can gather, but they just ain't enough by theirselves. We need a little meat to go with 'em."

"Jimmy, I'm going to give you something," said Will, untying the shotgun that he had carried all the way from Alabama but had never used. Handing the boy the saddlebags from the packhorse, he said, "Here's everything you'll need to load with. Make every shot count."

"Oh, wow!" said an excited Jimmy. "A double-barrel. T-Thanks Mister."

"Taking a twenty dollar gold piece from another saddlebag, Will handed it to Sarah. "I hope you and Jimmy will be all right. That should be enough to get you started." He then gave her nearly all his food from his saddlebags, keeping just enough to get him to McMinnville, less than a day's journey away.

"Mister, who in the world are you? Why are you doing this?" asked Sarah, with tears streaming down both cheeks and clutching the coin with both hands. "Did the good Lord send you here? Are you a angel or somethin'?"

"Ha! I've never been called that before, and if I told you my name, it wouldn't make any difference. You'll never see me again after today."

"Well, whoever you are, I thank you with all my heart. You've probably saved our lives."

As Will turned to leave, Jimmy ran along beside the horse. "T-Thank you, Mister, I'm real s-sorry I tried to rob you."

Will reined to a stop. "Jimmy, just promise me one thing. Promise me that you will never do anything that stupid again," said Will.

"I p-promise," said Jimmy, dropping his gaze to look at his feet. "I'm gonna take real good care of the shotgun, Mister," he added. Will noticed that this was the boy's first full sentence without stuttering since they had met.

"God bless you, Mister!" yelled Sarah, waving as Will rode away.

Don't bet on it lady, thought Will. If God had blessed you, I'd be twenty dollars richer right now. Still, he had a deep feeling of satisfaction in being able to help these unfortunate people. He would love to take Jimmy under his wing and guide the boy as he grew into a man, but there was no way that such a thing could be possible. He hoped Sarah, out of desperation, wouldn't latch on to the first no-account man that came along; she and Jimmy deserved something better after suffering the way they had.

By noon Will had made his way down the western escarpment of the plateau and was riding along beside Collins River. In a deep, still pool he could see a school of large suckerfish so close to the surface that their dorsal fins were barely under the surface of the water. The fish were enjoying the warmth of the surface water that had absorbed heat from the sun. Taking the Spencer, Will crawled to the edge of the bank keeping a low growing shrub between himself and the fish. He looked over the school of fish and chose as his target two fish that were so close together they were almost touching. Because of refraction, the fish were actually a little bit closer to him than they appeared. Knowing this, Will aimed an inch low and pulled the trigger. After the ripples from the bullet had dissipated, he could see that both fish had rolled belly-up, unconscious from the concussion of the bullet hitting the water. Will cut the tallest cane from a bamboo patch and maneuvered both fish to the bank before they could revive. He ran a forked stick into the gill slits and out the mouths of both fish and, tying the prongs of the stick together with a strip of bark from a nearby leatherwood bush, hung the fish over the saddle horn.

Will stopped in McMinnville only long enough to get more food staples, then turned west toward Murfreesboro. When he made camp that evening, he fried the fish in bacon grease--suckerfish have delicious flesh but are chocked full of bones—and gave Rex the heads.

Henry Thompson had been right about the dog; he surely could take care of himself. There were times when he would be gone for an hour or more--probably off somewhere trying to ambush a rabbit or squirrel--then suddenly, he would be back, trotting along the trail in front of the horse. Will fed him hardly anything at all.

The next day Will passed through Murfreesboro without stopping. He had met and passed many people since he had left the Selma, Alabama, area. Some were riding horses or mules, some riding in wagons, and others walking, but none had appeared as derelict as the man limping along just a few yards in front of him. Will slowed his horse in order to be able to observe the man more thoroughly. The poor fellow had on a tattered, once gray uniform and shoes bound to his feet with rags. He had a severe limp and was dragging his left foot somewhat, stirring up dust with every step. His beard and hair were dirty and in dire need of a trim. His appearance--his every move--exuded pain and suffering.

As Will drew abreast of the man, he raised his shaggy head enough to see who was passing. When he saw Will's captain insignia, he stopped, came to a semblance of attention, and saluted. "The war is over, soldier. You don't have to do that," said Will.

"Yes, sir. I feel that I do, sir," the man said, still holding the salute.

Will returned the salute and said, " At ease, private."

Will had ridden over this part of Tennessee several times during the war and knew the area intimately, making it easy to choose the better places to camp. But the soldier looked as if he hadn't been eating regularly, and Will wanted to tactfully invite him to a meal without insulting the man. "You know this area around here? I'm looking for a place to rest my backside and maybe grab a bite to eat in the process," said Will.

"Yes, sir. Know this area like the back o' my hand. My home is jist this side of Nashville. Stewart Creek is jist a little way ahead- -mighty fine place to stop for a while."

"Well, why don't we try to get you on that packhorse, and you can show me where this place is. Think you can hang on without a saddle?"

"I reckon I can ride jist about anythang that's got four legs, but you can't miss the creek; you'll have to ride right through it."

"Ride along with me, if you will. I never did like to eat alone," said Will, as he untied the packhorse and led it to the bank that abutted the road. "My name is Will Stanton," said Will, as he extended his hand.

"I'm Abraham Townsend. Abe to my friends," he said, as he shook Will's hand.

Abe, with Will's help, got astride the horse, sitting in front of the pack. As they rode slowly along, Will managed to get the man talking without seeming to pry. Abe had been severely wounded in the left thigh during the fighting near Atlanta, not long after Will and Buck had ridden away to rejoin Forrest. The wound had gotten badly infected, and the army doctor had insisted that the leg be amputated, but Abe had adamantly refused. It had been nip and tuck for days, before the infection and fever finally began to subside, but still, he had been laid up for months, as much of the left thigh muscle had been destroyed. It had taken many weeks of therapy to strengthen the leg enough to be able to walk again.

When Abe was finally able to hobble around, he started on his long trek toward home--on foot and without telling anyone that he was leaving. After more than two months, sometimes making only five miles per day and depending heavily on the charity of others, he was now within twenty-five miles of home.

When they arrived at Stewart Creek, Will and Abe turned upstream a short distance to a frequently used campground. Will sliced bacon into the frying pan, while Abe gathered firewood. After the bacon was fried, Will used the grease to fry potatoes. Abe sat down with his back against a tree, chewing on a slice of bacon while the potatoes were cooking. Within five minutes, he was sound asleep.

Will studied the frail figure before him. Obviously, Abe had at one time weighed much more than he now did--the tattered uniform hung loosely on his skeletal frame. Will felt disgust for himself because of the bitterness he felt, when it was obvious that this man had suffered so much more than he had. Was Abe bitter? If he was, he didn't let it show.

Rex came trotting into camp wagging his tail, sniffed inquisitively at Abe, and then lay down beside him.

When the potatoes were done, Will divided them, as well as the bacon, into two equal portions. Since he had only one metal plate and one fork, he would eat from the frying pan, using his knife, allowing Abe to use the plate and fork.

"Wake him up boy," said Will to Rex. Rising to his feet, the big dog barked once no more than six inches from Abe's ear. Abe came awake with his arms flailing the air.

"Guess I kinda drifted off," said Abe, feeling slightly embarrassed for having fallen asleep. "Where'd this barkin' horse come from?"

"That's Rex. He's my traveling companion," said Will, grinning at Abe's remark.

"How come you ain't got no saddle on him?"

Will figured Abe didn't expect him to answer the question as he handed him the food. Abe held the plate with both hands as he bowed his head and said boldly, "Thank you, Lord, for this food, and bless the hands that prepared it."

No, thought Will, the man is certainly not bitter. "Abe? Let me ask you something. How can you thank God for anything after what you've been through? How can you even believe in God?" asked Will, a little more intensely than he intended.

"Why, Cap'm, sir, how could I not be thankful? That piece of shrapnel could o' took my leg plumb off, or it could o' hit me in the body somewheres, or I could o' died from gangrene. But instead, I'm here, alive, with two legs to get around on. Well, almost two. Shore, I've missed a few meals, but I'm almost home, now. My wife and younguns are waitin' for me just a few miles down the road. Give me a month or two of my wife's good cookin' and I should fill out quite a bit. Yes, sir, I'm very thankful."

The fact that you have a wife and kids to go home to makes all the difference in the world, thought Will. He had no intention of letting go of his anger so easily.

"You about ready to move on?" asked Will, after he had finished scouring the frying pan and plate with sand from the streambed.

"I guess that means I get to ride that fine hoss some more," said Abe, jauntily. "That's mighty kind of you, Cap'm."

"Yeah, well, I'm going your way; it ain't no big deal," Will said, still a little chagrined that Abe could be so cheerful.

After riding only a short while, they entered the little town of Smyrna. Will stopped at the only general store and dismounted. "I'll just be a few minutes, Abe. You want to go inside or sit out here?" asked Will.

"Ain't no reason for me to go in, Cap'm. I ain't seen nothin' that even looks like real money in months. I'll be fine right here, sir. This here hoss sets pretty good."

"Don't go to sleep and fall off the horse. I won't be long," said Will, as Abe grinned a little sheepishly.

Will went to the dry goods section and picked out a shirt, overalls, socks and shoes that should fit Abe, that is, after he gained another thirty pounds. Abe was only a little shorter than Will, but his present weight was far less than Will's 185 pounds. The storeowner wrapped the purchase in old newspaper and tied it with string that had obviously been used before, since it had several knots in it. Will said nothing to Abe about the package as they resumed their journey.

At the next sizable creek, Will let Abe lead the way to a secluded area and helped him to dismount, thrust the package into his hands, and told him he needed a bath before he got home.

Abe's mouth was agape as the clothes and shoes tumbled to the ground when the string was broken. He stood holding the newspaper and string. Tears threatened to flow as he said, "Cap'm. I can't let you do this, sir."

"It's already been done. Now, wouldn't you like to look and smell a little better when you see your wife again?" asked Will, as he picked up a chunk of lye soap from the ground and handed it to Abe.

Abe was all smiles as he emerged from the bushes a few minutes later wearing his new clothes. His hair was still wet from the bath, and he smelled much better. "These clothes should be jist right after I put on a few pounds, Cap'm. Thank you, sir."

Will had been stropping his razor on his stirrup strap while Abe had been bathing. Now was the time for Abe to get a haircut, of sorts, and a beard trimming. He looked almost presentable after will got through with him.

As they neared Nashville, the sun was sinking low toward the western horizon when Abe said, "We turn left here, Cap'm. My place is on Mill Creek just a little way down this here road."

In less than thirty minutes they were looking at a two-story log house set back a hundred yards from the road. Fruit trees in full bloom lined the lane that ran past the left side of the house to a gristmill on the creek at the far side of the cleared property. This is a scene that an artist would love to paint, thought Will.

"This is it Cap'm. Looks jist the same as the day I left. Don't seem as if the war ever teched the place. Looks to me like Maybelle must've kept them two boys busy keepin' ever'thing nice an' neat. Right purty ain't it?" said Abe, as they rode into the yard.

When Will's horse snorted, a hound that had been sleeping in the shade of a rose bush began a loud, fervent baying. The hackles on Rex's back were raised, and he was growling deep in his throat. "Rex! Go to the road! Go on, now!" Will commanded, pointing back down the lane. When he turned back toward the house, Abe had dismounted and was almost to the porch when a woman and two teenage boys burst through the doorway, seemingly as one, and overwhelmed him. It was a melee with the dog barking and the whole family laughing and crying and jumping around.

After they all began to settle down, Abe turned toward the place where he had dismounted. "Cap'm, I'd like for you to meet... why he's gone. He's gone, Maybelle. The Cap'm's gone."

Will rode no more than a quarter mile from Abe's place before making his way into the woods to camp. It wasn't a real camp; all he wanted was a place to sleep. He didn't even eat anything before retiring.

Will was glad that Abe had such a nice place and loving family to go back to, but it made him feel so depressed and desolate to have witnessed such a homecoming, especially since he still missed Ginny so desperately.

Early in the morning of the fourth day after leaving the Sequatchie Valley, Will entered Nashville. Since he had eaten nothing the evening before, he was famished. Deciding to have something to eat other than trail fare, he chose an inconspicuous restaurant-tavern combination on a side street. He hitched the horses to the rail and commanded Rex to guard them. After standing just inside the door long enough to let his eyes adjust to the gloomy interior, he chose a table that allowed him have a wall at his back while facing the door.

The only other customers in the tavern were two Union officers seated at an even dimmer corner table. They stared at him for several seconds, but when Will began staring back, they turned their attention back to their drinks. Will was still wearing his stained gray uniform and felt no compunction at all about it. He had never surrendered or signed a pardon and considered no man his master. The war was over, and it would be better for everyone concerned if these officers left him alone.

This place sure was a shabby excuse for a restaurant; he hoped the food was safe to eat. The only reason he had chosen this place was because he thought there would be few customers. He certainly hadn't expected to encounter Union officers in such a dingy place as this. Common soldiers, maybe, but not officers.

The bartender-waiter promptly came to take his order, if you could call it that--there was only one dish available. So, Will had fried potatoes, cured ham, and cornbread, with a tall glass of buttermilk to drink and a piece of apple pie, made from dried apples, for dessert. The meal wasn't a whole lot better than what he would have had on the trail, but at least someone else had prepared it.

When he had eaten about half his meal, two roughly dressed characters entered the tavern. The larger of the two had the biggest knife on his belt that Will had ever seen. He had heard of Arkansas Toothpicks; this must be one of them. The two men were exact opposites in build—the larger one was grossly fat while the other was as skinny as a fence rail. The big man's upper body was so gross that his arms stuck out at an angle, and his head seemed to rest directly on his shoulders, with no visible neck at all. Will sensed trouble almost immediately. That feeling was fortified when the fat man looked belligerently at Will, then flashed a squinty-eyed smile in the direction of the Federal officers.

"Gimme a plate, Hank, and don't be stingy with the vittles," said the man with the knife.

"Make that two," chimed in the other.

When they had their plates in their hands, they turned and Knife-man swaggered over to Will's table.

"You're sitting at my table, Reb. This table is always reserved just for me. I'd consider it a personal favor if you'd take your eats somewhere else," said Knife-man loud enough for the two officers to hear.

Will looked up at the bloated face in front of him, which was even uglier up close, then forked another bite of potatoes into his mouth, acting as if he had heard absolutely nothing. The big man obviously wasn't used to being ignored. He took a deep breath and held it, puffing up like a large toad, which with his belly hanging over his belt, he had no small resemblance to.

Handing his plate of food to the skinny man and drawing the large knife, he said again even louder, "I said this here is my table!" Then punctuated the remark by sticking the knife into the table beside Will's plate with such force that the plate bounced and buttermilk sloshed out of the glass. "You got a hearing problem, loser? Maybe I oughta give you another cut down your left cheek!

Kind of balance things out, huh?" The skinny man, still holding the plates, giggled at the big man's supposed humor.

The fat man was bent forward over the table with his left hand, palm down, helping to support his weight, his right hand still wrapped around the haft of the big knife. Will calmly turned the fork in his hand around and stabbed the man through the muscle between the thumb and forefinger of his left hand, sinking the prongs of the fork into the table. The man yelped and jumped back, leaving the knife but dislodging the fork from the table. "Why you no account..." The man began but got no farther before the barrel of Will's revolver reached his temple. The man was out like a light. The table rattled as the big man hit the floor.

"Sit down, lieutenant! This is not our affair!" Will's attention was brought to the corner where the two officers were. The captain had his hand on the lieutenant's right arm, which was in the process of drawing a weapon. The young officer meekly sat down, but Will could tell that he really didn't want to. Will watched them a few seconds before holstering his own gun.

In Will's experience, lieutenants were an inflated lot, infatuated with their own sense of importance. By the time a man made captain, his ego had been punctured enough times to let some of the air out.

"I probably just saved your life, lieutenant. Maybe mine too," said the captain, just barely loud enough for Will to hear. "That man is obviously a veteran. That may not mean anything to you, but it does to me. He certainly knows how to handle himself, and I think it would be better all around if we just pretended that nothing happened. That troublemaker got what he deserved, don't you agree?"

Captain, he's still wearing a Confederate uniform, and I don't like it," said the lieutenant.

"Well, they could be the only clothes he's got. Ever think of that? The war just ended a few days ago, you know."

"Could I have another fork, please?" asked Will. He had lost his appetite, but he was not going to let it show. When he had finished eating, he inquired about his bill.

"Friend, you don't owe me nothing at all. I've been hoping somebody would stand up to that fat skunk for a long time. This ain't the first time he's tried to start trouble with one of my customers You're the first one he couldn't scare, though. Everybody else just let him have his way. My business has actually suffered because of him. Maybe he won't be so quick to push people around from now on. I tell you what, friend, that bit of action was well worth paying to see."

"Do you want some help with him?" asked Will, indicating the unconscious man whose shirt had ridden up exposing a pale, hairy belly.

"Naw, he'll come around after a while."

"What happened to his friend?" Will wanted to know.

"He lit out like he'd been scalded. He's probably half way to Kentucky by now."

"Thank you for the meal. Should I pull the fork out of his hand before he wakes up? It looks like the prongs are a mite bent."

"Naw, it'll be my pleasure," said the bartender, smiling and rubbing his palms together.

"Looks like the skinny one wasn't hungry after all," said Will, surveying the broken plates and spilled food on the floor.

"Ha! He didn't even take time to set the plates down, much less eat," said the bartender.

Will worked the large knife loose from the table, and bending over the unconscious man, cut his belt and took the scabbard that went with the knife. To the bartender he said, "He'll be less likely to get into trouble without this." Such a large knife may be of use sometime later on, he decided.

As Will reached the door, he thought of Rex guarding the horses. Turning back inside, he asked the bartender if he had a meat scrap he would sell. The man, refusing payment, brought a long bacon rind from the kitchen and tossed it to Rex. The big dog caught it in his mouth, but it was too tough to swallow without a lot of chewing. The strip of meat was flapping at both sides of his mouth as he trotted happily down the street beside Will's horse.

As he left Nashville behind, Will felt as if he were going to be sick. He shouldn't have finished the meal as excited as he had been. He had tried to put on a tough front, but inside he had been quite shaken, especially since he thought that he would have to defend himself against the young lieutenant. He certainly was beholden to the captain for keeping a rein on his companion. He didn't need the Union army on his trail.

Why did trouble seem to be seeking him out? Was it something about his demeanor? He really didn't think so. He never invited trouble, never acted first; he simply reacted. Maybe it was just that hard times breed hard people. He hoped that there was some place where he could find peace. He just wanted to live and let live. Was that asking too much?

XVI

"Billy," said Warren. "Your dad gave the Cleek woman twenty dollars and other things, and then thought that if God had blessed her then he could have kept the twenty dollars. Didn't he realize that his act of kindness was actually the blessing for that woman? And then there was the debt that he paid for Maggie Smith. And what about Abe? It doesn't rain manna from out of the sky any more. Your dad wants to hold onto his resentment and blame God, but at the same time, he does these acts of kindness. Doesn't that seem contradictory to you?"

"Yes, sir, I suppose it is contradictory. He could show compassion for those in need, while at the same time harboring a lot of anger and frustration. But because he had lost so much in such a short span of time, my dad was looking for someone or something to blame for all the bad things that had happened. God was just a convenient scapegoat, I suppose. Even though he was too angry at that time to be objective, he could look back later and see how he had let the anger blind him to his true self.

Down deep inside, my dad was basically a good man, despite everything that had happened to him. If someone wanted trouble, my dad was willing to give him all he could handle, but on the other hand, he was always willing to show compassion for the less fortunate. We'll see more examples of that as we continue with the story.

"Yeah, I'm sure you're right," said Warren. "I just thought I'd mention it. We can get back to the story if you'd like."

Will's next stop was Clarksville. It wouldn't be long until he would leave Tennessee for good. Most of Kentucky could be traversed in a single day at the western end, and on the seventh day after heading west, he was at Paducah, where he would cross the Ohio River into southern Illinois.

He had been to Paducah during the war, but every place north of the Ohio River would be new territory to him. He had to wait nearly an hour for the ferry to come back across the river from Illinois. He was so filled with apprehension about riding through what he still considered enemy territory that he almost turned his horses around and headed south, thinking to maybe go through Texas before heading toward the Rocky Mountains. The ferry returned before he made up his mind to leave. Paying the fare, he led his horses aboard.

If the people of southern Illinois thought it odd that a man dressed in Confederate gray was riding through their state, they didn't make an issue of it. Many were the people working in the fields that would stop what they were doing to watch him ride by, some with hostile stares, but a few with friendly waves. Then again, he remembered, there was no lack of Confederate sympathizers in Missouri, which was only a short distance to the west. Will had ridden all the way from Selma, Alabama, to southern Illinois, being challenged only once by anyone with authority. There were so many people on the move this close to the end of the war that travelers were commonplace. That suited Will just fine; he would have enjoyed being invisible, if that were possible.

Eleven days after embarking on his journey, Will crossed the Mississippi River into St. Louis--by far the largest city he had ever seen. He had never before seen such peacetime activity. The noise of the men loading and unloading the many steamboats and flatboats was almost deafening. He sat on his horse and watched the hustle and bustle until some of the workers began to stare back at him.

It was now over two weeks since he had been wounded, and the scab was beginning to peel. The itch was sometimes maddening. Will absent mindedly rubbed the scar as he meandered through the city to get the feel of it and was about to look for a place to spend the night, when a small crowd of laughing, cheering men caught his attention. He stopped his horse at the edge of the group and, standing up in the stirrups, peered over the heads of the men to see what was going on.

A short, slender man with a foreign accent, and dressed all in buckskins, was pleading with a much bigger man to return a pair of eyeglasses to him. Considering this none of his business, Will reined his horse to the left intending to ride on when he heard: "Please, *m'sieur,* I beg of you, do not break them. I am but a poor man. I cannot afford another pair."

"Why don't you just take 'em from me you little pip-squeak? Come on squaw-man, you don't look so good without 'em." Several men laughed, showing their approval of the pun. Will slowly shook his head and, with a sigh of resignation, dismounted. Pushing his way through the crowd, he walked up to the troublemaker, and looking the man square in the eyes and without saying a word, held out his left hand palm up.

The grin on the big man's face slowly disintegrated as his eyes followed the slightly swollen line of the scar on Will's face, then slowly descended to Will's right hand hovering over the butt of his revolver. "Why shore 'nuff, Mister, this here ain't nothing to fight about. Jist havin' a little fun is all," he said, as he laid the spectacles in Will's hand. The crowd groaned in unison at the ending of the entertainment, then began to break up.

Will, turning to the smaller man, said not too kindly, "Here, try to hang on to these, will ya."

"Aah, thank you, *m'sieur*, I am so very grateful to you. How can I ever repay you?"

"Forget it. You don't owe me nothing," said Will as he remounted.

"You are much too kind. If you would wait but for a moment, *m'sieur*, I will get my horses and ride along with you," said the little man, wanting the protection that Will afforded, at least until he was well away from the troublemaker.

"Do you know where would be a good place to spend the night?" asked Will, after the little fellow had caught up with him.

"I am camped beside the river just a little way north of the city, *m'sieur*. It would give me great pleasure to have you as my guest. My tent is large enough for four men to sleep in, and there is plenty of grass for all the horses."

"Well, maybe. I'll think about it. Right now, though, I've got to have a bite to eat. My belt buckle is rubbing against my backbone."

"*M'sieur*, I do not like to brag, but I, Jean Rene Gautier, am one of the best of cooks. If you will but buy the meat, I will cook for you the steak that you will never forget," said Jean, seeing the chance to keep Will around for a while, as well as an opportunity for a free meal.

Will chuckled then said, "Alright, John, you've got yourself a deal. My name is Will Stanton, by the way."

"I am very pleased to know you, Will Stanton, and my name is Jean."

"Yeah, John, I caught your name the first time around. It's an easy name for me to remember; my dad's name is John," said Will, not understanding why the little Frenchman was smiling and shaking his head.

They found a market and Jean chose the cuts of meat, the most expensive cuts Will noticed, and other items that he needed.

After they arrived at Jean's camp, the campfire was rekindled and the little Frenchman put potatoes in the coals to bake while the steaks were cooking. Will had been hungry when he had met Jean, now after all the waiting, he was famished. By the time the steaks were ready, he had eaten a half-cooked potato to quiet his stomach, burning his tongue in the process. He didn't know what Jean had used for seasoning, but after taking the first bite, he would have to admit that the steak was quite delicious.

As he looked around the camping area, he decided that he would much rather be here beside the river than to be in the best of hotels. Besides, he would have had to find a place where Rex would have been accepted. After four years of sleeping wherever he could and in all kinds of weather, even a tent was a luxury.

After so many days of riding, he figured he needed a rest, so the next day was just idled away talking to Jean Rene. He discovered that the little Frenchman lived in North Dakota in an Indian village on the Missouri River and had an Indian wife and two children.

"How did you come to live in North Dakota, John? It's been a while since I studied geography, but if my memory serves me right, that's a long way from France."

"This is true, *m'sieur*, but that is exactly what I wish. I want to be in the place where my father will never look for me. You see, my father is the military man, like his father and grandfather before him. As a teenager, I must attend the military school to please my father who, as a young man, was an officer in Napoleon's army. My father desired for me to also become an officer. Can you see Jean Rene as a commander of men? You saw yesterday the respect that men have for one of my size."

"I do not want to be in the military and I hate this military school, but I must attend or constantly fight with my father. While a student, my father would send to me a generous stipend every month, if my grades they are satisfactory, and my friend, I make sure the grades they are good, eh? I am not like my fellow students who waste money on wine and women. I save the money, and when I am twenty years old, I board this ship that is going to Quebec."

"I am there in Quebec for two years, teaching in the school, and then my father finds me. He has sent this man who is to take me back to France, but I am the lucky one to escape. I take passage on another boat going west. I make my way to Winnipeg, but before one month is past, this very same man, he is there also. Some traders are going south into the country of the Dakotas to trade with the Indians; I go with them, and that is where I stay."

"It is *wichohan washte*--the good way of life--but now and then I am overcome with the urge to travel, and so I am here. Two years ago I go to Chicago; before that I visit St. Paul. But, Jean Rene, he never goes north into Canada, even though there is nothing my father could do any more to make me return to France. There is no desire in my heart to see France ever again. My heart weeps that I also have no desire to see my father again, but it is true. I do not even know if he still lives. This vast land is now my home; I will never leave it. I have a wonderful wife and two sons. I am content.

When I am the student at the academy, I learn to love the books, and now and then, I must go to the city where I can buy books to take back to the village. I have two very inquisitive children and a wife who is also very eager to learn, and I teach them the English and French from these books. They also have learned to speak the English and French, as well as three native languages. Sometimes in their conversation the little ones will mix together the words of five different tongues. It is very comical."

"There is some similarity in our lives, John. I, too, had to get away from a domineering father, while I was still a young man. At the present, I'm not at all sure what I'm trying to get away from, but whatever it is, tomorrow I hit the trail again," said Will.

"Where do you go from here, my friend?"

"I'm heading west toward the Rocky Mountains, after that, I don't know. I'm just playing it by ear, as they say. I just want to lose myself in some secluded valley where there is plenty of game."

"I, too, am ready to travel once more," said Jean. "Since your plans are not so definite, my friend, why not come with me to my village, eh? You will see much wild game, I guarantee. You will see in one herd more animals than you have ever seen before in all your life, though, I am sorry to say, there are not now so many as there once was. The next year, if you still wish to continue your journey, you can get an early start for the mountains. Since we will be traveling north and west, I think maybe you will be just a little closer to these Shining Mountains, as the natives call them, when we get to my village. What do you say to this idea, Will Stanton?"

"Well, John, like I said, I've got no particular plans. It really makes no difference when I see the Mountains--this year or next. And, I'll have to admit, it is getting late in the year to start looking for a good spot to spend the winter. Since I don't know the mountain country, it would be pure luck to find the right place. Preparations for a winter dwelling would take a while, and the laying away of a supply of food would also take a lot of time. But look, John, I will still have to eat if I stay in your village. How are things going to work out any better if I go with you?"

"Ah, *m'sieur,* listen to me but for a moment, if you please. I foresee no problem at all. There is always enough food in the village. No one goes hungry. There will be a great bison hunt for the taking of much meat; there will be the dried vegetables from the field; the wild berry will soon be ripe for the harvest; there will be the nuts in the forest along the river for the taking. Do not concern yourself about food. As long as Jean Rene has food, Will Stanton will have food, I guarantee," Jean hurriedly exclaimed, afraid Will would choose to go his own way.

"Well, all right, I'll give it a try. Let's go into town and get supplies; I'm anxious to be on the trail."

"You will never regret this decision, I guarantee. But actually, *m'sieur,* I have another suggestion, if you would but listen for another moment. It would be much faster and easier to take passage on the riverboat. That is the way that I travel to the south, but I do not have the money for such a return," said Jean, hoping that Will might volunteer to buy the tickets.

"To tell you the truth John, I don't trust those riverboats that much. I've heard tell that the Missouri is an unpredictable river, with lots of snags and sandbars in it. Why, I heard that just a little while back a boat called the *Arabian* hit a snag and sank in about ten minutes. You hear anything about that?"

"Well… yes, *m'sieur,* I have heard a little something about such a boat, but there was no loss of life, except for one horse, that is."

"Is it true that the boatmen call the river Old Misery instead of Missouri?"

"Yes, that is also true, but…"

"I think I'll take my chances on land, thank you," Will interrupted.

With a downcast look, Jean shrugged in defeat, and then added, "There is but one more small thing. If we remain on this side of the river, we must go due west because of a great curve in the river until the whole state of Missouri is behind us, but if we cross the river now, we can strike a northwesterly course and save three, maybe even four, days of travel. What do you think about this, eh?"

"Which side of the river is your village on?"

"It is to the west of the Missouri on the stream called the Knife."

"That Missouri, or so I've heard, is a mighty big river, John, why not just stay on this side instead of crossing over now and back again later? A few days more or less won't matter. I'm in no particular hurry, are you?"

"No, *m'sieur*, I guess maybe I am not. It will take three weeks and more to reach the village, if everything goes well. As you say, a few days more will not matter," said Jean, resigning himself to a very long trip on horseback.

Since he wasn't heading for the Rockies anymore, Will didn't care if it took three weeks or three months to reach the village. He was content to just be riding again. After leaving the familiar areas of Tennessee and Kentucky, every place he had seen was new to him, and he was enjoying his journey very much. It also seemed that the farther he got from Tennessee the better he slept at night. Maybe it wasn't the distance but the passing of time that was dimming the memories he had of Ginny and Buck, but life was now just a little more tolerable than it had been. Even though the anguish over their loss wasn't as acute, there was still a lot of smoldering resentment just beneath the surface ready to spring forth at the least provocation. And there was a void in his life that needed to be filled. A void that would remain forever if he lived like a hermit in some far away secluded valley.

It took them five days to cross Missouri, and at Kansas City, after buying more supplies, they turned northwest. From St. Louis to Kansas City they had traveled on a well-established road, part of the Oregon Trail, but once they turned to the northwest, there was mostly open country with few roads and very few people—white or red.

As they traveled north, the signs of white civilization became fewer and fewer. The land had changed drastically since they had left Missouri, as trees had given way to grass--more grass than Will had ever seen before. One day as they neared a ridge that was much higher than the surrounding country, Jean insisted that they ride to the top. Will had never seen such a panorama in his life, as the one from this vantage point. In every direction, there was nothing but an endless expanse of grass, except to the east where a line of trees broke the prairie, undulating like a snake, where the Missouri River flowed. While surrounded by forest or in a city, Will had never felt insignificant, but here in this huge expanse of nothingness, he felt that he was no more outstanding than a flyspeck on a full-length mirror.

Will looked up at the clear blue sky. Not a cloud could be seen anywhere. Only one tiny black speck marred the perfection of the blue background. An eagle or a buzzard, he couldn't say which, was riding an updraft in lazy circles. The horses he and Jean were riding must look no bigger than ants to the bird at such a distance.

"This is the biggest waste of space I've ever seen, John. There's nothing much to see any way you look. I don't think I'm going to like this country a whole lot."

"It will take some time getting used to it, *m'sieur,* that is for sure. I have heard of men who have gone insane because of the emptiness of the prairie, but on the other hand, those that have lived their lives here would feel claustrophobic in a dense forest. If you stay long enough in this country, you will begin to notice things that you never suspected were there. It is far from empty. Look to the far northwest horizon. Do you see?"

Off to the northwestern where sky and earth seemed to blend together, there was a dust cloud that rose from the ground, indicating the movement of a large group of animals. Jean said it could be a herd of buffalo, an Indian village on the move, or a cavalry column on maneuvers. They were headed on a collision course with the dust cloud, so just in case it was hostile Indians, they would have to be especially alert toward late afternoon.

Will suggested that they veer a little more to the west, thereby cutting the trail behind the dust column, and then they could tell by the tracks what had passed. They kept to the lowland, away from the skyline as much as possible, to make themselves less conspicuous. When they finally cut the trail, they could plainly see the tracks of unshod ponies and travois drag marks--clear indications of an Indian village on the move. That night when they made camp there was no fire built, just in case there were Indian scouts about.

"Do you have any idea what tribe these Indians might belong to, John?" Will wanted to know.

"No, *m'sieur*. There are those who could look at the spoor left in passing and could tell you what tribe made it and how many Indians there were, but I am not one of them. I do know that this is Pawnee land and that they hate everyone—white and red alike. Any red man that we might meet should be considered an enemy. This is a big, sparsely populated land. It is my wish that we should meet no one at all."

The next morning they followed the trail for a while to make sure that it didn't veer from its northeasterly course. After traveling about five miles, they headed back toward the northwest. Will was amazed that one could ride for days and never see any sign of another human being. Except for the Indian trail, they had seen no other man-made sign in at least four days. Maybe Jean would get his wish. They passed Fort Lincoln, Nebraska, which lay miles to the west, and when they finally reached the wide valley of the Platte, Jean said that they had covered about half the distance to the village.

The Platte was wide but shallow. The only problem crossing was in keeping the horses from floundering in the loose sandy bottom. If a horse stopped even for a short time, its hooves began to sink into the sand, making the animal panic. Will was visibly relieved when the horses clambered up the north bank.

Where the Mormon Trail cut into the earth was plain to see on the North side of the Platte. It must have taken many wagons a lot of years to cut that deeply into the earth. Will thought that there must surely have been others besides Mormons who had traveled this trail--unless there were lots of Mormons.

The second day beyond the Platte, Will got to see his first Buffalo herd. Jean estimated a thousand animals--a small herd by past standards he said. In former times the animals were numbered in the millions. Now there were men who called themselves hunters that were slaughtering the animals for the hides, leaving the carcasses to rot. Jean predicted that in a few more years there would be no buffalo left. The decimation of the buffalo herds was one of the main grievances of the Plains Indians, who depended on the animals for food, shelter, clothing, weapons, just about everything.

After what Jean had told him, Will hesitated to say that they needed meat, but Jean hadn't meant what he had said to pertain to those in need. Will made ready the Spencer and rode slowly up to the herd. Jean Rene decided to stay a safe distance away from the dangerous looking animals. Will had no idea what would be the best way to take one of the beasts. The big, shaggy animals stared at him but showed no fear of him or the big dog that was following him, after all, they had seen plenty of wolves in the past.

He wanted a calf because there was no way two men could eat all of an adult animal, and he didn't want to waste the meat. The contrast in color of the animals was quite surprising to Will-- the calves were almost red, while the adults were nearly black. He tried unsuccessfully to separate a calf from its mother. If he shot the calf while it was with the herd he wouldn't be able to get to it. Giving up, he continued around the herd, giving the big bulls a wide berth, looking for an animal that was separated from the others. Besides, the stench of thousands of hot bodies and the dust raised by the milling herd was almost stifling.

When Will got to the up-wind side of the herd he took a deep breath of fresh air, then he noticed that some of the animals were sniffing the wind; they had gotten his scent. Those particular animals began to move away; Will slowly pursued them. Soon, more were moving, then that whole section of the herd was running. He spotted a recently born calf near the rear of the herd where the animals were more scattered. The little fellow was hard pushed to keep up with the herd. The mother was torn between the maternal instinct of protecting her baby and the urge to run with the herd. She would push the calf with her nose then run a little way toward the receding herd. She must have done this a dozen times before turning to run after the herd which was now nearly half a mile away.

Will urged his horse up beside the calf and dismounted. The little fellow gave out a plaintive high-pitched bawl, to no avail, toward the receding dark spot that was its mother. Taking the big knife, Will placed it under the calf's throat while holding the calf's nose with his left hand. Not wishing to look at what he was about to do, he turned his head and, with eyes closed, gave the knife a hard jerk. After releasing the calf, he stood for at least five minutes with his back turned toward the calf before he could force himself to look at his kill. Rex, with no remorse at all, was waiting expectantly beside the carcass.

Taking the big knife from Will, Jean Rene began to butcher the calf, putting aside the liver for their evening meal. Rex ate his fill on the spot as Jean threw him the less desirable cuts of meat. The big dog was already quite adept at catching rabbits and rodents on the open plains, but he wouldn't turn down an easy meal like this.

Before they were finished with the butchering, the calf's mother returned to look for her offspring. Will yelled and waved his hat in a vain effort to scare her away. She would run a short distance away, then walk slowly back. After several trials, he told Rex to drive the cow away, which the dog cheerfully did, not stopping until the animal was at least half a mile away. When she came back again, they would be gone.

They boned the meat where the animal lay, and using the calf's skin as a container, they carried the meat with them until they came to a stream where there were willow bushes growing. They built drying racks of green willow, and cutting the meat into thin strips, laid it on the racks to dry in the sun. The knife that Will had taken in Nashville was perfect for this kind of job. It was heavy enough to easily slice through a willow branch with one chop. He was almost glad for the run-in with the bully.

They then gathered all the dried buffalo chips in the area to burn under the meat to keep the flies away, and the smoke would add some flavor to the meat, as well as to facilitate the drying. Will spent most of the next two days atop the highest rise near the camp as a lookout, just in case the smoke attracted unwanted visitors. Rex was usually dozing within a few feet of him.

Just before dusk of the second day, Rex came quickly to his feet and, sniffing the air, stood facing down the slope. The dog's sudden movement alerted Will. He hadn't seen anything suspicious, but he trusted his furry companion explicitly. Will didn't change position, but his grip tightened on the Spencer that was lying across his thighs.

After perhaps half a minute, Will detected movement. Five prairie chickens darting from one clump of cover to another as they fed up a shallow gully that divided this rise from the next. Rex turned and trotted down the hill on a course that would put him well ahead of the feeding birds.

Will watched as the dog stealthily entered the gully at least a hundred yards ahead of his intended prey. Rex hunkered down behind a clump of thick grass, keeping his legs positioned under his body for a quick lunge. He waited patiently for several minutes, without once moving a muscle, until the birds darted from under low shrubs toward his hiding place. At exactly the right moment, he sprang through the grass directly at the nearest bird. Before the bird had a chance to turn, it was enclosed in a vice-like grip. Death came quickly with an explosion of feathers. That dog would have made a great guerilla fighter if he had been born a man, thought Will.

There was nothing much to occupy the time, so he was glad when the buffalo meat was finally dried. Jean and Will had lain around and dozed so much during the day that when darkness came neither of them was sleepy, so they lay and talked far into the night.

Will was beginning to like the little Frenchman, even though he felt that Jean was using him. Still, even if that was the case, it was good to have him as a traveling companion. At least, Jean knew the territory and the Indians, and the open plains were a stark contrast to the forests of the Southeast. Maybe it was good luck that he had met up with the little guy. What would have happened if he had struck out across the prairie on his own, knowing as little as he did? He could have lost his hair long before he ever reached the mountains.

The next morning they awakened to a completely overcast sky. The clouds and the terrain in the distance blended into one another. One couldn't tell where the land ended and the sky began. Without the sun, Will couldn't possibly navigate in this huge expanse with no landmarks, but Jean held a steady course without obvious concern. After hours of riding and wondering if they were continuing in the right direction, Will's curiosity got the upper hand.

"John, how can you possibly know that we're still headed north? We could be riding around in circles for all I know."

"It is a gift that I was born with, *m'sieur*," Jean said with a grin. "An unerring sense of direction. And also I have this," he said, as he removed an object from a string that he wore around his neck under his shirt. Jean stopped his horse so that Will could come up beside him. The object that Jean handed him was a fish emblem made of stone, with a hole in its back fin for the string.

"When preparing the site for my lodge, I find that another lodge has previously occupied the same location. In the ashes of an old hearth I find this emblem that you are now holding. At first I did not know what the purpose for it was, but when I discover that it is attracted to iron, then I know that it is lodestone and that it will ever point to the north. That is the way that I am able to stay on course."

"That's a very unique gift you were born with, John," said Will, with a smile. "Who in the village would have used such an object, I wonder?"

"I have questioned some of the older members of the village about whose lodge had occupied that site, and I was told that a man called Ninekiller, the uncle of Tall Man one of the villagers, had lived there before the smallpox epidemic of '37. Many lodges were burned to rid the village of any vestige of the dread disease. You will meet this Tall Man; he lives in my village with his wife and daughter."

"Ninekiller played the most prominent role in the defeat of the Sioux when they attacked the Mandan village many years ago," Jean continued. It is said that he was instrumental in turning the tide of the battle against the Sioux. He slew nine of the enemy with--how do you say--a single hand?"

"I think you mean single-handed."

"Yes, single-handed. How or why he had the fish emblem is a mystery to me. No one in the village had ever seen it before it was discovered in the ashes of the old hearth. There is also a steel arrow-head that lay beside the emblem, and I have judged from the pitted condition that it is apparently of very ancient origin. There is no way to account for it either. Of course I have my own theory about the origin of these two objects, but who will listen to Jean Rene, eh?"

"What was that, John?" Will asked absent-mindedly, still studying the fish emblem.

"Nothing, *m'sieur*, nothing at all.

XVII

As their journey continued northward, the prairie grasses gradually became shorter. When Will and Jean had first entered the prairie, the grasses were growing to the height of a man, but now they came only to the knee. The shorter the grass became, the more desolate the prairie seemed to Will. Riding through such empty terrain became such a boring routine that it would have been easy to lose count of the days. At first the vast openness of the plains had been fascinating to Will, but now it was becoming monotonous. He would love to see mountains and forests again. But riding along in this manner gave Will plenty of time to think, and the closer he came to the end of the trek the more apprehensive he became about what lay ahead.

"John, tell me about these Indians you live with. How are they going to feel about a stranger riding into their village uninvited, especially a white man?"

"I do not foresee any problem, *m'sieur*. These people have had contact with whites for many years and are very friendly, not at all like the fierce Sioux and Cheyenne. They can be ferocious fighters, mind you, but only if the village is attacked. They also will go to great lengths to exact revenge if they suffer a wrong, but they do not raid and steal from the other tribes as a way of life as some of the more nomadic tribes do. Riverboats make regular stops at the village. Many white men have visited the village in the past, and some of them have even lived there for a time, but nearly all the whites that the Mandan have been associated with have been traders, so it is natural for them to think of all white men as liars."

"The lodges are permanent, being built of timbers and covered with earth, and the people raise squash, beans, corn, pumpkins, and tobacco. Most of the lodges are big and house 10, 20, or even more people. My lodge is small and is adequate for my family only. As you know, most of our kind, white people that is, like privacy, but the villagers care nothing for privacy and have no sense of modesty. Modesty is a foreign concept to them. I have seen men, after enduring the sweat bath, run stark naked through the village and dive into the icy river."

"The village, she is protected on one side by the Missouri River and on the other by a palisade of logs. There is a trench dug on the inside of the wall that the warriors can stand in, while firing weapons between the logs at the enemy. This type of fortified village to my knowledge is unique among the Native Americans, although the palisade villages of the Southeast were somewhat similar."

"The Mandan, he is one skillful trader. Once he got the ornamental seashell from as far away as the Pacific Ocean and the Gulf of Mexico to trade to the other tribes. Before iron was introduced, obsidian from Wyoming was a very important trade item, as well as copper from the Great Lakes region. Now the products of the white man have replaced much of the old-time trade goods."

"Corn and other dried vegetables are traded to the Sioux for meat and hides, if there is need, but when the buffalo herds come anywhere near the village, the people will harvest their own meat. Since the great herds migrate north in summer and south in winter, some of them are sure to come within a day's ride of the village. The people will dance the *Bel-lochk-na-pic,* the Great Bull Dance, in order to lure the buffalo near the village. It will always work, for they will continue the dance until the buffalo arrive. It is a sight to see, this dance."

"With the rain dance, it is the same. The dance will continue until the rains come. It cannot fail. Once, when the position of Rainmaker became available, a certain young man greatly desired the office for himself. His magic is strong, so he claims. To impress the people, he climbs atop one of the lodges with his shield and lance. He thrusts the lance into the air; he dances and invokes the rain to come with much chanting of magic words. When the people hear a loud boom such as thunder would make, they become much afraid, because there is not a cloud in the sky. Since the rainmaker is higher up than anyone else in the village, he can see what the others cannot. A large riverboat is coming up the river and announcing its arrival by firing a cannon. The rainmaker shouts: "Ha! My medicine is very strong! I maybe did not bring the rain, but I did bring a thunder boat." Will thought that was quite funny.

"That part of the story is humorous, but later, a storm, with much lightening, actually did come, and a young girl was struck by the lightening and killed. The rainmaker explains that he has much inexperience and did not know how to limit his power. The parents of the young girl were mollified by this explanation."

"Do many riverboats make regular stops at the village?" asked Will.

"*Oui*, ah… yes, *m'sieur*, just about all of them stop. The villager, he has become quite dependent on the white man's trade goods. Steel, she has taken the place of stone, and the rifle has largely replaced the bow and arrow. In a few more years, the primitive way of life will disappear altogether."

"Couldn't you put in an order for books and have them delivered by riverboat almost to your door? It sure would save a lot of traveling."

"It could be done, if I knew in advance what books I would want. But if you can imagine what it is like to live in a lodge with only one door and no windows, then you will understand that to travel is sometimes a reward in itself. Jean Rene is no hunter or warrior, so he must break the monotony in his own way."

"But I also like to talk to the people who teach in the university, or those who have much knowledge and experience, even if they are not highly educated. I have learned much from the person that can barely write his own name. Also, there is much information in the old newspaper files that one can only access in the city where the paper is printed."

"That part about traveling is something that I well understand. Tell me more about the villagers. They sound like an interesting people," said Will.

"Well, you see, there was at one time three distinct tribes that lived similar but separate lives: the Arikara, the Hidatsa, and the Mandan. The woman that I have married is Hidatsa, but I know much more about the Mandan. Because they are such a mysterious people, much more has been recorded about them. White men have been curious about them since the first contact was made."

"The Mandan once numbered into the many thousands—fifteen thousand some have estimated. At the peak, there were eight villages between the Heart and the Little Missouri Rivers. There is so many facts about the Mandan stored in my head that the exact dates sometimes I am not so clear about, but I think it was around 1787, when the first smallpox epidemic killed many, many thousands. When Lewis and Clark wintered with the Mandan in 1804, there were only about 1250 that had survived in two villages. Thirty years ago, when the three tribes were still separate, the Sioux attacked and killed many, and then only three years later another smallpox epidemic hit the three tribes and came close to wiping out the Mandan altogether. Now, for mutual protection, the three tribes have combined into one village, though each has kept its own identity."

"I am always the curious one, *m'sieur* Will, I read the books, and I ask the questions. Whenever I meet an old one, white or red, I will glean from him whatever information is available. From what I have learned about the Mandan, they have been the object of curiosity and rumor for many, many years. The first document-ed visitor was a man from my own country named Verendrye. He reported in 1738 that many of the Mandan had blue eyes and blond, red, or brown hair. Also, he claimed that the males had facial hair, which is not the norm for the red man. When the Lewis and Clark expedition came back from the Pacific Ocean, their skins, from exposure to the sun and also from grime, were said to be darker than the Mandan's."

"A man named Maurice Griffith, a Welshman, was captured in Ohio in 1764 by the Shawnee. He became so well like by the Shawnee that he was treated as a guest of the tribe, and they took him along on an excursion up the Missouri River as a member of a hunting party. The Mandan took all of them captive. Griffith claimed that the Man-dan chief greeted him in Welsh, and when the chief discovered that Griffith also spoke Welsh, he was made the guest of honor. After Griffith made his way back to Virginia, John Williams, the historian, published Griffith's account in London. This inspired the rumor of a tribe of Welsh Indians, bringing others in search of the tribe."

There were so many reports of white Welsh speaking Indians circulating in the eastern states that President Thomas Jefferson gave the Lewis and Clark expedition the order to look for the tribe, during their trek to the Pacific Ocean. Jefferson even gave Lewis a map of the Missouri River which was draw by a Welshman named Evans who had visited the Mandan earlier."

"There was a black slave named York with the Lewis and Clark expedition. He was the first black man the Mandan had ever seen, and they were so in awe of the color of his skin that they named him Big Medicine. He had much fun with the village children by telling them that he was once a wild animal that had been captured and tamed by the whites. I am sorry, *M'sieur* Will, there are times when Jean Rene gets on the side track."

"Many traders and trappers came up the Missouri in the past looking for the tribe of white Indians that spoke Welsh. In fact, in 1792, as already I have stated, the Welshman named John Evans came all the way from Wales to St. Louis, bearing gifts, to find such a tribe. The Spanish, who controlled the Missouri country at that time, put Evans in prison, treating him as an English spy. He was able to convince his captors of his sincerity in wanting only to search for the tribe of Welsh Indians, so they let him go, giving back to him his trade goods. But his gifts were so inferior to what the Mandan were already used to that they chased him back down the river. Evans made the 1800 mile round trip in 68 days. He later had his revenge when he told everyone that there was no such thing as a tribe of Welsh Indians."

"It is true that the Mandan has light skin, and there is now and then the word that sounds like the Welsh word, and even has the same meaning, or so I am told, but there are many more words that do not. Of course much has changed with the tribe in the last few decades, but there is something besides their light skin and hair that shows Welsh influence. The bull boat, which is called the coracle in Wales, made of hide that is stretched over a round frame and the great earth house of the Mandan are unique in America, but both are known in Wales."

"There is the legend about a Welsh prince named Madoc who supposedly arrived in America in 1170, more than 300 years before Columbus. The prince had made the initial voyage to the new land, possibly as a scouting expedition, but he then returned to Wales. He had left behind 120 men in a fortified settlement in

America, but when he returned many years later with 10 shiploads of colonists, which he led to Mobile Bay, the garrison is missing, apparently it has scattered among the native peoples of the area."

"There seems to have been white explorers and settlers in this country long before Columbus received credit for the discovery, would you not agree?"

"That is a subject I know absolutely nothing about, John. What you are telling me is the first I have ever heard on the matter."

"I read the books, *m'sieur;* I read the books. And I ask the questions. Jean Rene is as curious as the proverbial cat."

"There are many accounts by the early explorers of the Welsh speaking Indians in America. In western Florida, after the Spanish claimed that area, a tribe of white Indians flees to the north. That is near Mobile Bay, is it not? For the next two hundred years, the early frontiersmen tell stories about their encounters with these people. The Creek nation called them the people of Madawg. Very similar to Madoc, eh? And not so very far from Mandan, either."

"In 1834, a German prince by the name of Maximilian visited the Mandan. He wrote that some members of the tribe were almost white. He also noted that some of their traditions had a remarkable similarity to stories from the Bible. Noah and the ark; the Deluge; and the story of Sampson, to name but a few."

"Some people believe that the Mandan are descendants of Vikings who came to the Minnesota area hundreds of years ago. There is documentation in Rome that tells of Henricus, Bishop of Greenland, who visited Vinland, the Viking name for America, in the year 1117. He complained to the Vatican that the Norse in Vinland were marrying natives, giving up Christianity, and living like savages. European explorers found natives with light skins and blue eyes in the sixteenth century as they sailed along the northeast coast of America. Could these people have been descendents of

Vikings who sailed to Vinland hundreds of years before and mixed with the natives? It is an intriguing possibility, is it not?"

"Yes, but North Dakota is a long way from Florida and New England," said Will.

"That is true enough, but the point is that there were Europeans in America before Columbus. There is a trail of evidence that we will follow from Mobile Bay to the Missouri River. This evidence may not convince some people, but I have lived with the Mandan and know that they are not an ordinary people, even now that they have mixed with the other tribes and lost much of their white features. Since the last smallpox epidemic, they have intermarried with the Arikara and Hidatsa to the point that there is probably no pure blood Mandan left, that is, if the Mandan can ever be referred to as pure blood. They seem to have been a mixture all along. The white influence has been diluted but still evident, even today, however."

"Also, besides the legends of Welsh and Norse, there is the story of Saint Brendan of Ireland who sailed in a large boat made of hides stretched over a wood frame and waterproofed with sheep fat. He went to the Faeroe Islands north of Scotland first and then sailed westward past Iceland and Greenland to Newfoundland. It took seven years for him to make the round trip."

"Even though it has nothing to do with the Mandan, there is the story of Henry Sinclair, Prince of the Orkney, Shetland, and Faroe Islands. He sailed to New England in 1398 with 300 men, mostly monks and fugitive Knights Templar. They landed in Newfoundland, but the natives repulsed them. They sailed on to Nova Scotia and explored that area, but the sailors became disgruntled. Sinclair allowed most of the men to sail back to the Orkneys, but with two ships, he explored south as far as Rhode Island. There, he is said to have build what is known today as the New Port Tower. A Micmac Indian legend tells of a god with blond hair and blue eyes called Glooscap, no similarity to Sinclair, eh. They also said the tower builders were fire-haired men with green eyes. To me, that could only mean that some of them had red hair. Sinclair sailed back to the Orkneys and was assassinated shortly thereafter."

I personally do not think that these stories are fanciful, because there is correlation on this side of the Atlantic of white presence prior to Columbus. If you are becoming bored with all this trivia, *m'sieur,* just tell me so, and I will stop."

"Not at all, John. This is all new stuff to me. I was taught nothing of this sort in school," said Will.

"No, of course you were not. What I have told you is not accepted as history, but maybe in a few years, after more research is done, credit will be given where credit is due. But now, let me get back to the Madoc story."

"The people of Madoc migrated from Mobile Bay up the Alabama and Coosa Rivers to north Georgia and Tennessee, where they built stone fortifications on Lookout Mountain, Fort Mountain, and at the Duck River near Manchester, Tennessee. The Cherokee claim to have driven a white race from the Valley of the Tennessee as their tribe was migrating toward that area sometime in the 1600's. In 1792, Oconostota, a 90-year-old Cherokee chief, told John Sevier, Governor of Tennessee, that white people, called Welsh by his grandfather, built the stone fortifications throughout the area. The leader of these people, who had crossed the Great Water in ships that move without oars, was named Modok."

"Now, John, first you tell me that Madoc landed in Mobile Bay in the 1100's, then you say their leader is Modok in the 1600's. That would make him pretty old wouldn't it," said Will with a grin.

"Well, of course it could not have been the same man, but maybe each new leader of the whites took that venerable name as his own, much like the kings and Popes do in Europe even today."

"Anyway, the Cherokee, who are slowly migrating toward Tennessee from South Carolina, fight with these whites for a number of years. Upon discovering that the white people are building large boats to escape down the Tennessee River, the Cherokee move ahead and ambush them at Muscle Shoals, Alabama. The battle went on for some time, but there was no clear victory for either side. The white leader asked for a truce, and after an exchange of prisoners, the whites agreed to leave the area never to return. They eventually settled a great distance up the Missouri River, Oconostota said. Who could that possibly be but the Mandan?"

"You're covering my home territory here, John, but what you're telling me is completely new to me, although, during the war, I visited the Old Stone Fort at Manchester. I was told it was built by Indians," said Will.

"Aah, but of course you were. White people were not supposed to have been in this country at that time, so the historians tell us that the Indians must be the builders. The Madoc story is not common knowledge, *M'sieur* Will, and is not taught in the schools. Maybe someday enough information will become available to make the subject better known."

"I am not sure of the time period, but the Shawnee in Ohio claim to have exterminated a white race that lived in Kentucky. The Shawnee could not live in the land south of the Ohio River, they say, because the ghosts of the dead whites would not permit it. In fact for a long period of time, the Kentucky area was devoid of all human habitation. The Shawnee would even ask the ghosts for permission to hunt in that land. The Kentucky area, as you know, is directly between the Cherokee in the south and the Shawnee in the north."

"All of the whites were not killed by the Shawnee, of course, but they were driven out of the Ohio-Kentucky area. The survivors then migrated up the Missouri River. Obviously the Mandan, eh? There is some similarity between the Cherokee and Shawnee accounts, would you not agree?"

"Yeah, I'll have to admit they're similar. Do you think the two stories are one account told by two different tribes, each one wanting the credit of being the main force in driving the whites out?" asked Will.

"There is no way to know. The events happened too far in the past to be sure of anything. The Cherokee attack was at a shoal in the Tennessee River, and the Shawnee attack was at a shoal in the Ohio. Very similar, but I personally believe different, accounts. It is my opinion that the Cherokee drove the whites from Tennessee, and they settled on the Ohio River before being driven west to the Missouri."

"In 1773, Chief Black Fish of the Shawnee told Thomas Bullitt, a man who wanted to settle in Kentucky, about the white race that came from the eastern sea and had settled in the Ohio country before the Shawnee arrived.

In 1778, the son of the Shawnee chief, Tobacco, told General George Rogers Clark of a great battle that took place at the Falls of the Ohio River, where many white men were killed. Clark and his men found skeletons stacked like cordwood on Corn Island above the falls. After the Revolutionary War was over, Clark returned to the falls to establish a settlement called Fort Clark, now known as Clarksville, Indiana. Later, people from the settlement found six graves a few miles upstream from the falls that contained skeletons that had been buried with breastplates of brass. These breastplates had been cast with the Welsh coat of arms and had a Latin inscription on them. Clark himself was convinced that these were some of Madoc's people."

"Now that is pretty strong evidence, John. That should be enough to convince any skeptic. General Clark was a man of integrity."

"Alas, I am afraid, *m'sieur*, the evidence has all disappeared, leaving nothing but the story as proof."

"Other people think there might have been a connection between these whites and the lost English colony of Roanoke Island. Do you know of this story, *m'sieur*?"

"No, John, I don't have any idea what colony you're talking about. I finished the first eight grades of school, but I haven't read a single book since then. I simply don't have the knowledge that you have."

"Aah, yes, my friend, I understand. As for me, if I could not find new books to read, I would surely go mad. But let me continue with the Mandan."

"Years ago, before I came to the village," Jean continued, "there was this white man named Catlin that came to live for a while with the Mandan. He was an artist and painted the important men and women of the tribe. They think that since their likeness is captured on canvas it will make them immortal. At first they are afraid because a rumor is circulating that their very souls will be captured in the paintings and that Catlin is an evil magician, but Catlin convinced them that anyone can, with enough practice, learn to paint portraits just as well as he. This man, Catlin, has given the most complete description of the Mandan that I have yet found. When he was living in their village there were maybe 2,000 Mandan; after the smallpox epidemic of '37, there were only a few left--some say two hundred, others say even fewer."

"In Catlin's day, ten percent of the *Numakiki,* the People, as they call themselves, have silver-gray or white hair with the texture of a horse's mane. Even small children could be a *cheveux gris,* as my countrymen call the gray hairs. These gray hairs were in addition to those that have the blond, brown, or red hair. This Catlin, he believed the Mandan were of a different origin than the other tribes of the region. They are certainly one very intriguing people, *non*?"

"Yes, quite interesting. What do they say about their own history? Don't they have any oral traditions?" asked Will.

"*Oui, m'sieur,* but nothing about the white influence that is truly clear. According to their own testimony, they came from the east, from the Ohio Valley, and migrated slowly up the Missouri River. There is evidence of old abandoned villages down river from the present site. That confirms the Cherokee and Shawnee traditions, would you not agree? The Mandan and the Winnebago tribe of the Wisconsin area seem to have had a connection some time in the distant past. At least it is said that their languages have common roots. But the whites could have intermarried with the Missouri tribe. The Missouri are a branch of the Winnebago tribe that migrated south many, many years ago; therefore, they are of the same root language. The white influence must have come, at least in part, from the Welsh speaking white race that I mention before that lived in the Ohio-Kentucky-Tennessee area. It is a probability that the Mandan are actually descendents of a Welsh and Indian mixture, though it cannot be proven."

"Catlin was told by the Mandan that they are descended from a white man, called Lone Man, who sailed in a big canoe that came to rest on a high mountain after a great flood destroyed everything on earth. There is a symbolic representation called the Big Canoe in the very center of the village as a reminder of that deluge. A dove was sent out to search for dry land. It came back with a willow twig in its beak. A story much too similar to the Bible account to be mere coincidence, do you not agree?"

"Yes, practically the same story," Will answered.

"There is more. They even have a story of a child of virgin birth who later in life performed miracles, including feeding a multitude with a small amount of food. After everyone is sated, there is plenty of food left over. This miracle worker fed the people with buffalo meat instead of fish and bread, but the basic story is the same. They also believe in a personal devil and a fall from grace due to the transgression of a primal mother. Their heaven, of course, is a paradise, but oddly enough, hell is described as a place of ice and cold instead of a hot, fiery place."

"I believe that the accounts that I just told you came from the Welsh influence. Another creation story has them coming out of a hole in the ground, somewhere many miles east of the village near a lake. One story seems to stem from the white influence, and the other from the Indian influence, would you not agree?"

"Yeah, it would seem that way," Will agreed. "Must be confusing, though."

"Catlin found the Mandan such an interesting and peculiar people that 16 of 58 chapters he wrote about the North American Indians is devoted to the Mandan.

"In 1784, long before Catlin visited the Mandan, there was an article in a Pennsylvania newspaper reporting the discovery of a new nation of white people 2000 miles west of the Appalachian Mountains. These people, it is said, are acquainted with the principles of the Christian religion and extremely courteous and civilized. The Mandan have always been very friendly with white people."

"As I told you earlier," said Will, "I lived in Knoxville for eighteen years. Not too far north of Knoxville, on Clinch Mountain, there lives a mysterious dark skinned people called the Melungeons. According to their own account they are descendants of Portuguese, but no one knows how they came to be in the Tennessee mountains long before the first documented white settlers arrived. What about the Arikara and Hidatsa? What kind of history do they have?"

"Melungeons you say? Yes, I have heard of these people, but I know only a little about them. There was an Englishman named James Needham who was exploring the Tennessee Valley in 1673,

I believe it was. He finds a tribe of hairy, dark skin people who speak neither English nor an Indian tongue. Somehow, they relate to him that they are descended from a group of Portuguese that were shipwrecked on the east coast. How they came to live in Tennessee is a mystery. I can tell you that the Portuguese supposedly fished at the Grand Banks off Newfoundland before Columbus ever sailed the Atlantic, so a shipwreck on the east coast is not out of the realm of possibility. And the fact that they call themselves Portyghee should mean something, also."

"Now, to return to your question. There is not so much that I can tell you about the other two tribes. Like the Mandan, the Hidatsa, too, migrated from the east. They show some white influence, but not nearly as much as the Mandan. They have been associated with the Mandan for a very long time, so intermarriage would be one explanation for their white features. When the villagers acquired horses, the Hidatsa split into two groups. The breakaway tribe, the Crow nation to the west, became more nomadic, giving up permanent homes to live like the Cheyenne. War has always been part of the Hidatsa lifestyle, although they have never to my knowledge been hostile toward the Mandan. The Crow and Hidatsa still visit each other because of family ties."

The Arikara are a branch of the Pawnee nation to the south. They were the last to join the three tribe union, if you want to call it that. They also once numbered in the thousands, being even more numerous than the Mandan. And they were once deadly enemies of the Mandan. Smallpox decimated their numbers also. Other than that I do not know."

Will then decided to tell Jean his own story. It took a while, but they had plenty of time. As he related the last few months of his life, the smoldering anger once again came to the surface. Jean Rene tried to placate Will with soothing words, but Will wanted to vent his anger, causing him to direct his anger toward Jean. He didn't appreciate being treated like a child, but he didn't say anything hurtful to Jean, although he felt like it at the moment. Much later, after he had calmed down, he felt ashamed for losing his cool, but the pain from the loss of Ginny and Buck was never far below the surface of his mind and too easily came to the forefront. He decided then and there never to discuss that part of his life with anyone ever again.

How could Jean Rene understand how he felt? He hadn't been with Ginny at the hour of her greatest need. And it was his decision that had gotten Buck killed. There were twenty good men in his command that day, and they were all dead because of him. No, soothing words would never take away the guilt that gnawed at his tortured mind. He withdrew within himself and said not a single word for the next two hours as they rode steadily northward.

Staying in the saddle ten or more hours between dawn and dusk was letting them cover an average of forty miles per day. They had been on the trail eighteen days counting the two days to dry the meat. By Jean's estimation they should be no more than two hundred miles from their destination. Just five more days of riding, if everything went well, and they could take a well deserved rest.

They had just forded the Cheyenne River and were going to take a brief noon break on the north bank when Rex gave a low, rumbling growl. Will looked intently at all the available cover to the west, the direction that Rex was facing, but he saw no sign of life. A light breeze was blowing from that direction, so Will had no doubt that the big dog smelled danger. He was especially alert as they resumed their journey, continually scanning the surrounding area for any sign of human activity.

In mid afternoon Will and Jean were riding parallel to a low ridge when Rex, with hackles raised, again gave a warning. Will decided to take a look at what lay on the other side of the ridge. The fact that there had been no further sign of danger bothered him greatly. He dismounted short of the ridge crest, and after telling Rex to stay back, bellied up to a clump of grass growing near the top. A quarter mile away and slightly ahead of his own position, Will counted eight mounted warriors. He motioned for Jean to join him. During the short interval it took Jean to reach Will's position, the warriors had turned to the right and were coming up the far side of the ridge.

"I know these young men, *m'sieur*. The one in front is called Badger. He is a young, how do you say, hot-blood Sioux that was adopted, when still a very young child, by a Hidatsa family. He refuses to live the peaceful life of the other villagers. He is intensely proud of his Sioux blood and desires to be a fierce warrior and would very much like to be a war leader, but no one of maturity will follow him. They know that he has no experience, and there are plenty of proven leaders already. The others that are with him are some of the more easily influenced youngsters from the village. They have the promise of scalps and glory if they will accept the leadership of Badger. Everyone in the village knows that these youngsters are rushing headlong into trouble if they do not change their ways. These young men know me; I will talk to them."

"John, I don't like the way this is shaping up. They don't look exactly friendly to me," Will cautioned. "I believe they have ridden a parallel course to us ever since we crossed the Cheyenne River. They wouldn't have done that unless they're up to no good."

"They will be banished from the village forever if they do harm to me, *m'sieur*. They know this," said Jean.

"They won't be banished if we're killed and our bodies are never found, John. These young men are certainly not going to return to your village and tell on themselves," Will added.

"Please, *m'sieur*, give to me just a little credit. After all, it is I who know and live with these people," said Jean Rene, drawing himself up just a little taller in the saddle.

"Yeah, you're right of course. I can't argue with that," said Will. "Go ahead, but be careful."

Jean mounted his horse, leaving the packhorse with Will. The braves topped the ridge from the opposite direction at the same time that Jean Rene did. They weren't expecting to see Jean and Will already at the top of the ridge. They hesitated just long enough to have a quick conference. After giving Will a reassuring nod and a smile, Jean urged his horse toward the warriors.

Two of the braves reined their horses around and rode away at a fast gallop. The other six formed into a line and sat their horses, waiting. When Jean was about fifty yards away, Badger yelled a loud war cry, and with lance extended, charged toward Jean. The other five followed in a ragged line a horse length behind Badger.

Jean was too stunned by this unexpected action to immediately respond. Realizing that escape was impossible, he tried to dodge, but the lance literally lifted him from the saddle. Encouraged by Badger's success, all six of the young warriors then charged toward Will, gleefully yelling as they rode.

Will was greatly distressed to think that Jean Rene had been killed. He was an experienced soldier and had sensed danger. Why hadn't he been more forceful with the little Frenchman? Angrily he untied his packhorse and let him stand ground-hitched while he calmly drew the Spencer from its boot. Dismounting and going to one knee, he took careful aim and fired at the brave on the left of the advancing line. Working the lever, he again took aim and a second brave fell. The other four were quickly closing in.

Not wanting to be caught on the ground at a disadvantage, he quickly rebooted the rifle and mounted the gray. Will didn't wear his saber at his side any more but kept it attached to his saddle. Drawing the saber, he rode directly toward the middle of the charging line. At the last second he reined his mount to the left putting all four warriors to his right. Timing was everything in this type of fighting, and Will had years of experience. He doubted that these young men had ever been in a battle before, but he wasn't going to be soft with them, after all, they had killed his friend and were trying to kill him. Will parried the lance of the nearest warrior and immediately twisted his wrist so that the saber sliced across the warrior's chest and right bicep, causing him to drop the lance.

The force of the blow caused the brave to lose his balance. He struggled to remain on his running horse, but his right arm was useless. With every jolt that came from the galloping steed, he slipped a little farther to the left until he was hanging on with only his right heel over the horse's back, and his left hand entwined in its mane. After riding about fifty yards in this fashion with no hope of righting himself, he let go and hit the ground. Feeling utterly defeated, he simply lay where he had fallen, awaiting his fate. The wounds weren't mortal if the bleeding was stopped, but the young man was definitely out of the fight.

The three remaining braves had stopped a short way from where their comrade had fallen and turned their mounts to face Will. They were having second thoughts about the battle; it wasn't going the way they had planned. Half their number was already down. They had believed the soldier to be armed with a muzzle-loader. After his one shot was expended, they had expected to ride him down. Badger was the leader, and he obviously wasn't eager to continue the fight, but what else could he do? Things weren't going exactly as he had envisioned them in his mind, but if he turned tail and ran, he would completely lose face and become a laughing stock. No one would even consider following him again. It would be better to die like a warrior than to live in shame.

The three warriors were sitting on their horses watching Will when suddenly Badger let go a war whoop and charged. This action was so unexpected that the other two braves and their mounts were startled. Resheathing the saber, Will again took the rifle and dismounted. Badger was riding in a fully upright position, exposing as much of his body as possible. Taking careful aim across his saddle, Will waited until Badger was only a few yards away before pulling the trigger. It seemed as if an invisible hand swept Badger from the back of the horse. He hit the ground flat on his back, bounced once, and lay still. The other two warriors rode quickly away, lying low on their horse's backs in case a bullet was sent their way.

Badger had attacked Jean and caused the deaths of two of his companions and the wounding of another. Now he had paid with his own life. It was such a senseless waste. Absolutely nothing had been gained by the attack--no scalps, no glory, nothing. Will had been in many battles and had taken many lives, and he could see no glory in killing or dying for anything except a just cause, and after all that he had suffered, the only cause he now considered to be just was self-defense or the defense of another.

Will wasted no time in going to his friend. He was overjoyed to find Jean still alive. The lance had made a severe wound in his right shoulder, but he would live. It was bleeding steadily, instead of spurting, which was a good sign. Jean was very pale and in obvious pain, but barring infection, he would be fine in a few weeks. As he cut the sleeve from Jean's shirt, Will could hear him praying in French and saw him make the sign of the cross with his left hand.

"I am dying, my friend. Would you do a favor for me and tell my wife and children that my last thoughts were of them?" asked Jean, in a voice barely audible.

Will could barely keep a straight face as he bandaged Jean's shoulder. The blood, coming in a steady flow, was already abating, making the flow much easier to stanch.

"Try to hang in there just a little longer, John. You don't want to give up just yet. Do you think you might be able to sit in a saddle for just a little while?"

"I can only try, *m'sieur.*"

As gently as possible Will helped Jean into the saddle. Next, Will checked on the young brave He was very weak from the loss of blood, but he was still defiant. Rex was keeping watch over the young man without even having to be told. Will had Jean Rene--once Jean was convinced that he was going to live--explain to the wounded man that he wasn't going to hurt him, that he only wanted to help.

He bandaged the warrior's wounds as best he could and put the young man on one of the Indian ponies. That was no easy task since he was very weak from the loss of blood and the horse had no saddle to facilitate mounting. The brave had use of only one arm with which to help, but the task was finally accomplished. Both of the wounded men had their right arms in rope slings, requiring Will to keep a close watch over them in their weakened conditions, especially Jean Rene, to make sure they didn't topple from their horses.

The brave seemed astonished that Will would help him after what he and the others had tried to do. Since he was already feeling remorse for his actions, he co-operated with his captors. Will had tied the other Indian ponies behind the packhorses and was leading all of them himself. The dead braves were left where they had fallen. Will rode slowly, because of the wounded men, as far as the nearest stream and made camp.

After they had settled down, Jean asked the warrior, Broken Feather, questions and translated the answers for Will. It seems that Badger had convinced all but two of the young braves that they should kill Jean and Will and take their guns and horses, and then the horses would be traded for more guns. And besides, who knew what treasures they would find on the two packhorses? That would be an added bonus.

When they had scalps and guns, more young men would want to join them, and soon, they would be a force to be reckoned with. The fierce Sioux or Cheyenne that everyone feared would then accept them as fighting men. Were they to become warriors today, or did they want to go back to the village and help the women raise squash and beans?

The two young men that rode away would have nothing to do with killing a man from their own village, even though he did have white skin. If Will had been alone it would have been a different matter altogether.

After they had eaten, Will retrieved his sewing kit from his saddlebags. The wounds made by the lance and saber were gaped open and needed very badly to be closed to facilitate healing and avoid an ugly scar. Will decided it would be best to work on Broken Feather first. He was sure the Indian would tolerate the pain without flinching; Jean Rene's reaction was questionable.

As Will had expected, Broken Feather showed no outward sign of pain as the needle passed through the skin. Jean Rene on the other hand fainted at the first stitch, making the task much easier for Will.

That night, Rex kept guard over the wounded brave. Having the dog around sure made life easier for Will. He could sleep in peace knowing that Rex would wake him if danger arose.

XVIII

Meanwhile, at the village on the Knife, Shadow Woman, Tall Man, and their daughter, Lone Dove, were sitting and talking as their evening meal was simmering over the fire. Tall Man held a long stick with which he occasionally stirred the hot coals under the kettle. After a time the conversation lapsed and Shadow Woman seemed to withdraw into herself while staring into the flames. After maybe thirty seconds had elapsed, Shadow Woman's body started with a sharp intake of breath. She looked around as if she didn't quite know where she was. Tall Man and Lone Dove had seen this happen before and were not unduly alarmed. Shadow Woman had had another vision; they would learn of it when she was ready to talk.

After a few seconds of looking at her surroundings as if to orient herself, Shadow woman began talking in a halting manner. "There is a man...on his way to this village," she began, in a voice barely loud enough to be heard. "A man--a white soldier--wearing a gray uniform and riding a gray horse. He has hair the color of straw. He could not see me, nor was he aware of my presence, but I could see him as plainly as I see the two of you. I looked about in every direction and saw many dead soldiers in blue uniforms lying about. There were also the bodies of three of our own people lying there. I seemed to drift closer, and I looked at the face of one of the bodies. It was the face of Badger. This gray soldier seemed sad because of all the dead bodies lying about. I could sense that he was responsible all these deaths, but he does not enjoy the taking of life, as some soldiers seem to.

When I moved closer to this gray soldier, I could see a scar that ran from the center of his forehead across his face to the corner of his mouth. Then I looked into his eyes--into his very soul--and I could feel sadness and anger and loneliness. His soul is in such a state of confusion that he doesn't know what he wants to do with his life. He seems to be a good man who has suffered much anguish. He thinks no one, not even the Great Spirit, cares for him. As I reluctantly began to drift away, I looked back, and I saw a young woman running toward the gray soldier. He dismounted and they embraced. There was a smile tugging at the corner of his mouth. The countenance of his face began to change. A look of happiness was beginning to show on his face for the first time in a long time."

Tall Man, whose full name in Mandan means Man Tall as a Tree, merely grunted, showing his full acceptance of what his wife had just divulged. After all, she had gotten her name through her ability to visit the realm of *wanagi yatu,* the place of souls and spirits. He doubted nothing that she had said. Lone Dove, her curiosity greatly piqued, wanted to know more about the young woman in the vision.

"Mother, did you see the face of the young woman?"

"Yes, Daughter, I saw her face quite clearly."

"Was it someone we know? Someone from this village?"

"Yes, my Daughter. Yes... to both questions."

"Who was it, Mother? Tell us her name," said Lone Dove, barely able to contain her excitement.

"Her name is...Lone Dove."

Lone Dove's mouth dropped open she was so astonished. Twice she tried to speak, but no words would come. Her vocal cords seemed to be paralyzed. Tall Man chuckled at her reaction.

Both Tall Man and Shadow Woman doted on their daughter. They had been man and wife for eight years, and had already given up on having a child, when Shadow Woman became pregnant. Now, twenty years later, they were both past fifty years of age, and their daughter was still unmarried. Tall Man would love to hold a grandchild in his arms before he died, preferably a grandson. Lone Dove had had many suitors, but none of them had captured her affection. So many young men had been turned away over the years that for the past year or more not a single warrior had tried to win her approval.

Daughters of the village tribes were treated the same as property and often had no choice about the man they married. There had been white men who had bought a young girl and lived with her for a season before abandoning her, and then her father would sell her again to another man. Tall Man could have sold his daughter to any number of men for many horses and other goods, but he loved his daughter more than life itself, and her happiness was the only thing that mattered to him. Besides, he had no use for horses, wealth meant nothing to him, and he was neither warrior nor hunter any more.

Shadow Woman's vision had rekindled the flame of hope in his heart. Hopefully, this gray soldier would be the man that would finally capture his daughter's heart. That this man was white made not one bit of difference to Tall Man; he was simply anxious for the gray soldier to arrive. The possibility that there might be no such person as the gray soldier never entered his mind. He had complete faith in his wife's vision.

The next morning Lone Dove told her best friend about the vision, that friend told another friend, and soon the whole village was abuzz with talk and speculation about the arrival of the gray soldier. The villagers, too, had no doubt that there was such a man on his way to the village. They were as sure of his arrival as they would have been if someone had actually seen him in person and heralded his coming.

At twenty years of age, Lone Dove was by far the oldest unmarried woman in the village. Most girls were married by the age of fourteen, so most of the speculation was about whether or not she would accept the stranger or reject him, as she had done with all the other suitors.

Most of the villagers looked on the vision as simply a fact that the Manitous, the guiding spirits, had already ordained Lone Dove's future; therefore, she could do nothing but accept what was to come. Since the soldier and Lone Dove had embraced in the vision, the people were ready to accept a man they had yet to see as Lone Dove's future mate. In fact, they refused to think of him in any other way.

Lone Dove was also beginning to lean in this direction. It was ironic to her because she was beginning to fantasize about life with a man that she had never met. There were times at night before she went to sleep that she would imagine herself embracing the stranger, just as her mother had envisioned. At five feet and eight inches, she was the tallest woman in the village--height inherited from her father. She hoped that the gray soldier was also tall.

The villagers hardly noticed when the two young men, Antelope and Otter, having left Badger five days earlier, rode in from the prairie. Both were totally astonished to learn within the hour that the whole village knew about a soldier in a gray uniform who had killed Badger and two of the warriors with him. Before Antelope and Otter had ridden away from the others, they had seen the gray soldier with Jean Rene, but they were well out of sight before the shots were fired. Badger was still very much alive when they had departed, and they were positive that no one had arrived in the village ahead of them. True, they had heard the distant sound of three rifle shots. Then it must be as everyone was saying. Badger was dead and the gray soldier was coming here to the village. But how could the villagers themselves know all these details?

When Antelope and Otter were told that Shadow Woman had seen all of this in a vision, they went immediately to the Wolf Chief, the village headman, to tell him everything that they knew about the incident. They didn't know the extent of Shadow Woman's vision, so in order to absolve themselves of any blame, they cooperated in every way. And, until they could see what the consequences of having been associated with Badger would be, they intended to walk a very straight line. They avoided Shadow Woman altogether. What else might this woman have seen that they would not want revealed?

XIX

Three days later Will, Jean, and Broken Feather rode into the village. Even with two days of rest and riding at a leisurely pace, it had still been a difficult journey for the two wounded men. Broken Feather had no idea what fate awaited him, but whatever it was, he was resigned to accept it like a warrior. He had been wrong; he had been a fool to listen to Badger, and now, he was ready to face the consequences. If only he could go back in time one week, he would travel a different path, but why even have such a thought; the past cannot be changed.

They had been observed riding toward the village while still some distance away, and word of their arrival had spread like wild fire. In a very few minutes the whole village was waiting to meet them and get a good look at the gray soldier. Jean was in the lead, with Will bringing up the rear. Rex stayed close to Will and bared his teeth at the village dogs that sniffed his trail but dared not get too close to the big dog.

Everyone pretty much ignored Jean and Broken Feather and concentrated on Will. He realized that he was a white man and a total stranger to these people, but their actions--with whisperings and open-mouth stares, the pointing and the nodding of heads-- made him feel like a freak in a sideshow. Was it the scar on his face; his strange uniform; or simply being a white man that made him the center of attention? Did any of those things make him look that much different? Or was it a combination of the three?

Since Will had no understanding of what was being said, he overtook Jean and asked why the villagers were acting so peculiar. Why were they pointing at him and whispering about him? "It seems, my friend, from what little I can overhear, that the People were expecting you," said Jean. "They call you the gray soldier, and they say that you look exactly as Shadow Woman has described you. I understood one woman to say that the gray soldier and Lone Dove would make the perfect couple. It must be, for some reason that is unclear at the moment, that you have already been paired with this woman, Lone Dove, which you have yet to meet," Jean said, with a sly smile and the raising of his eyebrows, as he glanced sideways at Will.

"I'm afraid I don't understand what you're talking about, John, these people don't even know me. You know yourself that I have never met anyone named Shadow Woman. Not one person in this village, to my knowledge, has ever seen me before, and there is definitely no woman in my life," said Will, with emphasis.

"I will have to gather more information before I, too, can understand all of it, although, I do know this Shadow woman--and Lone Dove, also."

They rode between large earth-mound dwellings, unlike anything Will had ever seen before, without stopping until they came to Jean Rene's lodge. There, his wife, Corn Tassel, seeing for the first time Jean's right arm in a sling, waited anxiously to minister to him. Corn Tassel was even shorter than Jean and almost as wide as she was tall. She had a round face, and her dark eyes peered out of mere slits, giving her the appearance of squinting. Will was certain that Jean Rene hadn't chosen this woman because of her looks.

Will dismounted and carefully helped Jean to the ground. Broken Feather nimbly threw a leg over the back of his horse and slipped to the ground without help. Will handed Broken Feather the reins of the pony he had been riding and asked Jean to tell him that he was free to go, if he wished. Broken Feather was astonished. What manner of man was this gray soldier to let one who had tried to kill him walk away?

Corn Tassel began immediately making a fuss over Jean. Her hands were fluttering like butterflies as she removed the old bandage with a continuous singsong chanting that Will couldn't understand. Will smiled as Jean Rene seemed to become more helpless by the moment, thoroughly enjoying the attention he was getting.

The Wolf Chief, the principal leader of the village, having heard the rumors concerning the deaths of three of his people, called for a meeting in one hour. He wanted Will, Jean, Broken Feather, Antelope, and Otter to attend, as well as the village elders and respected warriors. Each one of the five people involved in the recent altercation would be allowed to tell his version of what had happened, then the chiefs, of which there were four, would decide who was guilty, and what punishment was to be meted, if any.

While they were waiting, Jean asked a youngster to take the ponies that had belonged to the dead warriors to their respective lodges. The relatives of the warriors could decide what was to be done with the animals, even though, by right of conquest, they belonged to Will.

While Corn Tassel rebandaged Jean's shoulder, adding an evil smelling poultice to the bindings, she brought them up to date on the village gossip concerning Shadow Woman's vision. She spoke in broken English for Will's sake, with a smattering of other languages that Jean had to translate.. After she had finished, Will thought the whole story so strange that he had a hard time accepting it. Yet, he couldn't deny that the villagers seemed to have recognized him on sight. Things like this just didn't happen. He had heard of people having premonitions, and there had been soldiers that he had been associated with during the war who had known they were going to die and when, but since there was a war going on that didn't seem so strange to him. A man could be killed at any given moment in battle. But nothing close to this had ever happened to him before. It was all so foreign to his way of thinking that he would find himself shaking his head in disbelief while deep in thought, and then quickly looking around to see if anyone was watching him.

"John, tell me about this Shadow woman. I'm having a hard time accepting what I've heard about her," said Will.

"I do not know what to tell you, *M'sieur* Will, except that it is a fact that this woman can sometimes see into the future. Her name was given to her because she is a gifted visionary. It is whispered in the village that she has even wandered in *Wanagi Yatu,* the place of souls."

"Do you find this so strange? All the tribes that are known to me have shamans that seek visions to guide them and their people. Even the young men, when they reach a certain age, will leave the village to fast and pray until they have a vision. They will usually go to the top of some isolated hill that is exposed to the hot sun. Sometime they fast for many days, taking nothing but water. It could be said, of course, that their deprivation causes a hallucination. I do not know. That is not exactly the same as Shadow Woman's gift, though."

"What I am trying to say, *m'sieur,* is that these people live close to the spirit world. Much that you and I would scoff at, they accept as fact. I have seen so many strange and unexplainable things during the past years that I now, ah, how do you say, keep my mind open."

"Keep an open mind."

"Yes, I keep an open mind. When I am first come to the village, I am also the skeptic, but now it is different. I do not judge whether it is right or wrong, mind you, I simply accept that it is the way of life for them. You and I were brought up in a completely different society. We were taught to frown on such goings on. Remember what was done to the so-called witches in Salem? No doubt some people died there for no other reason than being just a little strange."

"Most white people do not question that there were prophets in the Bible, but they think that is different because God was working through them, and so I, too, believe. But the villagers do not have the Bible for a guide. They seek guidance through the dream and the vision. I do not know about the accuracy of some of the other dreamers, but I do know that Shadow Woman is definitely among the best."

"What about some of the more famous prognosticators such as Nostradamus? Have you never hear of him? No? What about Tecumseh, the great Shawnee leader? Yes? Did you know that he accurately predicted the appearance of a comet, the great New Madrid earthquake, and his own death? He once had a brother called Prophet who made many, many predictions, but most people believe that Tecumseh was the true prophet while letting his brother take the credit for the predictions."

"Tecumseh predicted the great earthquake at least nine years before it actually happened. He visited all the tribes north, south, east, and west of his home territory in Ohio, trying to convince others to join the Shawnee tribe in a confederacy to oppose the white man's encroachment. He even came to the Mandan. The great earthquake was to be the sign to rise up and attack the white man everywhere at once. His power hungry brother, the Prophet, destroyed Tecumseh's dream by launching an attack at a time of his own choosing, and much too early."

"Of course you and I know that nothing will ever stop the westward expansion of the white man, but maybe the red man could have won some kind of concession, like perhaps a territory or state of his own, instead of the few scattered reservations that he now has. If they could have laid aside their differences and lived together as brothers., they could have had much power, but some tribes hate one another even more than they hate the white man."

"Forgive me, *m'sieur*, I digress again. And as you know, when Jean Rene gets started on a subject that he enjoys, he is hard to stop. We were discussing prophecy. There can be no doubt that Tecumseh was a gifted prophet. Predicting the great earthquake so accurately would have been enough by itself to establish his reputation as a seer."

"Is that the earthquake that formed Reelfoot Lake back about fifty or so years ago?"

"Yes," said Jean, "a little more than fifty years ago--in December, 1811, to be exact."

"I've heard of the earthquake. My dad used to talk about it. He said it shook the Knoxville area pretty good, but I didn't know that Tecumseh had predicted it. And I've even seen Reelfoot Lake, personally."

"A great greenish-white meteor streaked across the sky from north to south at the very time that Tecumseh was born. I am sure that you have seen falling stars as people call them. They last only a few seconds, but it is said that Tecumseh's meteor lasted for a full 20 seconds. That was a sign to the Shawnee that he would be a special person and attain a high position within the tribe. They call the meteor The-Panther-Passing-Across."

"Forgive me, my friend. It is very difficult for Jean Rene to have a single mind. I know little of Shadow Woman's past, but she is an accepted visionary in this village, although, she has never predicted an event as great as an earthquake. Her visions are on a more personal basis, but you will have to admit, after her description of you, that she is quite accurate."

"Well, alright. I don't have the knowledge to argue with you. You've convinced me that it's possible for certain people to see the future, but I'll tell you, it's a little disconcerting to be personally involved," said Will, grudgingly.

"I read the books, and I ask the questions, *m'sieur.*"

It was time for the meeting. Will attended only because Jean assured him that everything would be all right. Although he didn't know the protocol of such a meeting, he went armed with revolver and knife tucked under his shirt. He didn't know these people or what they would do, but he would not stand for any kind of personal chastisement. He had done nothing except defend himself. If they tried anything, then he would go down fighting.

Will sat through the other four testimonies without understanding the first word that was said. These Indians sure liked to talk. Maybe that was why Jean Rene was a little long winded at times. Then, it was his turn, with Jean translating. "Just tell to me what you want for me to say, *m'sieur*, and I will say it. They want to hear your version of why you killed three of their young men."

"Tell them that we were attacked by six young warriors led by Badger. You were wounded. Then, I wounded one man and killed three others. The other two ran away."

Will watched to see what kind of reaction the chiefs would have to his abbreviated version. One of the elders, a very tall man with a pockmarked face, from smallpox no doubt, tried to stifle a smile. The others seemed disappointed at such a terse speech. After some discussion with the other chiefs, the headman spoke to Jean. "They want to know what we, you and I that is, wish to do about Broken Feather," said Jean. "He is the only one present that they can find fault with. The two that ran away will be banished from the village, forever. I, as well as they, will abide by your decision, *m'sieur.*"

"Look, John, I don't know about you, but I don't want anything done to this young man. Though, it should be more your decision than mine--you were the one that got wounded--he did nothing at all to me. As far as I'm concerned, he made a bad mistake and he has paid dearly for it. He will carry those scars as a reminder of his folly for as long as he lives. I think he has learned his lesson. But if you want me to make the decision, then I say let him go unpunished."

After Jean had translated, the chiefs looked at one another with raised eyebrows, and then with nodding heads, they grunted their approval. The tall, pockmarked man was looking at Will solemnly and very slowly nodding his head, as if he had arrived at some personal decision concerning Will. This man was different from the others, not only was he much taller, probably six and a half feet, he was also much lighter in skin tone, and his hair wasn't jet black either. Actually, it was more of a dark brown shade than black, with the fringes tending toward red.

As the meeting began to break up, Broken Feather stopped Jean and Will and humbly thanked them for being so generous in their clemency, and he would always be in their debt. Will didn't know what would be the appropriate thing to do, so he simply laid his hand on Broken Feather's good shoulder, smiled, and nodded. He hoped that would show there were no hard feelings.

Broken Feather stood and watched as Will and Jean walked toward the lodge door. If there were any possible way that he could repay these men he would do it, even if it meant laying down his own life for them.

XX

The tall man with the pockmarked face was waiting outside the door for Jean and Will to exit the lodge. He began to talk and Jean translated. "This is Tall Man, *m'sieur*, the nephew of the great warrior Ninekiller, and he says that if you will consent to abide at his house, he will be much honored to have you as his guest. To be totally accurate, the dwelling belongs to Shadow Woman. Women are actually the homeowners of the village. But anyway, he thinks that you are truly a noble warrior to have shown such generosity toward Broken Feather. He says that his lodge is much too big for his family of three, and there is also enough room for your two horses, since he has no horse of his own. I did not tell you before, *M'sieur* Will, that the People keep the horse inside the lodge at night, to prevent the stealing, you see. It would be the best of all arrangements, *m'sieur*, especially since I would have to put you in the tent. Winter is not so very far away, and the tent, she would be very cold, especially when the winds blow. Jean Rene's lodge, she is small and already crowded. What do you say to this, eh?"

"I don't know, John. These people are total strangers to me. And besides, how would we be able to communicate with one another? I haven't understood one word that has been spoken by these people since we arrived in the village, except for your wife that is."

"If anything important should arise, Jean Rene will be only a short distance away, *m'sieur*. I am sure it will be fun for everyone to learn a new language. You can learn together, one from the other, *non*? It will be a good way to pass the time, and one never knows when another language may be of use."

"You know what, John, I do believe that you are the most persuasive man I have ever met. You have manipulated me like a puppet on a string since the day that we first met. You seem to have a gift for it. All right, tell the man that I graciously accept, but you have to come with me until I'm settled in. I'm not saying how long I'll stay in his lodge, mind you. I may take off for the mountains tomorrow, understand?"

"Yes, but I think that you will not regret your decision, my friend. In fact, I am sure of it," said Jean, immensely proud of himself for making such an arrangement.

"My decision, huh. Yeah, right," mumbled Will.

Tall Man proudly led the way to his lodge, his head held high, looking neither right or left at the curious onlookers that had gathered to get another look at the gray soldier. Will's horses had to be left outside until the stall was made ready--it was presently being used as a storage area. Jean made formal introductions all around, repeating the names until Shadow Woman, Tall Man, and Will could say them reasonably well. Lone Dove wasn't present at the moment; she was working in the cornfield.

So, this is Shadow woman, thought Will, the woman that had seen him in a vision. She seemed quite ordinary to him, although he didn't know exactly what he had expected--a hag with a wart on her nose perhaps? She was an attractive woman and must have been quite pretty in her younger days. Her hair, eyes, and skin were even lighter than Tall Man's was. Will had noticed several light-skinned, light-haired people in the crowd earlier in the day, but no true blonds or red heads, all of them Mandans he supposed.

After Will was settled in, Jean Rene said his farewell and left the lodge. Will made an involuntary step to follow him before he remembered that this would be his new home, but only, he reminded himself, if he decided to stay. He had never felt so alone before in his life, even though two people were standing within arm's reach of him. Why was he here, he wondered? How did he get to be in this situation? Why did he let that runt of a Frenchman twist him like a string around his little finger? He had absolutely nothing in common with these people. There was no way this arrangement could possibly work.

Tall Man and shadow woman stood there apparently at Will's command, pleasantly smiling and nodding their heads, making Will feel even more disconcerted. For the past four years he had told others what to do, but this was different. This home didn't belong to him; he was merely a temporary sojourner on his way to the Shining Mountains.

Will took a moment to scan the interior of the lodge, something he had been too busy to do until now. There were four heavy upright poles with beams from one to the other to make a square at the top. Smaller poles were placed close together from the wall to the top, and finally a thick layer of soil covered the outside. The only opening other than the doorway was a smoke hole in the center of the roof, making the interior quite dim. A fireplace of upright stones in a circle was directly under the smoke hole. There were articles of clothing hanging from pegs on the upright beams and baskets of goods were arranged around the perimeter of the lodge. Skins to form sleeping quarters partitioned off room-like cubicles to give a semblance of privacy. The floor was lower than the earth outside the lodge, leaving a circular ledge all around the inside wall that could be used to sit on. Overall the place was quite neat and clean.

Will didn't know that Indians built such dwellings. He knew that the Cherokee had adapted to the white man's way of living and built log homes for themselves, but the tepee, so he thought, was the home of most red men, but then, he knew almost nothing about Native Americans.

Will stored his saddle and gear near, but not too near, the family's bedding area. A cubicle of his own would be necessary if he wanted a semblance of privacy, although, total privacy was impossible under these living conditions. Maybe he should just go on to the mountains, even though it was getting late in the year. He wasn't used to living in such close proximity to other people, not even during the war, and especially with strangers who spoke a different language.

Rex went sniffing all around the lodge then chose a spot near Will's saddle for himself. There were lots of dogs in the village, all of the same breed, apparently, but none looked quite like Rex. He was as big as any two of the other dogs combined. His size alone, so far anyway, had kept him from being seriously challenged by any of the others.

Will had finished with his belongings and was going to visit with Jean--even though it had been less than an hour since he had last seen him--when he almost collided with a young lady coming through the doorway. She was carrying a hoe, made from a bison scapula, in her right hand. She laughed and stepped lightly aside in order to let Will pass, but he just stood there dumbstruck. He certainly hadn't expected to see such a strikingly beautiful woman way out here in the middle of nowhere. There had been lovely women on the streets of Nashville and St. Louis, but Will had hardly noticed them in their finery and made-up faces. But here before him--barefooted and wearing doeskin clothes, with auburn hair and hazel eyes--was completely captivating natural beauty.

The young lady said something that brought Will back to his senses. He was a little embarrassed at having stared at the young woman with his mouth agape, and mumbling an apology that she didn't understand, he hurried out the door. After he had regained his composure, he was angry with himself for losing control and acting like an idiot because of a pretty face, no matter how unexpected the meeting had been. Ginny had been dead for--what was it--three months? And he was already betraying her memory by acting like a fool.

He had intended to go and talk to Jean, but now all he wanted was to be alone for a while. He simply had to do some thinking. Things were piling up; things that he had no control over, and he didn't like it. He and Rex walked beside the great, muddy river--Will angrily kicking sticks, stones, whatever was in his way--until they came to a large log. He sat on the ground, leaned back against the log, and watched the muddy Missouri flow by many feet below.

Rex lay down beside Will and rested his head on his right thigh. He seemed to sense that his master was unhappy.

Will's goal in coming to this spot had been to decide whether to remain in the village until spring or to leave immediately and take his chances in the Rockies. But every time he tried to concentrate, his thoughts kept coming back to the beautiful girl. What was it about her? It wasn't her beauty alone; there was something else about her that he couldn't define. His mind was drawn to her like a magnet. If he did decide to leave, could he bring himself to go through with it? He honestly didn't know. Even now, as he tried to make up his mind whether or not to leave, he wanted to see the beautiful woman again. He tried to replace the Indian girl's face with the image of Ginny, but for some reason he couldn't remember exactly what Ginny looked like, making his anger even more intense. He finally gave up and just let his mind wander.

Will held his head in both hands and moaned aloud. He immediately looked all around to see if anyone was close enough to hear, but even though there were many people not far away, he was as much alone as he felt. Although he had been a loner much of his life, he desperately needed companionship at this moment more than any other time in his life. Jean Rene had his family and friends; the villagers had each other; Will had no one but Rex. Absent mindedly, he stroked the big dog's head as he tried again to reach a decision about leaving.

He knew that in the mountains winter would come early. A shelter would have to be built and food would have to be stocked. He would be lucky to survive if he delayed leaving any longer. He might have already waited too long, but his mind refused to cooperate. What would it matter if he didn't survive? No one would miss him. No one would ever know what had happened to him. So what if he froze to death or starved. He had heard that freezing was not a bad way to go. You simply went to sleep and never woke up. Will suddenly realized that he was wallowing in self-pity and became even angrier.

When the gray soldier had first entered the village, Lone Dove (more accurately translated as Unique Dove) had been at the back of the crowd where she could observe everything without being conspicuous. She wanted very much to get a good look at this man; after all, she had been anxiously waiting several days for his arrival. He had been at the center of her thoughts for days. And now here he was. He was exactly as she had pictured him in her mind--there was no disappointed at all. She even liked the scar; it gave him the look of an experienced warrior. She closed her eyes and imagined embracing this man as in her mother's vision. Her heart raced with the thought. She believed she loved this stranger already, even though she had never even spoken to him. No other man had ever stirred such feelings in her breast.

And then, just now, they had met in the doorway. His appearance was so sudden that there was no time to think, only to react. She had tried to be friendly, but he had seemed to be angry with her. What had she done? Maybe it wasn't her that he was angry with. She would follow him at a distance and see what she could learn.

At the river she watched the gray soldier from the cover of a tree that stood at a safe distance behind him. He seemed so forlorn and lonely that Lone Dove's heart ached for him. She wanted to go to him, take him in her arms, and comfort him, but that would be inappropriate, and besides, how would she communicate with him? Standing here watching him was accomplishing nothing, but she couldn't bring herself to abandon him here alone. Maybe his friend Jean Rene could do something to help. She hurried away to find Jean.

Jean found Will at the log where Lone Dove had last seen him, even though the sun had gone down and darkness would soon fall. "Will, my friend," he began as he sat down on the log, "we were getting worried about you. You have been gone from the village for such a long time now. Is it something that is bothering you, *m'sieur?*"

"Yes… Yes, John," said Will, with a touch of anger in his voice. "As a matter of fact, there is something bothering me. My mind is in total confusion, and I seem to be unable to make even a simple decision. I don't know exactly how to explain it, since I don't completely understand it myself, but it seems that I've some-how totally lost control of my life. Since the day that I met up with you, it seems that I have been maneuvered toward this village, even though my original intention was to lose myself in the Rocky Mountains. And then when I get here, I find that the whole village is expecting me--including some woman who obviously thinks that we are already a couple. My life seems headed in a direction that I have no conscious control over. I've always thought of myself as a very decisive man, but right now I feel powerless to make the simplest decision."

"John, do you believe there is such a thing as destiny? Could it be possible that I was destined to come to this place? If so, then was my wife destined to die giving birth? Was my friend, Buck, destined to die one week before the end of the war? Do we have control of our own lives, or are we simply actors in a predetermined plot? Are we merely puppets with someone else pulling the strings? It seems that I can never say no to you, or have you noticed?"

"*M'sieur,* I do not think..."

"The day that I left my father's house," Will interrupted. "I felt that I had finally taken control of my life. I believed that day that I had finally taken the reins away from my father, but now I'm not so sure any more. Someone or some thing seems to have taken over those reins, and it bothers me. I don't know whether to stay here or go on to the mountains. My mind is in total confusion, and it makes me furious. Up until now I've always thought of myself as a clear thinker, but tonight, I don't have the ability to direct my thoughts in any direction. I have never been this frustrated before in my entire life." This was one of the longest speeches, without pause, that Will had ever made in his life.

"I do indeed believe, *m'sieur,* that we have options in our lives," Jean answered. "I know in my heart that you can ride away this very moment, if you truly wish, and go to the mountains, never looking back. Although, if you make such a decision, I believe that you will later come to regret it—in more ways than one."

"It is true that the people were expecting you here in the village, but you were already almost here when the vision came to Shadow Woman, is that not so? Maybe I did play just a small part in your decision, but it was your decision, was it not? I could not possibly have tied you like the hog and brought you here against your will. Is this not also true?"

"You have been estranged from your parents, lost your wife and best friend, and fought for a lost cause, but your life, it must go on. Do you know the story of Job? He lost much, but he was given back even more. You have lost much, my friend, but you could be about to receive much more in return. Who is to know? I think that you question life too much, *non*? Why not be more like Jean Rene, trust in a benevolent God, and simply accept things as they are. I was born into a very devout Catholic family. Faith comes easy for me. Can you not find just a little faith somewhere down deep inside you that everything will turn out for the better?"

"We can beat our heads against a brick wall and gain nothing but a headache. I feel in my heart that our Creator has something wonderful in store for you, Will Stanton. Be patient, my friend, and wait upon the Lord."

Job? Why did that name ring a bell, Will wondered? "I have always been pretty much a loner and took care of myself, John. I've never seen much evidence of a loving God; never had any reason to trust in anyone other than myself, but you could be right about one thing. Maybe I am reading too much into this situation, but what about this woman thing? How am I supposed to handle that? My wife has been gone for only three months, and I certainly am not looking for another woman."

"Then you have not met this woman, *m'sieur*?"

"No, not that I know of, John. Who is she?"

"Her name is Lone Dove."

"Yes, you mentioned her name when we rode into the village, but who is Lone Dove?"

"I thought that I had already told you, but maybe I have not. She is the daughter of Tall Man, *m'sieur*."

Will's face registered his surprise. "Aah, I see that you have met her after all. Is she not the beautiful one, eh?" asked Jean Rene, with a sly smile.

"Yes…I have met her, and yes, she is beautiful. And, also, I see that I have been maneuvered right into the same house with her. How so very convenient," said Will, looking angrily at Jean.

"*M'sieur* Will, do not be angry with me. What I have done was with your benefit in mind. Please listen but for a moment. What is past cannot be changed. The rest of your life you can live alone, and you will gain absolutely nothing from it. You cannot bring back your wife, but here is a beautiful woman who has spurned the advances of all other men. It is as if she has waited all her life just for you, and she is ready and willing to be your woman. God made woman to be the companion for man. He does not want for you to be alone, my friend."

"Are you going to be offended and pass up this opportunity for happiness? Tell something to me. If the situation, she is in reverse, would you want for your wife to waste away her days in the mourning for you? I know that you had…ah…have much love for your wife, and you are trying to be true to her memory, but you must remember that she also had much love for you, and she would want for you to be happy. You have many years ahead of you; you should live them to the fullest extent. Life, she is like the bull, my friend. You should take this bull by the tail and live."

Will had to smile in spite of the turmoil that he was going through. "I think you mean take the bull by the horns, John."

"It will be much safer my way, *m'sieur,* I guarantee. Come, let us walk back to the village together. Everything will be fine if you will but give it a chance."

"Thank you, my friend, I feel a little better now. You have given me something to think about. Once again you've made me see things from a different perspective. As usual, you seem to have known exactly the right things to say. You go ahead; I'll be along shortly. There's something that I need to figure out first."

After Jean had gone, Will tried to remember what it was about the name of Job that had pricked his memory. He knew the story of Job and had heard several sermons over the years preached about his great suffering and patience. That was it! The sermon at Hicks Chapel about people and their problems: when there is nowhere else to turn, call upon the Lord and give your problems to Him and He will lift you out of despair.

That was easy to say, but how did one go about doing such a thing? If problems were tangible, if they were objects, it would be as easy as throwing a stick into the river. With that thought, he picked up a stick and threw it as far as he could into the darkness over the water. Hey! Why not? He turned and tore a large piece of bark from the log.

Will had never talked to God on such a personal basis before. Sure, he had done just what most people had done when in a fix-- made promises to God that were promptly forgotten when the crisis had passed--but he didn't even know how to begin a real prayer. What was it the preacher at Hicks Chapel had said? Call upon the Lord and cast your cares upon Him. Was that it? There had to be more. Oh, yes, and He will lift you up from out of despair, or something along that line. That seemed much too simplistic to do any good. Well, he had nothing to loose and everything to gain by giving it a try.

Mentally, he went through the list of burdens and cares that he wanted to be rid of and mentally placed them on the piece of bark, one at a time. As humbly and sincerely as he knew how, Will began, "Lord, as you already know, you and I have never exactly been pals. I've always been pretty much a loner and never depended on anyone but myself, but now, I've reached the end of my rope, and I can't handle things by myself anymore. I really don't know how to put my trust in you, as Jean Rene says to do, but I am going to try. And if you can bring peace to my burdened soul, I surely would be grateful, but it beats me as to why you would want my problems in the first place. Oh, yeah, uh, thank you and amen."

He stood up and stepped to the edge of the steep riverbank. Holding the piece of bark by the end, he sailed it like a skip rock out over the black surface of the water. Since full darkness had fallen, the bark disappeared into the gloom, the sound of it hitting water never reaching his ears. Hopefully, his problems had disappeared along with the bark.

Deep in thought, Will stood several seconds staring into the gloom. He hadn't heard thunder or seen lightning strike or anything as dramatic as that, but he definitely felt better. Is that all that had been necessary? Just simply letting go? If that was all that was necessary, why had he been so stupid? He should have done this a long time ago. As Jean Rene had said, Ginny would want him to be happy, just as he would want her to find happiness if the tables were turned. What would he gain if he continued as he was going? Absolutely nothing. Jean Rene was much wiser than he looked.

As he walked back toward the village, he felt as if a great weight had been lifted from his shoulders. He could even smile with nothing humorous taking place. He hadn't felt this free from burden since before the war had started, and now, he realized that the place of peace that he had ridden hundreds of miles to find had been within his own soul all along. He now knew that he had hidden that peace under a blanket of bitterness of his own making. How could he have been so blind? Everything seemed so clear to him now, and all because his friend had been wise enough to show him the way.

As Will walked, he continued to berate himself for being so dumb these past few months. Yes, he was happier than he had been in a long while, and with Ginny's memory being no less precious to him now than before.

Even Rex appeared to be in a lighter mood as he jauntily trotted ahead, leading the way back to the village.

XXI

Jean had been right. It was actually fun to learn a new language, and within a week, Will and his new family--as he now considered them--were able to communicate, up to a point, in a mixture of simple English, Mandan, and sign language. Sometimes, they would laugh until they cried at the way they would pronounce each other's words and the silly sentences that they constructed.

Tall Man and Shadow Woman, in fact all the villagers, accepted Will as a fully-fledged member of the family. Lone Dove and her mother served him as if he were helpless, wanting to do even the simplest things for him. A man could get used to this kind of treatment. Will didn't realize that this servile attitude was all part of a female's upbringing.

It was most difficult living in the same lodge with such a beautiful young woman, now that his attitude had changed, and especially so, since both of them used every excuse to be close to one another—and to touch at every opportunity. So, after another week of language lessons and some special coaching from Jean Rene, Will asked Lone Dove if she would accompany him on a walk along the river.

He led her to the log that he now thought of as his own private sacred place, reveling in the feel of her hand in his. Facing her and taking both of her hands in his—the touch of her flesh felt almost electric--he asked haltingly if she would consent to be his *mitawicu,* his wife. She immediately let go of his hands, and throwing her arms around his neck in a tight embrace, gave him the only answer he needed. When Will tried to kiss her, Lone Dove, not understanding at first, turned her head aside. Kissing was a white man's custom that she was unfamiliar with. But Will, taking her face in both hands, managed to brush his lips against hers. After that first kiss, she was hooked for life.

"I am so happy that you never found a man that you liked *tekihila,* my love. In just two weeks, I have grown to love you so much. I believe I loved you the first time I laid eyes on you, but I wouldn't admit it to myself at the time. There is no way for you to know how wonderful it is for me to feel love again, instead of the bitterness that had been my constant companion for so long. You can't imagine the change that has taken place in my soul in just the last two weeks, and you, my love, have played a big part in it. I'm going to spend the rest of my life making sure that you never regret this day," said Will, as he held her as closely as possible. The feel of her body against his, combined with the smell of her hair, gave Will such a heady sensation that he felt dizzy. He felt as if he could drift away with the breeze. How could he have ever contemplated riding away and leaving this beautiful woman behind?

Will had spoken mostly in English, but Lone Dove had understood enough to grasp the meaning of what he was saying. "I love you also, Will Stanton, and I would be honored to have you as my *higna,* my husband. I now realize in my heart that it was you that I waited for all these years. There never has been and never will be any one else for me as long as I live," she answered in Mandan. They didn't have to understand one another perfectly; love is a language unto itself.

Will thought that life was again worth living, and that he could face anything with such love in his heart and this beautiful woman at his side. To have a reason to live once again made all the difference in the world.

When they went back to the lodge, Will managed with Lone Dove's help to ask for Tall Man's approval of the marriage. Tall Man was in his favorite spot poking in the ashes. At Will's question, he jumped to his feet and grabbed Will by the forearm in the Indian style of handshake and said, "Yes, you have my permission, Will Stanton, and I am so very happy that you came along before she got too old to bear children." They all laughed heartily at this banter.

And that was all there was to it. They were now married. Will's only possession that Tall Man considered desirable was the large knife, so Will presented the knife to him as a gift. "*Pilamaya*, thank you, Will Stanton, but gifts were never necessary to begin with. I am happy that my daughter has accepted you as her *higna*; nothing else matters."

The villagers had already accepted Will as Lone Dove's mate days before he had even arrived at the village. To them, the announcement of the wedding was a mere formality.

The villagers, impatient because the young couple had waited two weeks to be married, decided to celebrate with a feast and dance. Will donned clothes that he had brought from St. Louis and never worn. He took the gray uniform to the log by the river and ceremoniously burned it--the time had come to break completely with the past. He was no longer the gray soldier; he was now Will Stanton, *higna* of Lone Dove, the most beautiful woman in the world. He had to take part in the dancing, and the villagers thought his awkward antics were hilarious. The festivities continued so far into the night that everyone slept a little later than usual the next morning. For a honeymoon, Will and Lone dove decided to borrow Jean's tent and ride up the Knife and camp for a few days.

As he helped Will load the tent on the pack horse, Jean Rene could see the change that had taken place in Will and commented on it. When Will explained how, after their conversation at the river, the transformation had taken place, Jean gave him a hearty slap on the back and said, "Did I not tell you that you would not regret the decision that you have made?"

"Yes, I am happy to say that you were totally right, my friend," said Will. It was good to have someone on whom he could depend for advice, especially now that he had a newfound respect for Jean Rene's judgment. But he was not at all sure just how much of the decision was of his making. The belief that he had been the object of manipulation was still present, but it no longer mattered. He was too happy to care any more, and actually glad it had happened.

XXII

After sleeping in the open the first night, the happy couple rode slowly the next morning along the little river, enjoying each other's company as they looked for a place to camp. In mid-afternoon they found what they considered the ideal location. About a mile up a small tributary of the Knife they found a clear, deep pool about twenty feet across, with willows and cattails growing around the edge. Thick willows also grew along the little stream that drained the pool. Two large cottonwood trees grew close beside the pool where Will pitched the tent. The whole setting was in a secluded little valley between low hills that afforded some protection from the wind and the cottonwood trees gave shade from the hot sun. They couldn't have found a more perfect location.

"*Hinhanni waste, mitawicu.* Good morning, wife," said Will, as they awakened the second morning as man and wife.

"*Hinhanni waste, higna.* Good morning, husband," returned Lone Dove, with a very seductive smile. They both agreed that since there was nothing on the agenda for that day, there was really no reason for them to get out of bed.

By mid-morning, the tent had become too stuffy to be comfortable, so after a refreshing dip in the pool, and a hearty breakfast, they did some serious napping in the shade of the cottonwood trees. That whole day was filled with devotion to each other, and they were deliriously happy.

Just after dawn of the morning of the third day, Rex alerted Will to a small herd of antelope that were meandering down the far side of the little valley. The animals couldn't see the tent behind the willows or catch scent of the camp, since the breeze was blowing away from them. Will, with the Spencer at the ready, waited patiently behind the cover of the willows until the antelope were well within range before shooting one of the smaller of them.

There were many edible prairie plants and roots in the meadow and along the stream, and the roots of the cattails growing in the shallow areas of the pool, when boiled down to a mush, to Will, tasted like mashed potatoes. They ate well enough without the food that they had brought with them. Rex had fun chasing rabbits and actually seemed happier here than in the village. He had taken to Lone Dove and watched over her like a hawk. Every time she went swimming the dog went swimming, too.

Will and Lone Dove had five glorious days of nothing but each other, and it was wonderful. Will couldn't possibly love this woman more, and she seemed to reciprocate fully. But on the morning of the sixth day, the idyll was shattered. They had just finished eating a leisurely breakfast when Rex sniffed the air and growled, looking toward the willows downstream. A light breeze, barely strong enough to rustle the tree leaves, wafted from that direction. Will grabbed the Spencer and hurriedly took Lone Dove into the thick willows beside the pool, using the tent as cover between themselves and the willows down stream. Ordering Rex to stay with Lone Dove, Will left the extra revolver—with which he had already familiarized Lone Dove--and circled upstream around the pool, using the willows to mask his movements. He hurried through a gap in the ridge on the far side of the pool, and wended his way up the backside of the ridge almost to the top. Crawling on his belly the last few feet, just far enough to peek over the top, Will had an unobstructed view of the whole miniature valley.

The top of the tent was in plain view from this vantage point, as well as the horses grazing near it, but he could see nothing of Lone Dove in the thick willows by the pool. She seemed to be well hidden.

Shifting his gaze downstream, Will at first saw nothing out of the ordinary, but then, from behind the willows at a bend in the stream, came five warriors in single file and carrying bows. It would be easy to let them get closer and pick them off one by one, but he had no desire to kill these men. He let them advance to the foot of the hill, less than a hundred yards away, before standing up and making his presence known. Speaking as well as he could in Mandan, which he had been told was akin to the Sioux language, he told them, in no uncertain terms, to return the way they had come and to keep going, or they would die where they stood.

They talked among themselves for a few seconds, and then spread out, staring up the hill at Will. Their arrows would be ineffective at this range. It appeared that they were considering an attack, probably thinking that he was armed with a muzzleloader. After one shot to their thinking, he could be overwhelmed. To show them that they would be making a big mistake, Will fired five quick shots over their heads. At the first shot, two of the braves hit the ground behind tall grass; the other three dived for the willows. Immediately, Will realized that he might have made a terrible mistake? There were only two rounds left in the rifle and six in his revolver. In his haste, he had forgotten to bring extra cartridges for the rifle, but to fool the warriors, he went through the motions of reloading. Once again he told them to leave or the next time he would shoot to kill. The two warriors in the grass slowly stood up and the apparent leader said something toward the willows. The other three men emerged from the willows and all five headed downstream, slowly at first, to show their defiance, but when they were well out of range of the rifle, they began to walk faster.

Will waited until he saw, in the distance, five mounted horses climb the ridge on the far side of the valley. Then realizing it was possible that the warriors might charge the camp on horseback from the other side of the little valley, he was almost in a panic as he hurried back to camp by the shortest possible route. He quickly topped off the rifle magazine while explaining to Lone Dove about the five warriors. While he was hurriedly striking the tent, Will had Lone Dove round up the horses.

When everything was loaded on the packhorse, they headed in the opposite direction taken by the warriors. Will wanted to eliminate any possibility that something bad might happen to his new bride. That would be more than he could bear. After about an hour of riding and seeing no sign of pursuit, they turned toward the village. They rode on into the night, slept on the ground for maybe two hours, and then continued their journey.

When they arrived at the village toward the middle of the next day, they were so tired that the first thing they did was sleep for an hour before starting to unpack. It was good to feel safe again. During the ordeal, Will had never once been concerned for his own safety, but if Lone Dove had been harmed, he would never have been able to forgive himself.

XXIII

Will couldn't say exactly when the anger and depression had completely left him, but he definitely was more lighthearted these days, and laughter came more often and much easier than in past months. When he thought of Ginny these days, they were always happy thoughts of the good times they had shared. It was now hard to believe how tightly he had held on to the anger that had been eating at his soul. He realized now that he had wallowed in self-pity like a pig in a mud puddle. There must have been thousands of soldiers in the war who had suffered even more than he had and handled it much better. And to think that all that had been necessary was to simply let it all go.

He had felt himself changing slowly, day by day, ever since the talk with Jean Rene beside the river. The fact that he had avoided shooting those five men yesterday was proof of the change that had taken place within him. Even one month ago he probably would have provoked those men to attack and then made them fully regret their actions. Maybe his bad attitude in the past had brought trouble his way after all, like iron filings to a magnet.

Could he have avoided killing the three brothers in Alabama? He went over the details in his mind and couldn't see any other course of action that he could have taken. They really hadn't left him any choice. Their plan was to follow him and take what they wanted at his expense. If he hadn't gotten the drop on them, they probably would have killed him that night while he slept.

The five Union soldiers? They obviously would have kicked and stomped him to death. What other course could he have taken?

What about the three young warriors? Possibly, if he had taken out Badger first, the others might have ridden away. Or, if he had simply shot their horses out from under them, they might have stopped their attack. Then again, they might have continued their attack on foot. Besides, he would rather shoot a bad man than a good horse. Men were accountable for their deeds; horses weren't. It was much too late to do anything different now. No one in the village seemed to blame him for what had happened—not even Broken Feather, or the parents of the other warriors.

The face of the young Union soldier still haunted him every time he let his mind drift back to the battle in Alabama, but if he had hesitated even one second, he would have been the one to die. He fervently hoped that he would never again have to face such a situation. He wanted never to have to take another human life, even in self-defense, but he would of course, if forced to do so.

The next time that he talked to Jean Rene, Will mentioned the fact that the deaths that he had caused were bothering him a great deal lately. "*M'sieur* Will, do you feel that you were at fault, that you were the transgressor in any of these cases?"

"No, of course I don't, John, but it still bothers me."

"You are having--how do you say--a bout of conscience, my friend. It is only natural in your changed attitude, but do not let it get you down. A murderer you are not. What you have done was either your duty or in self-preservation. Fully accept the fact that you have turned over a new leaf, *m 'sieur,* or your own mind will rob you of your newfound happiness. Do you understand what I am trying to tell you?"

"Yes, John, I do understand, and I am thankful that I have you to talk to. I really don't know what I would do if I didn't have you to help me. You have taught me a great deal."

"When the student is ready, the teacher will be sent. This is something that I truly believe," said Jean. "I was born to be a teacher. If my father had not forced me to run away, I am sure that today I would be a schoolmaster in France. But I am not in France, yet I am being used."

"Are you saying that we were somehow brought together so that you could help me in overcoming my anger?" asked Will.

"But of course. Think about it, my friend. After everything that has happened, is it so incredible to believe this?"

Will did think about it, and often. It made sense. How could he possibly have gotten rid of the anger on his own? Without Jean, he would have gone to the mountains and lived like a hermit and probably died an angry man. It was comforting to think that maybe there was a guide somewhere upstairs watching over him. Lone Dove, in fact all the villagers, he found out later, believed in guiding spirits—manitous, above beings, they were called by some people. Were they the same as guardian angels? One thing he now knew, his mind was no longer blind to the spirit world like it once had been, and he no longer felt that he was all alone in the world.

As Will became more fluent in Mandan, he broached various subjects with his new wife. He found that she had a quick mind and was a willing student and very eager to learn. He borrowed a book that Jean had used to teach his wife and children the fundamentals of reading and writing. The concept that conversations and thoughts could actually be conveyed through marks on paper simply amazed Lone Dove. It bordered on magic to her. That the stories in the Bible--the longest existing book that Will could find--had been written many hundreds of years ago, and that the thoughts of people long dead could be made known to anyone that could read, completely astounded her. To convince Lone Dove that the marks made on paper conveyed the same meaning to anyone that could read them, Will wrote a few words with a burned stick on a piece of leather. The message was: "Lone Dove is the most beautiful Woman in the world, and I love her very much." He told Lone Dove what the words said and handed the piece of leather to her.

"Now, take this to Jean Rene and ask him to tell you what it says."

When she returned, she wanted to learn to read more than ever.

The Plains Tribes had a form of picture writing by which a story could be told. Each figure used was a reminder to the story-teller of how the story was to unfold. Unless someone explained the meaning of the figures, a stranger might not get a full under-standing of the story from the pictures drawn, yet all who learned to read the white men's marks came to the same conclusion. Even the minutest detail could be made clear to the reader.

In one week Lone Dove memorized the sounds of the alpha-bet and could recognize many of the individual characters by sight. With Jean's help, Will hoped to be able to teach her to read simple words in a few weeks.

Will found that Lone Dove's sense of time was quite differ-ent than his own. He habitually thought of the past in hundreds or even thousands of years. Whereas, with no written history to refer to, the past beyond the time of her grandparents was vague to Lone Dove. She could make no distinction between a thousand years and ten thousand years. Will had a difficult time getting her to perceive the distant past. After she learned to read, he would introduce her to numbers, Will decided.

Tall Man, Shadow Woman, and Lone Dove all had a well-de-veloped sense of humor, and loved practical jokes. Life around them was never boring, and Will was happier now than he had ever been before, happier even than he had been with Ginny, though he would never consciously admit it.

The months passed and language ceased to be the barrier it once was. He could even speak some Arikara and Hidatsa now. The three tribes were so closely associated that it would be impossible to learn Mandan and leave the other two out.

Village life so well suited Will that he had absolutely no regrets about letting Jean Rene talk him into coming here to live. He fully agreed with Jean Rene that this was *wichohan washte,* the good way of life, and he could no longer imagine living any other way. And a future without Lone Dove was unthinkable. Whether it had been destiny or an accident of life that had brought him here no longer mattered. That he was here was enough.

Along with learning the language came more knowledge of village life and the customs of the People. Will studied the curious object, shaped somewhat like a barrel, in the very center of the village that the people seemed to have so much reverence for, and he asked Jean about it one day. "That is the representation of the Big Canoe that I told you about as we were riding north, do you not remember?" said Jean. "It is a reminder of the Great Flood." These people never ceased to amaze Will, but then again, he had always supposed that white people had a monopoly on the Flood story. But then, according to Jean Rene, the Mandan were partly white. It was hard to grasp everything that Jean Rene had told him about the Mandan.

There was one rite, though, the *okipa* ceremony, also known as the sun dance, that Will would not watch or have anything to do with. Young men who were being tested for manhood would have skewers of bone or wood stuck horizontally through the skin of their chests or backs, one on either side, and with rawhide ropes looped around the bones they were lifted off the ground to hang all day or until the holds tore loose. This was totally senseless torture as far as Will was concerned. If this had been required of him in order to become a man, he mused, then he probably would have failed miserably.

From a Bible that Jean had given him, Will one day read to Lone Dove the story of Jesus and how He had been nailed to a wooden cross and left there until He died. He was surprised at how readily she accepted the story. The suffering of the young men of the village she had witnessed many times. The suffering of Jesus she could relate to through the suffering of the young men, but she didn't quite grasp how the sins of all mankind could be paid for by a single sacrifice.

Time was passing much too fast for Will now that he was enjoying life again. Winter was just around the corner and meat must be harvested. A large buffalo herd came within scouting distance of the village later that fall--after the Great Bull Dance--and Will managed to harvest enough animals to keep the family in meat for the rest of the winter. Many of the other villagers had gotten all the meat they needed also, but if a family didn't have a capable hunter, extra animals were shot for them. Whereas, most white people were close to the members of their own immediate families, the villagers were more like one large extended family— no one would be allowed to go hungry as long as there was food to share.

Practically the whole village turned out for the hunt. The men rode ahead to catch up with the heard before it left the vicinity. The women, children, and dogs trekking along in a long ragged line would arrive after the buffalo were already down. There was a holiday spirit with women talking and laughing; children running and playing; and dogs--pulling empty travois--yapping and barking. Only the elderly and the younger children remained at home and some of them under protest.

Will, Jean, Broken Feather, and three other men were riding some distance ahead of the main body of hunters when four bison were seen to disappear over a distant rise. The six riders rode at a fast clip to the top of the rise, but there were no bison to be seen, anywhere. The perplexed hunters had stopped and were discussing where the animals could possibly have disappeared when a group of eleven screaming Sioux warriors burst from a gully at the bottom of the hill. The hunters then realized that they had almost been lured into a trap. If they had ridden a little closer to the gully searching for the fake buffalo, the ruse would have worked.

When the hunters dismounted and prepared to do battle instead of turning their backs and running away, the Sioux stopped their charge. They had probably heard of the straw-haired white man with the repeating rifle. He alone could kill three or four of their group. It wasn't worth the risk to continue. After the Sioux had ridden away, Will and the others joined with the main body of hunters, but everyone kept alert to the possibility of attack. The fact that the village had been left almost defenseless was on every warrior's mind. As soon as the hunt was over, nearly half the warriors quickly returned to the vulnerable village.

The method of taking animals was much the same as Will had discovered by accident when he took his first calf. The hunter would pick an animal out of the moving herd, ride along beside it, and then shoot it behind the shoulder. Those that had bows could at times bring down an animal, particularly a cow, with only one well-placed arrow. Bulls, on the other hand being bigger and tougher, were much harder to kill and, as Will was about to witness, very dangerous.

A young man, who only recently had become a warrior, was on his first hunt and wanted the tough hide of a large bull to make his first war shield. The youngster had placed three arrows behind the shoulder of one huge animal, but he showed no sign of slowing, even though bloody froth was blowing from his nostrils with every breath. Will, following immediately behind the young warrior, had emptied the Spencer into other animals and would have to stop in order to reload. It was much too dangerous to attempt reloading while riding along at full speed. One mishap and a man would probably be trampled to death in seconds. Sensing danger, he decided to wait until the bull went down before riding to safety to reload.

The young man had placed the three arrows only inches apart exactly where they would do the most damage, but the big animal refused to go down. The bull had covered a quarter of a mile since taking the first arrow and was losing more blood at every exhaled breath. Finally, he seemed to be slowing, when yet another arrow was placed beside the others. The bull, probably sensing death, decided to take the battle to his adversary and swerved into the horse running beside him. The horse was thrown off balance and went down. The young rider, thrown free and apparently unhurt, came immediately to his feet.

The bull, being such a huge animal and becoming weaker, ran on a short distance before he was able to stop and turn. He seemed to know instinctively that the horse was not his antagonist and started toward the young man, head down. The Indian pony, being frightened by the ordeal, shied away from its owner, who was trying to remount and watch the great bull at the same time. Will rode up and yelled for the young man to grab his hand. In one graceful motion, the youngster, using Will's arm, bounded onto the horse behind Will. The Indian pony followed as they rode to safety. The bull, having finally come to a halt, stood with his head lowered and forelegs splayed, too weak to give chase. The huge animal soon went to its knees, rolled over, and died.

The young warrior, who had regained his horse and bow, was soon beside the huge beast, but he was visibly shaken. As a way of helping the young man save face, Will told him that he had claimed a fine trophy. The young man's chest expanded with pride as he struggled not to smile.

On the way back to the village, the dogs--bellies distended by meat scraps and pulling travois loaded with meat--were forced to rest often, their burdens were so great. The women also employed Rex, who looked at Will as if his heart was broken. Every horse, led by the owner, had hides filled with meat draped across its back, and women and children alike carried as much meat as possible. The People would feast, and then the process of preserving the remaining meat would begin.

Winter came early to the northern plains, and was a lot more severe than Will was used to. A lot of time was spent indoors and the women worked with the animal hides that had been harvested. From the hides of deer and antelope that Will had harvested prior to the buffalo hunt, Lone Dove made a buckskin outfit for him that cut the wind quite well and, with cotton long-handles underneath, kept him quite warm except in the coldest of weather. The moccasins that she made for him were so comfortable that he didn't know how he could have ever worn boots.

His hair had gotten long enough that he now wore a head-band to keep it out of his eyes. He chuckled when he thought about what his father would say if only he could see his son now. A squaw man (he smiled to himself at that thought), with no regular job and few earthly possessions, who was undoubtedly much more content than his father had ever been in his life. What kind of life would he now be living if he and his father had had a closer relationship? Well, there really was no point in thinking about it because there was no way to know the answer. The thought of a lifetime in his dad's warehouse made Will shudder. The happiness he had finally attained was all the consolation he needed as compensation for his unhappy childhood. He knew one thing for certain: the mistakes his father had made, he would never make with his own son, if he had one. And he just might, for Lone Dove was pregnant!

Sometimes in late winter, when the weather permitted, Will would ride out looking for deer or antelope, and one day Broken Feather asked if he could go along. Will readily consented, and they soon developed a close relationship. Will was learning to use a bow and Broken Feather the rifle and pistol. Will made Broken Feather a gift of his extra revolver, but he would have to wait to get powder, caps, and bullets from the next riverboat that arrived. Though Will seldom fired his other revolver, there wasn't enough ammunition to share.

"As Will became more settled into village life and grew closer to Broken Feather, he spent less and less time around Jean Rene, not that he didn't liked Jean any more, but his interests were tending toward other directions. He had less need for Jean's guidance now than in past days, and Jean would never be a hunting companion as Broken Feather was.

One sunny day in late February when the temperature was warmer than it had been in weeks, Will and Broken Feather went riding into the country west of the village. They had ridden to the top of the highest hill in the vicinity and were admiring the scenery when Broken Feather pointed toward a pony tied to a bush at the bottom of the hill. The only trees in the area were growing along the banks of a small stream that meandered down a little valley between the hills. Movement from upstream caught Wills eye. A lone whitetail doe was making its way slowly toward where the pony was tied. The deer would stop periodically to browse the low branches of bushes along the way.

Suddenly, the deer bolted back in the direction it had come, and Will could barely make out the feathers of an arrow protruding from the deer's ribs. He hadn't seen the hunter at all, but soon a young man walked out from the cover of the trees to examine the ground where the deer had been.

From his vantage point, Will had a clear view of the whole miniature valley below him. He followed the deer with his eyes as it crossed the little stream and headed up a draw between two hills on the other side of the valley. The doe tried to ascend the nearer hill, but the effort seemed too great. Growing weak from the loss of blood, she decided to take cover in a clump of bushes at the bottom of the draw. The path the deer had taken made a large arc of maybe half a mile with the ends only half that distance apart. The youngster, Will could see, was making slow progress as he patiently tracked the wounded animal.

Will and Broken Feather rode to the young man's horse, untied it, and led it across the creek before the hunter emerged from the trees beside the stream. When they got to the clump of bushes, they could see the doe lying partially hidden in the shadows, looking as if she were peacefully sleeping. Will tied the pinto to the backside of the bushes, and he and Broken Feather rode up the draw a short distance to watch.

In a few minutes the young hunter came into sight, as he slowly made his way toward the bushes with arrow nocked and ready. Will saw a happy grin spread across the youngster's face when he saw the dead deer under the bushes. The young man laid his bow on the ground and began to crawl into the thicket to retrieve his prize when he saw the legs of a horse on the other side. He quickly backed out from under the bushes, knocked another arrow, and cautiously made his way far enough around the bushes to see the pony. Will had to laugh at the expression on the youngster's face when he discovered his own horse standing there before him.

As Will and Broken Feather rode up to him, the youngster was standing slack-jawed, looking from the two men to the pinto and back again. "We thought we would save you the trouble of walking back to get your horse," said Will.

"H-how…how did you know where to bring him? How did you know about the deer?"

Will closed his eyes and put his index fingers up to his temples. "I watched in my mind as you shot the deer. I saw where the deer went to lay down, and so, I brought your horse here," said Will, as Broken Feather sat stone-faced beside him.

"Wah! You must have the same gift that Shadow Woman has!" the youngster exclaimed.

"Well, either that or I was watching the whole thing from the top of that hill over there," said Will with a big grin on his face.

It took the young man a few seconds to appreciate the joke, but then he began to laugh. "That is good. That is very funny." Even Broken Feather was now laughing.

"Let's get that deer on your horse and get back to the village. You'll have time to skin it before it gets dark."

They placed the deer on the horse in front of where the youngster would sit so that he could keep it in place with his knees and left hand. After they were all mounted, Will again closed his eyes and with his fingers at his temples said: "I see fresh venison for the evening meal at your lodge tonight."

"The young man laughed and said: "I do believe you have a true gift." Will had made another friend.

Sometime along about the first of April--Will didn't even try to keep up with the exact date, time no longer mattered--Lone Dove gave birth to a robust baby boy. Will was walking on air, but he was hardly any prouder than Tall Man and Shadow Woman. He was so happy now that he could hardly remember how dismal life had been only a few months ago.

He didn't have a lot of chores to do around the lodge, so attending to baby Billy was his favorite way to pass the time. Billy never lacked for attention with both his parents and grandparents making him the center of their lives. Even a minor whimper usually had two or three adults checking to see what the problem was. Will couldn't remember a time as a child when his own father had spent any personal time with him. There was so much pleasure and satisfaction in tending to Billy that it made Will sad to think about what his father had missed by not developing a close relationship with his own family.

As time passed and Billy continued to grow, Rex took on the responsibility of guarding him and tolerated all the hair pulling and ear biting with calm aloofness. Wherever the baby was, the dog was always nearby. It was a common sight to see the two of them curled up together, sound asleep.

XXIV

"Growing up in an Indian village was an ideal life for me as a boy," said Billy to warren Hathaway. "There were practically no chores or responsibilities to speak of. My days were spent participating in games of competition with the other boys to hone future hunting skills, although, I never got to go on a real hunt. My family moved to Montana Territory when I was still very young. The only wild game that I was able to take with my little bow was rabbits and other small animals."

"When I was eight years old, both of my grandparents fell ill at the same time during the winter. We never knew for sure what disease they died of, though the villagers called it the winter fever. Their bodies were put on scaffolds until there was nothing but bones left, then their skulls were taken and placed in a circle along with the skulls of others that had passed on. That is the way of the Mandan, and each person knows which skull belongs to his particular loved one. My mother allowed the villagers to take the skulls of her parents to the reservation with them when they were forced to move north to Fort Berthold."

"Well, Mr. Hathaway," said Billy, " that just about does it for life in the village. Things were changing at a rapid pace on the Northern Plains. More and more whites were settling in the Dakotas, dooming the free-roaming Indian's way of life. There are still isolated instances of trouble with the Indians, even now, but everybody knows it's only a matter of time before all the tribes will be completely pacified, as the white man likes to say. You'll have to forgive me if I sound just a little bitter, but there is good reason for it."

"The railroad that ended at Bismarck in 1873 would be extended westward to join the Union Pacific line in just a few more years. We lived in the village on the Knife until shortly after the three tribes were forced to abandon the site, then, as I said before, my family headed for Montana."

At that time the Sioux still controlled the area that we would have to travel through, although their hold would be largely broken before long. But at the time of our journey they were very agitated and dangerous to any strangers found in their territory, especially anyone of white blood. Remember now, this was shortly after Custer made his big mistake at the Little Bighorn that we traveled through this area. The Sioux and Cheyenne were jubilant at their success over Custer, but they also knew that retaliation would be swift in coming."

"Dad had acquired another horse for my mother, while I rode the old packhorse. The old fellow was on his last legs, but I was his only burden, and I didn't weigh very much back then. Mom and Dad's horses had to pull travois loaded with our belongings, which wasn't much. Broken Feather decided to go with us, as he and my dad had become almost inseparable."

"Rex, by this time, was quite old and had slowed down to the point where he could hardly catch his own food any more. One evening, while we were enroute, he didn't show up when we made camp for the night. The next morning Dad and Broken feather separated and searched along our back trail, but they didn't find any sign of him, although they did find wolf tracks in the area. It was like losing a member of the family."

"If Rex had been around, he probably would have warned us early one afternoon that a party of Sioux was nearby. Before we knew what was happening, we were surrounded by Indians." Billy chuckled. "You know, it sounds funny for me to be referring to the Sioux as Indians when my dad was the only fully white person around. But anyway, there were an even dozen of them painted for war. My dad had barely enough time to hand my mother the revolver and unsheathe the Spencer before they were upon us. Broken Feather also had his revolver ready. We wouldn't have stood a chance had a battle erupted, but the Sioux would have paid dearly, and I think they knew that. We sat quietly, waiting for them to make the first move.

"Finally, after several very long seconds, one of the warriors rode forward to within a few feet of my dad. I don't know if he was the leader or not, but he obviously was a man of some import. The others held back while he did the talking.

"'You are the one known as the gray soldier who lived with the Mandan.' It was a statement, not a question."

"Yes, I am the one," said my dad.

"You fought the bluecoats in the white man's war." Another statement.

"Yes, that is true."

"I also fight the bluecoats." To this, my dad said nothing. "I have seen you before. Years ago near the Knife River. There were four others with me. We were going to attack your camp." My dad said later that at this point he was sure that we were in very dire straits.

"You could have killed all of us that day, but you did not."

"I had no desire to kill you then. I have no desire to kill you now."

"During this whole time, my dad held the Spencer with his thumb on the hammer and his finger on the trigger so that it could quickly be brought into play. This didn't go unnoticed by the warrior."

"Where are you going?" the man asked, pointing at the travois the horses were pulling.

""We are going west to the Shining Mountains. The Mandan have been forced to move to a reservation. I cannot live that way."

The warrior gravely nodded his agreement. "Go then," he said, as he reined his horse around and galloped away, the others following.

"My dad finally got to see the Rocky Mountains, after a delay of several years. We made camp in a beautiful little valley with plenty of game, while Dad searched the surrounding area for miles, looking for the ideal place for a permanent home. He searched for weeks for a special place that he really liked. He had no intention of settling down without being completely satisfied. And then one day, many miles to the south of our camp in the foothills of the Bighorn Mountains, he found it: a gorgeous little valley that cuts back into the mountains for about five miles. There, a stream filled with trout drained the valley, and near where this stream headed up, it split into three branches, widening the valley into a basin. Dad knew at first sight that this was where he wanted to live out the rest of his days. The valley being narrower at its mouth makes it much easier to keep our cattle from straying. A simple barrier of piled brush at the narrow outlet is all that is needed."

"There is lush grass growing throughout the valley, and plenty of trees higher up the slopes that we used to build our house with. At first we built a dugout near a spring at the mouth of the valley and lived in it the first winter, but the next year we started our house. I say we, but actually, at my age I wasn't much help in the actual building. There were plenty of flat broken slabs of stones at the base of a near-by cliff. Using a sled that Dad had made, I hauled enough of the stones—with my dad loading and Broken Feather unloading the sled--to build a seven-foot high foundation enclosing the spring. With the natural lay of the land, the western end of the house is at ground level, while the eastern end rests on the rock foundation. Dad said there was no need to carry water from outside when the spring could be right under the house. We use the basement, if that's the right term, as a root cellar and the spring as a cooler for milk and butter."

"Even after the house was finished, Broken Feather continued to live in the dugout--even though Dad protested--until he met a young Crow woman and got married. He now lives on the Crow Reservation, which is only a few miles away. We visit each other regularly."

"We run a few head of cattle back in the valley, bought with the money that Dad had carried with him all those years. It's really a nice place. Our herd will grow since there's enough elk, deer, and antelope in the area to supply our needs, but we'll never be a big outfit. We just want to raise enough cattle to have a comfortable living."

"I remember the day my dad killed his first elk. He sat down beside the animal and rubbed its neck and shoulder like it was a sleeping dog. He had such a far away look in his eyes that he seemed to be in a trance. At the time I thought he was sorry for shooting the animal. But after I learned more about my dad's life, I came to realize that he was thinking back to the time, as a young boy, when he had fantasized about hunting elk in the Rocky Mountains. His fantasy had finally come true."

"You got room out there for a Tennessee newspaper man, Billy?"

"In Montana or in the valley?"

"I'm joking of course. I can't imagine myself as a rancher," said Warren. "Neither can I see myself leaving Tennessee."

"Billy, there is something that I've been wondering about. Where did you get your education? Did the Frenchman teach you like he did his own children?"

"Yes, that's it exactly. My dad taught my mother and me to read and write, and then Jean Rene took over. Not many boys get to go to school with a parent, but it was really fun learning alongside my mother. We were required to read every book that Jean had. After we finished each one, we were questioned to make sure that we understood what we had read. Of course, my dad read quite a lot during the winter months himself; a Bible that Jean Rene had given him being his favorite book.

"That's really interesting to think of people living so far from civilization getting an education, while there are lots of folks around here that can't read and write. What ever happened to Jean Rene and his family?"

"As riverboat traffic increased on the Missouri, Jean had the foresight to take advantage of the situation. Before the tribes were removed, he built a trading post on the Missouri just a little way south of the Mandan village. A little community grew up around the store and it was called--now listen to this--Stanton. It's still called that today. I rode through there on my way east. The place had changed so much since I was a boy that I hardly recognized it. Many of the old earth lodges have fallen in, making the village a place of desolation. I couldn't make myself stick around very long. The community of Stanton has actually grown into a small town. Jean has passed on, but his wife and one of his sons still run the store. I grew up with his children, but now, after so many years, we are like strangers. They were happy to see me, of course, but we don't have much in common any more"

"Stanton, huh? Don't that beat all. Some coincidence, huh?" said Warren. "Tell me, Billy, are you heading back to Montana soon?"

"There's something I've decided to do first, but yes, I'll be leaving shortly."

"Well, Billy, it's really been a pleasure knowing you, and I hope this story gets published. You'll have to give me your address so that I can write you. You do get mail out there don't you?"

Billy laughed, "Yeah, but it takes a while. We get into town maybe once a month. The address is Billings, Montana. That should be easy enough to remember. Well, sir, I'll say good-bye to your wife and son and be on my way. It's been a pleasure knowing you and your family, and please do write. We--my dad and I--will always be interested in news from this area."

XXV

Billy stopped in Cheekville just long enough to say good-bye to Jed Thompson and his family, and then he was off to see Gracie. It had been two days since he had seen her, and he could hardly wait. Her beautiful face was always in his mind, and food and sleep didn't seem nearly as important as they once were. Gracie was waiting expectantly. The second that Billy's feet touched the ground, she was there to greet him with a short kiss, then taking him by the hand, she led him around the corner of the house and gave him a tight embrace and a lingering, passionate kiss. Billy was reluctant to let her go, but there was an important subject he had to broach. "I've got something very important I want to ask you when your dad gets home," he said, almost breathlessly.

Gracie thought she already knew what was on Billy's mind, but she wanted to hear him say it. "Oh, Billy, you just said that to pique my curiosity. You should know you can't do a woman this way. Go ahead and ask me now."

"This is something that concerns your whole family," said Billy, enjoying himself.

"Billy! You're killing me with suspense," said Gracie, stamping her foot and trying to appear angry. "Ask me now and we'll confront Mom and Dad together."

"Alright. I'm on my way to visit my grandparents in Knoxville. I'll be gone about a week, and when I come back, I'll be going home to Montana. I want you to go with me--as my wife of course. Before you say anything, I have to tell you that if you say yes, we will have to live in the same house with my parents until we can build a home of our own."

"Well…I don't know, Billy. This is…so sudden. I'll have to do some serious thinking about it," said Gracie, frowning and pausing for about five seconds. "Okay, that's long enough. Yes, Darling, I'll marry you and go to Montana with you." They both laughed as Billy lifted Gracie off the ground and swung her around in a circle. "And I don't care if we have to live in a cave, as long as we can be together."

"A cave, huh. I think that can be arranged. There just happens to be an old dugout on our place, and with a little work, a few flowers, and new furniture it could be turned into a nice cozy hole in the ground," said Billy, with a grin.

"It'll take more than that to discourage me, my love."

They spent the afternoon sitting on the porch holding hands. After Herman came home, they waited until everyone was seated at the supper table, and then Gracie could wait no longer. "Mom… Dad… Billy has asked me to marry him and go to Montana with him! I said that I would!"

"Well, I can't say that this was totally unexpected," said Maggie. "And, Billy, if you were anyone else but Will Stanton's son, you two would never get my approval, especially since you've known each other for such a short time. But solely because you are Will's son, I trust you, Billy, to take good care of my daughter."

"I really don't want you to live so far away, Gracie, but I guess it's time for you to leave the nest. What do you think, Herman?" asked Maggie, as silent tears began coursing down her cheeks.

"Yes, you're right, Mag, that's a long way off, and we'll certainly miss you, Gracie, but we won't stand in the way of your happiness. You are old enough to make up your own mind. You have my blessings also. When is the happy occasion?"

"After I visit my grandparents in Knoxville; it'll be about a week," said Billy. "If you will let me sleep in the barn tonight, I'll get an early start in the morning."

"Yes, of course you can, Billy. I just wish we could be more hospitable," said Margaret.

"Think nothing of it. You have no idea the places I've slept in the last few months." They didn't know it, but Billy would have slept on a bed of nails just to be near Gracie.

XXVI

Using the money that Warren Hathaway had given him, Billy bought new clothes and stored his buckskins in the barn. His thinking being that his grandparents, especially his grandfather, would receive him more readily if he looked a little more conventional. He didn't know why it was so important to him, but he really wanted his grandfather's approval.

Billy traveled, in reverse, essentially the same route to Knoxville--up the valley and around the Crab Orchard Mountains--as Will had traveled 28 years earlier on his way to the Sequatchie Valley. If Billy had known the exact location of Junior Hawkins' cabin, he would have, out of curiosity, visited that site, since he would be in the vicinity. Surely, Junior would have passed on before now; he was getting old when Will had come this way. Billy hoped that Junior, in his old age, had enjoyed a few years of rest in Alabama; he probably deserved it.

Billy had no trouble at all finding the Knoxville river-docks and began asking where he might locate John Stanton's warehouse. He was guided to a long, low building not far away. Inside he was informed that John Stanton no longer owned the warehouse, and in fact, was no longer living, but his widow lived just a few blocks down the street. Now, he would never know how his grandfather might have received him—if at all.

The house that he had been guided to was old but well kept. It appeared to have been recently painted. A white picket fence enclosed a yard of recently trimmed grass, adding to the neat appearance of the residence.

Billy was very nervous as he knocked on the door. The woman that came to the door gave Billy quite a shock. He didn't know what he expected his grandmother to look like, but it wasn't like this woman before him. She was a tottering, scarecrow of a woman, wearing a shawl about her stooped shoulders even though it was a very warm day. If his reckoning was correct, Clare should be in her middle sixties. This woman looked twenty years older. "Yes, what can I do for you young man? If you're selling something, I'm not interested."

"Are you Clare Stanton?"

"Yes. Yes I'm Clare Stanton."

"I--I'm--my name is Billy Stanton, Ma'am. Will Stanton is my father."

"Oh, my gracious Lord! Yes, of course, I can see that you are! I should have recognized you immediately. You look so much like Will did the day he... Oh, please, do come in," said Clare, so excited that her hands were fluttering.

"How is Will; there's nothing wrong is there?"

"No ma'am. When I left Montana, he was just fine."

Billy went inside and had to start answering questions from the moment he sat down. He hit the highlights of Wills life, not wanting to go into detail so soon after all the dictating to Warren Hathaway. He had already told Will's story three times in as many weeks. Mostly, Clare was just happy to know that her son was alive and well.

Clare placed her chair close to Billy so that she could hold his hand while they talked. "Oh, Billy, you don't know how many times I've prayed for some word from Will. He has been on my mind constantly for all these many years, and now my prayers have finally been answered. I have wished a thousand times that I had stood up for him that last day--the day he walked out of here with your mother. I have become an old woman before my time because of the worry and guilt that I have had to live with. I'm not trying to get your sympathy, Billy; I deserved every bit of the anguish that I have suffered these past years. And your grandfather went to an early grave because of his idiotic stubbornness. He was wrong, and he knew it, but he never once admitted it."

"What kind of father is Will? I hope he isn't anything at all like John was. Your grandfather was a good man in many ways, but he never knew how to show love. He seemed to think that the showing of tender feelings was an expression of weakness."

"First, let me bring you up to date on something, Grandmother. The woman that Dad brought here with him was not my mother. That lady was my dad's first wife. She died during childbirth while he was away during the war. Believe it or not, my mother is a woman of the Mandan Indian tribe. You can't tell it by looking at me, but I am one-half Indian. Now, to answer your question, I really couldn't ask for a better father. He and I are more like close friends than father and son."

"Oh, I am so glad to hear that, and I don't care one whit if you're half Indian. How do you get along with your mother?

"She is truly wonderful. I've got the greatest parents in the world."

"I am so glad that you--all of you—get along together. That means so much to me," said Clare breaking into sobs. After she regained her composure she continued: "I never knew that Will was in the war. If he had been killed, I might never have known about it. There is so much that I've missed out on. All these many years, I never knew whether he was alive or dead."

"Dad regretted, at first, that he didn't write you, Grandmother, but after a while he thought it best that you think of his as dead. He intended to lose himself in the Rocky Mountains, and never come back to Tennessee again."

"I understand how he must have felt. I don't hold it against Will for not writing after the way John acted, and the way I let him down."

"Billy, I want you to do something for me. I sold the warehouse after John died. I got 22,000 dollars for it. I want you to take Will 5,000 of it. Some of it I've had to spend already, but there should be more than enough left to last me the rest of my life. I'm going to get a lawyer to fix it up all legal like, so that when I die Will inherits what money is left. And whatever this house brings will go to you, personally. That is the very least that I can do for Will and his family, after the way I let him down. I would have already had it done, but like I said, I didn't even know if he was still alive."

"Thank you, Grandmother, but you need to know that Dad never had any hard feelings toward you. He considered you as much a victim as he was. And he harbored no ill will toward Grandfather, either. He just felt a terrible sadness that Grandfather was the way he was."

"Well, it was sad, alright, very sad. But if I had stood up to John years earlier, maybe things would have turned out differently. At least I can die more contented now, just knowing that my son is all right. It feels like a band has been removed from around my heart," said Clare, with a fresh flow of tears.

"Grandmother, Dad has tried to teach me to accept things the way they are. I know that is easy to say and difficult to do, but he said that sometimes questioning things too much and holding on to grief can only lead to more misery. For the past twenty or more years, his philosophy has been to trust in God and be patient. Worrying doesn't change anything, Grandmother, except the one that is doing the worrying. We can't undo the past, so try to be more content and don't blame yourself any more."

"Yes, Son, that is easier said than done. I will try, nevertheless."

"Maybe you would consider going to live in Montana with us, Grandmother."

"No. No, Billy, it's too late in life for that. I would be nothing but a burden, now, in my condition. I would never dream of imposing on Will after the way I've treated him. If I was younger and in better health so that I could be of some use, I would do it, but not now. Though, I would like to write a letter for you to take to him, if you wouldn't mind."

"No, of course I wouldn't mind. I'll be leaving shortly. I'm going to surprise Mom and Dad. I'm getting married in a few days, Grandmother, to the daughter of one of Dad's old friends."

"Oh, that's wonderful, Billy! I'm so happy for you. I'm sure that she's a lovely girl. I wish that I could have met her. Would you accept a wedding present from me?" she asked, as she went to the bookshelf and took a hundred-dollar bill from between the pages of a Bible. "Please, buy your bride-to-be something nice with this."

"Thank you so very much, Grandmother, that's really very kind of you. This is truly a blessing. I didn't even have enough money for a ring. When I came to Tennessee, I wasn't planning to get married; it's just something that happened," said Billy, as he hugged his grandmother for the first time. "Should you be keeping this much money in the house? Some people wouldn't hesitate to rob you, you know."

"It pleases me to know that I am able to help you, Billy, and I can afford it. Now, don't you worry none about me getting robbed. That money would have been in the bank soon. I'm selling everything that I don't absolutely have to have, some things John had that I have no use for, so there won't be any loose ends when I pass on. It was merely a coincidence that I had that money here to give to you."

Clare talked Billy into spending the night. He could use the extra bedroom, the one his dad had slept in as a boy. He had to put his horse in the livery stable down the street and walk back to the house, but it wasn't far—Knoxville wasn't that big of a town.

Billy and his grandmother talked far into the night, as Clare wanted to hear every detail about Will's life over the past twenty-odd years. After they retired for the night, Billy slept well because he was tired from riding, and Clare because she finally had peace of mind.

The next morning, after his business at the bank with his grandmother and a visit to a jewelry store, Billy was eager to be on his way back to see Gracie--with a wedding ring in his pocket.

Clare was smiling and crying at the same time as she waved goodbye to Billy.

XXVII

Billy and Gracie were married at the church in Hicks Chapel community the next Sunday afternoon, so that Maggie and Herman could attend. The same church that Will had attended with Ginny so many years ago. The same church that they had also been married in. Gracie looked radiant in a new white dress that accentuated her shiny, black hair. Billy used some of the money his grandmother had given him to buy the first suit that he had ever owned. Everyone who attended the wedding agreed that they made a lovely couple.

Gracie left her tearful mother in the churchyard, as she and Billy left for Jasper. The horses were sold to Tucker Walden, and with the money, Billy bought train tickets to Montana. Billy had originally planned to ride a horse back to Montana, the same way he had left, but now that he had a wife, that was no longer an option. They asked Warren Hathaway to drive them to Shellmound Station, across the Tennessee River, to catch the train--that being the closest railroad station to Jasper.

They had to board the ferry at Rankin Cove in order to cross the river. Gracie had never seen so much water before in her life; in fact, she had never departed from solid ground before. Wading in the shallows of the Sequatchie River was her only experience with water outside of drinking and bathing. She hadn't even learned to swim. The Tennessee River was only a dozen miles from Hicks Chapel, but Gracie had never traveled that far before. As the ferry began to move, she was standing at the rail looking down at the water, which seemed to be rushing by. Her knees became weak, and she almost swooned, but Billy put his arms around her to steady her before she collapsed. Billy walked her toward the center of the ferry, where she held onto the buckboard until they were across the river.

Gracie was having mixed emotions about the future, as she sat on the bench outside the little train station. As with anyone who is about to venture into the unknown, she was a little frightened at the prospect of leaving home on a permanent basis, but she was also excited about the new life that she was about to embark upon. Her love for Billy was the deciding factor, but she was already having more fun and adventure than ever before in her life. The ferry ride itself was quite an experience.

After bidding Billy and Gracie good-bye, Warren left the newly-weds at the station and started the short ride back to Jasper. The train was late, but they didn't mind—they were in love and happy just being together.

The arriving train was the biggest, noisiest machine that Gracie had ever seen. She had seen locomotives only in pictures, and would never have gotten on board without Billy's insistent coaxing. Initially, for Gracie, looking out the window of the railcar had the same dizzying effect as the ferry ride, but her mind soon made the adjustment that put her at ease. Riding in a buckboard had no such effect on her, but she was too excited to waste time trying to figure out why. The railroad bridge across the Tennessee River at Bridgeport, Alabama, was so narrow that Gracie kept her eyes tightly closed until the train was again on solid ground. When the train entered the tunnel under the Cumberland Plateau at the head of Crow Valley, Gracie unconsciously held her breath until her starving lungs forced her to gulp air. Billy laughed until his side hurt when he realized what she had done. She was just getting used to the darkness when the train burst into sunlight on the other side of the mountain. What a relief to see daylight again; Billy was also relieved, even though he didn't let on.

The honeymoon was one very long train ride, and Gracie was thrilled to be seeing so much strange, new country. She had never been more than a few miles from home before, so everything was new and exciting to her. She thought the vastness and emptiness of the Great Plains was fascinating, but the awesome majesty of the Bighorn Mountains took her breath away. The Cumberland Mountains on either side of the Sequatchie Valley were mere hills in comparison.

In Nashville, Billy had bought a money belt in which he carried the five thousand dollars that belonged to his dad. The only time he took it off was when he was in bed or bathing. When they got to Billings, he and Gracie had to hire a buckboard to take them the rest of the way home. Billy had almost run out of money, but he would never spend his dad's money, so the driver took them home with the promise to be paid later. Out here, a man's word was as binding as a signed contract.

Will and Lone Dove were so happy to see their son that at first they unintentionally ignored Gracie, but when Billy finally could get around to introducing her as his wife, they gave her such a warm welcome that it made her feel right at home. That she was Maggie's daughter meant something special to Will, and he was so very happy for Billy. If Gracie had also been Buck's daughter too, everything would have been perfect.

Gracie could already feel the love that was in this family, and she knew that she and Lone Dove would be close friends and not have just a mother-in-law--daughter-in-law relationship. They already had one great bond between them. They both loved the same man--Billy.

The letter that Billy had delivered saddened Will's heart. He would have to write to his mother and somehow convince her not to blame herself for what had happened. Will didn't know how he could be more contented with the way his life had turned out. He wished his mother knew just how happy he now was. Only one thing could he wish for: that the rift between his father and himself could have been mended. Nothing, not even reconciliation with his father, though, could have convinced him to go back to Knoxville and the warehouse. His present life, he had fanaticized about as a child, and now it was a reality. He couldn't possibly be happier.

Will had searched diligently for months for a place where he could find peace, suffering much anguish before realizing that place had been in his heart all along. And now, when he compared his life of old with the present, there was such a contrast that he still had a hard time believing it. He once had nothing but a horse, a dog, and a gun and a heart filled with anger, and now, he had a comfortable home, a loving wife, a wonderful son and daughter-in-law, and money to build with.

Not that anyone could ever be a replacement for Buck, but Broken Feather was as good a friend as Will could ever hope for. What more could any man possibly want? He was reminded of what Jean Rene had said about Job, and how he, like Job, had been blessed, and beyond his wildest expectations. He looked up, and with his heart full to overflowing, said: "Thank You."

www.ingramcontent.com/pod-product-compliance
Lightning Source LLC
Chambersburg PA
CBHW021230130626
46554CB00004B/1414